DRAGON FATED

PRINCE OF THE OTHERWORLDS

CASSIE ALEXANDER

KARA LOCKHARTE

To Mr. Lockharte and Mr. Alexander for supporting us with ice cream and cheese!

ABOUT DRAGON FATED

Andi Ngo tried to walk away but destiny kept calling. Time will tell if fate made the right choice.

Although she tried to make the right decision to protect herself and her heart, Andi couldn't resist the pull of Damian Blackwood, billionaire, dragon shifter, and secret assassin. Now both she and Damian (and his dragon) couldn't be happier. She's certainly not complaining about dating a gorgeous, intense, and savage man who fulfills her every fantasy. For the first time in her life Andi feels treasured. Despite their many differences, like her Chinese-American upbringing and his life in another realm, one with magic and dragons, she and Damian fit together like two pieces of a puzzle.

But the edges of a harsh reality are creeping in fast. Dark secrets from her family's past, truths they never told her, are threatening to destroy their newfound love. Danger lurks around every corner in Damian's complicated world. And the weight of their collective pasts might drag them down before they have the chance to soar.

CHAPTER

ONE

"Wake up and say yes," a rough voice advised Andi as she felt strong arms encircle her, pulling her back against someone's chest.

Her eyelids fluttered, blurrily revealing her own room, and all the events of the prior night came rushing back—her uncle, her brother, and *him*.

Damian. The man holding her now and murmuring in her ear, nuzzling his face into her hair. She stretched against him, waking up. She felt so well rested—likely because he'd exhausted her last night —but also because she hadn't dreamed. The entire time she'd been asleep by Damian's side, she hadn't had a single nightmare. It felt like it'd been weeks since she'd last slept well.

Damian used the opportunity of her stretching to tighten his arms around her, one underneath her and up across her chest, beneath her breasts, the other possessively around her waist. He was deliciously warm against all the places that his arms touched, and where his chest pressed against her back too, his neck against her shoulder, his chin against her neck—but no place more so than the stiff cock he had nestled between the clefts of her ass.

1

"Wake up and say yes," he suggested again, his voice thick with desire as he smoothed her hair away to begin kissing her neck now that he knew she was rousing.

"Hmm, yes to what?" she asked, reaching up to run her fingers through his straight black hair.

He didn't answer her; he just rocked her with his hips, and she laughed. "Damian, I can't," she said, as his kisses started to run higher up her neck and along her jaw.

He paused to mutter, "Why not?" sounding absolutely petulant —like a boy whose favorite toy had just asked to be put away.

Andi laughed. "Because...I'm gross...I have dragon breath."

He chuckled melodiously near her ear and said, "Like I care," before resuming course.

Andi grinned in the half-light of her room. Of course, he didn't. Because he *was* a dragon. And, right now, he was *her* dragon.

"Yes," she said definitively. "Yes and yes and yes," she went on.

Damian practically purred; she felt the rumble inside of his chest. "Save some yeses for later," he said and reached for her thigh.

HE PULLED her top leg up and over his hips, making her feel like she was falling back against him, but she knew he'd catch her. The hand on her chest beneath her breasts reached to cup her nearest one and stroke her nipple with a thumb, as his tongue ran up the shell of her ear.

"Let me kiss you," he demanded, the need in his voice as raw as his erection.

She twisted her head to meet his, so his lips could find hers and part them, tongue pushing in. Once again, she felt surrounded by him, and soon, both of her hands were in his hair, holding herself to him, feeling his hips thrust against her in time with his fingers stroking and his tongue pushing, and she gasped out a moan next time he let her breathe.

"Yes," he agreed, his voice low, rocking himself against her again.

She felt the warm velvet smoothness of his hard cock slide against her ass—and the aching emptiness of the space between her legs where she wanted it, where it belonged. She squirmed against him in anticipation, and he chuckled darkly. "Does my princess need something?" he asked her slowly, rocking into her.

There was the temptation to pretend and fight and lie, and then there was the temptation to just admit it and give in. Both would wind up feeling good, but only one of them felt easy. And the longer he kept rocking against her in promise, the more firm his attentions on her breasts and nipples became, the heat radiating out from his mouth where he'd gone back to kissing her on her jaw and throat....

"I want..." she said, her own voice just as husky as his. "You. Inside me. Now."

He easily hitched her leg higher on himself, stretching her wide open, as he sank the hand on her chest down to press her hips back. His position behind her changed so that his own hips were below hers, and now the head of his cock was free to arch up and nudge against her, and he did so. She felt the heat of him push over her folds and rub against her clit, and she whined as he did it again and again instead of pushing in.

"Say you need it, princess," he told her, teasing her, pushing her open only to then not enter. Each time the thick head of his cock rubbed against her clit, she groaned. "You're so wet, I can feel it. I know you want me, but I want to hear you say you need it," he whispered in her ear between kisses.

She bit her tongue to deny him, even as she knew that he was right. Her nipples were hard and her hips were shaking and she was so turned on. It wasn't that she wanted to fight him so much as it was just what she was used to—being stubborn and doing exactly what she wanted to at all times.

But what she wanted right now was for him to *do* her, and she did need it, *fuck it all*, as long as he was fucking her.

"I need it—*dragon*," she said, almost spitefully, and Damian growled near her ear.

"Good, *princess*," he said, in the exact same tone, and held her hips still with one hand as his finally pushed up.

DAMIAN COULD FEEL the exquisite soft heat between Andi's legs part to take him as she moaned and roiled against him, and at her use of the word "dragon," his own was instantly present inside. *Does she mean that?* it asked him.

Does it matter? he snapped back, trying to maintain control of himself. Andi was wet, but still so tight—and likely sore, after last night. He didn't want her body to ask him for more than she could handle.

His dragon didn't answer him, and then Andi hissed, "Oh, God, Damian," and the moment between him and his beast was gone, replaced by his concern for her.

"Are you all right?" he asked, stopping everything to stroke her hair.

"It's good-bad," she confessed. "This position—I'm so tight, and you're freaking huge—"

"Why thank you," he quipped.

"It's not a compliment; it's just a fact," she said with a pout and an eye roll. "And after last night, I'm so sore—"

Damian kissed her forehead softly. "It's okay. There're a million other things we can do," he said and started to pull out.

"No." Her top hand rushed to his hips and stopped them. "Don't. Not yet. Because...it's still good too. Just...give me time?"

He saw her dark eyes searching his. "So much time. All the time in the world," he told her and meant it with all of his heart.

"Okay," she said and nodded, then started to rock her hips against his, moving fractionally up and down his cock, and it was his turn to hiss.

She felt so fucking good, and what was more—as he watched her bite her lips and screw her eyes shut to concentrate on taking him—

had anything a woman ever done for him before been so hot? She wanted to be his so badly it was making her shake; she wanted him to make her feel good; she wanted nothing more in the world right now than to be able to fit him—not knowing that as his mate, she already did and that it was his job for the rest of eternity to pleasure her.

Damian wrapped an arm around her loosely enough that she could easily push it back and reached his hand between her legs to stroke. Her hands found his there, and he expected them to make him stop, but instead, they pressed his fingers tighter to her, showing him how she liked it, rubbing the soft nub of her clit beneath its hood just over the spot where his cock stretched her wide. Her hips moved more surely now, and quicker, and he whispered, "Oh, princess," in her ear. "You're doing so well...you feel so good...keep going."

Her pulse fluttered at his compliments, so he continued, his voice low and full of promises as she worked herself against him, as he, in turn, worked his fingers against her clit. "I know you can take me, Andi. You fit me. And I fit you. And in just a little bit, you're going to have me all the way inside you, and then I am going to fuck you and make you feel even better." The wetness where they met slicked his fingers, making them slippery, and he used that to rub her faster as she whined his name.

"Damian...Damian," she said as her voice went high and begged him. He didn't dare move. He didn't want to hurt her, but she was going to come for him, just halfway down his cock, because she couldn't help herself.

"God," he growled, gritting his teeth, doing his best to remain still as she writhed against him, her stomach muscles clenching beneath the heel of his hand as her hips beat against his harder, all of her tensing, ready to give it up.

"Damian...I...oh!" she shouted and then moaned and thrashed in earnest as the waves hit her. He held her tight to his chest, following her hips with his hand, his fingertips on her clit incessant, demanding. Her orgasm was as much his as it was hers because she was his—she belonged to him. It was all he could do not to bite her neck and hold her down and fuck her madly. When she was wild, it made him wild. Blinding need seared through him, and he wanted to drag her hips down onto his and impale her there, to feel his own cum shoot inside her. The only thing that stopped him from doing just that was a lifetime accustomed to control.

But he was there, with her, beside her, inside her. He felt her pleasure ripple through her body and moaned as she did, grunting as her hot wet heat grabbed at his cock. He wound his hand down in time with the end of her flutters, until she lay panting against him, and he stilled his fingers. She was dripping now; he could both feel it and scent it in the air and knew that the second she was ready, he could slide her down his shaft and shove his way inside. He licked up the line of her jaw in an animalistic manner without thinking.

Andi sagged back with a contented sigh. "Oh...I'm sorry."

Damian blinked, his vision for their next few minutes momentarily disrupted. He wrapped his arms tight around her anew. "What've you got to apologize for?"

"Nothing. Everything." She twisted to look up at him, her gaze soft with sex. "I think I'm just used to apologizing is all."

"Well, stop it."

"Sorry," she said intentionally, with a laugh. He felt it pulse around him and groaned. "Sorry-not-sorry," she said, squeezing him again, this time clenching her muscles around him on purpose.

He growled a warning in her ear. "I think you will be sorry if you kill me."

She pushed a hand up into his hair. "And how could I manage to kill a dragon?"

He felt so safe and open with her there that he was actually tempted to list them—all the ways that she could flay him—one by one. By leaving him, by not taking all that he had to offer, by hurting him intentionally—nothing that would kill the scaled beast inside him, but all things that would wreck his much more human soul.

But he knew that was too much for right now, in her small bedroom in her small apartment on her small penguin-sheeted bed. So instead, he told her the obvious answer: "By not finishing what you started."

"Dragons get blue balls?" she mused, with a flash of her dark eyes.

"We do. And it's so much worse. Because our balls are so much bigger."

She laughed, and he felt each peal of it roll through him and then he was laughing too and his mouth was at her neck again, at the angle where throat met jaw, just below her ear, and as he kissed it, she shivered on him.

"Damian...I," she began and started to move against him again.

"Oh, princess, yes, fucking take it," he murmured as she rocked back, and he carefully—oh, so carefully—thrust up until they met, and all of him was wrapped by her at last. He let out a low moan. "You let me know...okay? Say the word, and I'll stop."

"No, it's good, it's good," she whispered hoarsely.

Damian allowed himself to finally thrust then with her permission, feeling the tight glove of her pussy squeeze around him. He held her to his chest so tightly, so possessively, arching his hips up and into her, relishing the sensation of her sliding up and down his cock, the way she made every inch of him feel grabbed and held and pulled. And when her hips started urging his faster, he growled.

"Fuck, you turn me on," he whispered roughly in her ear, and Andi thrilled at hearing it. Now that she was stretched out and could take him, now that every inch of him was wet, his hot breath against her neck made her shudder. His hand on her breast, his fingers playing with her nipples...she needed to hear him say it because what he could do to her so easily seemed entirely unfair. She wanted to have some small power over him, even if that power was making him lose control.

"Everything about you," he went on, landing deep in her with a satisfied grunt. "Just this...fuck," he moaned through another stroke. "I want to come in you again, princess. I want you to come for me, and then I want to—"

They both heard it at the same time—a key at the front door, and then that same door opening.

"Shit...it's Sammy," Andi whispered, tensing, and then Damian's hand moved from her breast to latch across her mouth, where she could taste the salt of his palm.

"Shhh," he whispered in her ear. He took another stroke, and his other hand reached between her legs again to rub her just how she'd showed him.

"Oh, God, oh, God," she whispered—or tried to—but she couldn't get any words out. Damian chuckled behind her, stroking her wetness up her belly in a line up to a nipple. He circled it for a lazy moment, then pinched her, hard.

"Mmmm!" she complained, squirming against him. The muffled sound came clearly out, and she could feel him trying not to laugh.

Sammy's footsteps came down the hall. "Andi, are you up?" She could hear Sammy taking off her heels. "If you are, girl, I've got to tell you all about last night," she said in her lovely Irish lilt.

Damian rocked forward, stroking into her again, and she had to fight not to moan. Then he let go of her mouth, and she took a ragged breath.

"Andi?" Sammy asked with concern, as Damian kept on torturing her. His hand against her clit sped up, and his strokes became more insistent.

"I'm up...it's just...don't come in; I have a cold," she got out in between being rocked by him, biting her lips to stop from making any other noises, no matter how much she wanted to.

"Oh, no! I'm so sorry!" Sammy said, from safely down the hall.

"Yeah, it's awful." Andi feigned a hacking cough.

"My princess is a bad liar," Damian whispered with amusement in her ear.

"Fuck you," she whispered back at him. He punished her with another stroke, arching his hips so that it felt like she could feel the crown of him dragging inside her and she rolled her head back, gasping out, "I'm gonna go back to sleep now, Sammy...we'll catch up tonight?"

"Oh, God, you sound awful. Yes, feel better." They heard Sammy's footsteps depart down the hall, then just as quickly return to stand right outside her closed door. "Just know that for once, you're not the only one who needs sleep!"

Damian pulled himself out quickly and then plunged just as fast back inside, and one of Andi's hands fisted in her sheets, trying not to scream. "Congratulations!" she gritted out cheerfully.

"Thanks!" Sammy said with a giggle, and Andi could almost hear her hair-flip, as she padded back down the hall.

"You are the worst," Andi whispered hoarsely, the second they heard Sammy's bedroom door close.

"The worst what?" he asked her back as she twisted to look up at him. His grin feigned complete innocence like it was entirely separate from the rest of his still-fucking-her-slowly body.

"The worst everything," she said with a head shake.

"Oh, I don't know about that. Does this feel like the worst to you?" he asked her, then thrust into her deeply again, catching her mouth with his hand again to muffle her moaning. "I like to think I'm quite good at some things, princess," he said and started taking her more quickly.

Her hips started working against his of their own accord, letting him land deep, and she brought up both hands to keep his hand over her mouth because otherwise there was no way she could stay quiet, and Sammy would instantly know, as would their neighbors and Eumie's customers below, just what was happening in her bedroom. He purred at that, keeping his own sounds soft, but Andi could hear his rough breathing in her ear. One of his hands pressed between her legs again, half to keep her hips back, and half to touch her, rubbing her so perfectly, and she could feel her heart speed up and taste the salt of his palm and her nipples were twin points of ache, so she gave up on holding his hand in place to grab her breasts and pull them only to feel him tense up as he watched her.

"Give it to me Andi," he demanded quietly, his commands hot in her ear. "Give. It. To. Me."

He punctuated every word with a thrust and the combination of everything—his breath, his hands, his cock—undid her. She moaned her way through a long release. She couldn't help it; not even a saint could've managed it quietly, thrashing against him, and heard his own accompanying hissing as he valiantly tried to stay quiet and also failed as he lost himself inside her, pulsing hard, thrusting up, making her ride him to completion. His hand slid down her face, and as the edge of his fingers pressed between her lips, she bit them to keep them there as she gasped.

"Fuck," she whispered when she next had breath to do so. "How...?" She went on, shaking her head, unsure what she should say next. How did he do this to her every time? How come everything with him always felt so right? How could it feel this good?

How on earth would she survive if this ever stopped?

"I don't know, princess," he said, kissing her as he slowly, regretfully pulled out of her. "All I do know is that a moment when I'm not with you is a moment wasted."

Andi felt herself flush. He wasn't supposed to say things like that —it was unfair. It was not what normal people did.

But he wasn't normal, was he?

He situated himself around her so that she was flat on the bed, and he was leaning beside her protectively, one of his thighs across hers, one of his arms underneath his own head, with the other hand roaming her body. "What would you like now?" he asked her. "More sleep, breakfast, or round two?"

Andi looked up at him and found his golden eyes staring kindly down. The coolly imperious man she'd been in turns excited by and frightened of had softened, though she knew that man was still inside Damian, same as his dragon was. "All of the above, I think."

He smiled and laughed. "Pick an order." Just then, her stomach rumbled, choosing for her. "Breakfast it is, then," Damian grinned, and began pulling away.

"But then rounds two through twelve?" she said, sounding just as petulant as Damian had earlier.

"There'd better be more than twelve," he said, reaching for his jeans on her floor, and she watched him bend over, every single muscle on his abdomen rippling, as he pulled on his boxer briefs and jeans—which was why it was taking a while for the less sexed parts of her brain to come online.

She sat up. "Wait...where are you going?"

"Through the mirror in your bathroom," he said, gesturing with his chin as he swept his shirt up.

"To cook me breakfast?" she questioned.

"No. Sorry, cooking's not a skill I possess; I hope that's not a huge disappointment," he said as he tugged his shirt on. "When I'm out in the world, I use money for food, and when I'm at home, I use my magic cat."

Andi clapped her hands to her face and tried not to giggle.

"What? You've seen him!" Damian quietly protested, looking amused.

"I know!" She'd met Grimalkin a week ago at Damian's when she'd been saving his friend's life, and she'd seen him change himself from a normal-sized seal-point Siamese into a tiger in under a second. "It's just, you look super manly, and then you go and say the words 'magic cat' like that's not absurd—"

"I'll show you some absurd things," he whisper-threatened, lunging meaningfully toward her bed with his hand on his belt buckle.

Andi squealed softly and skittered backward, almost off the bed, and he grabbed her ankles to yank her back toward him, before falling over her himself and catching himself with his elbows. She was hyperaware of just how naked she was beneath him and all the things that they could do and keep on doing, and he leaned down to kiss her gently, before pushing himself to stand straight again.

"Stop thinking so loudly...it's distracting," he said teasingly.

"What? You can't read my mind," she said, rolling over on her bedsheets, suddenly concerned. "Can you?"

"No, but I don't need to when you're looking at me like that." He gestured at all of her, sprawled out atop her bed.

She coyly stripped a sheet over her with one hand, hiding half a leg and a breast. "What am I thinking now, then?" she asked and pouted at him.

He grinned at her lasciviously. "I'll tell you after breakfast. And, if I'm wrong, I'll keep guessing until I'm right."

Andi pouted. "I feel like there should be penalties."

"I could definitely come up with some."

"For you, not me; I'm not the one bragging I can read people's thoughts." She shrugged as cutely as she could and then slow-rolled herself over, winding the sheet around her body.

"Fuck me," he muttered as he watched her, before stepping away from the bed with purpose. "Stop that. Just let me feed you. I'll be right back."

He turned on his heel and walked toward her bathroom, and after a second, she jumped out of bed and followed him, curious how the whole thing worked, wrapping herself with the sheet along the way. She caught up with him as he put a knee up on her counter, though at seeing her, he paused and tsked her name. "Andi."

"What? I just want to watch is all."

He groaned. "So many other circumstances in which I want to hear that, but," he said and took her in, "what's the sheet for?"

"Well, now that I know that anyone can be looking through the other side...." She hitched the penguin-patterned sheet higher under her arms, looked at herself in reflection, and fought not to laugh. It was a good thing he was so enamored with her because she had some serious, serious sex hair.

"Most people can't. It's an upper-level power." He rocked off the counter and turned around to sit on it instead. "And it's even harder without a connection to the person on the other side." He reached out to her with his arms and she walked into them, letting him loosely wrap them around her hips.

"Will you be able to see me?" she asked with a serious squint.

"I could, yes."

Her squint doubled. "Did you look? Before?"

"Not really?" She heard the strain in his voice and remembered that she'd made him promise to never lie to her the prior night.

"Damian!" she hissed. "You did! Didn't you!"

He looked up at the ceiling for forgiveness and then returned his gaze to her. "Only twice. Once, when you were waiting at the bus stop for that *man*," he said, and Andi heard the snarl in his voice at David's memory. "And then again—not in here, I swear—but in your bedroom. The other night I saw you smiling at your phone as you messaged someone, and it nearly killed me." Pain flickered across his face at the memory.

"You mean my roommate? I'd say it serves you right, but I suspect you already know that."

"I do, believe me." He let go of her to lean back against her mirror and run his fingers through his hair. "I wouldn't have even been looking if my dragon hadn't wanted to see you so badly."

"Oh, so that's what you call it?" she said, gesturing between his legs, and he laughed then reached for the sheet around her, using it to tug her close to him again.

"I won't look anymore. I promise. I know you need your privacy."

"Good because I do. Especially in here. Except for maybe when I don't, but I will tell you when that is, mister." She reached for the sheet he held and shimmied it loose from his hands, before dropping it to kick it aside. "Like now, for instance. Because I am going to take myself and my ornate hairstyle into the shower."

She stepped into her tub and leaned over to turn on the water. Andi heard him mutter, "Trying to kill me," again before the sound of the water drowned him out—but when she looked over, he was gone.

DAMIAN PULLED himself through Andi's mirror with clear intent before he could talk himself out of it again. After breaching the surface of the glass, he was in the howling void of the between-places for a second—a cold space filled with what felt like grasping hands—and then he was pushing through the glass of his own travelling mirror on the far side, stepping out from the dead chill into the warmth of his own bedroom.

All the other mirrors on his wall were closed and fogged except for the one he'd just walked through. He took a moment to look back and saw Andi's form barely hidden by the glass door of her shower. It made her blurry, but he could still see the outline of her curves and the wave of her now wet hair cascading over her shoulder. He hadn't showered with her yet, had he? They'd been in his dragon's bathing pond together, but he'd been trying not to look at her the whole time—it hardly counted. One more thing to look forward to: being in a shower with her—maybe even his shower—where he could pick her up, and....

What kind of dragon doesn't provide food for his mate? his dragon chided him. *Feed her soon...or I will.*

I know, I know, he said, waving a hand and closing their connection. At the thought of his dragon taking charge and getting food for Andi *Game of Thrones*-style, he snorted, and then his own reflection caught his eye.

He hardly looked like himself. Everything on the outside was still the same—he was tall, well-muscled, had black hair, and women seemed to like his appearance. But a tenseness that'd been riding his shoulders for far too long was gone. And even though it felt foolish, he was smiling—not at himself, but just smiling—because he couldn't help himself...because of her.

14

He had an urge to tumble back through the mirror to her side and tell her—to show her—that this new him was all her fault, in a good way. But it would only take a few seconds longer to do it with breakfast in tow, as he'd promised.

"Grimalkin?" he said aloud, and the cat appeared into existence beside him.

"Present," Grim meowed and sat back on his haunches to primly eye Damian. "You smell like the nurse. Did you have fun?"

Damian got the distinct impression that his 'magic cat' was judging him. "I did. Why do you ask?"

"Because Austin got up in the middle of the night last night," Grimalkin reported.

"And?" Damian asked, fighting down old habits. His life in the Realms had been one of waiting for the next blow to land, and fears of backstabbing and betrayal came rushing back—none of which Austin deserved, he knew. Damian forced himself to rein in his fears the same way he reined in his dragon and wondered if he'd ever stop being haunted by his childhood.

"And he *went* to the *kitchen,* and he *ate* all my *cheese.*" Grimalkin said every other word with a hiss. "He didn't even try to hide it, Damian! He did it right in front of me! Bite after bite!" The little cat visibly shuddered. "He put my twenty-year-old Wisconsin cheddar on saltines!"

Damian sighed in relief. "Grim...you're...a hugely powerful magical entity. Why didn't you just teleport it away?"

"I couldn't!" Grim said with a pained yowl. "I was just watching him, and I couldn't believe he'd do that—I mean, he's a dog, how could he know how good cheese tastes?—and by then, it was too late." Grimalkin flopped to the ground dramatically, as if someone had just stolen all his bones.

Damian almost groaned. All he wanted was to go back to Andi's side with a palatial breakfast, but that required Grim's help. At least he was getting a 'magic cat' story out of it to tell her—he could already hear her laugh about this in his mind. "I'll buy you more, Grim," he promised.

"It's not that." Grim lifted his head like it cost him all his strength. "It's the principle of the thing."

Damian knelt down to gently pet the cat's side. "Do you want me to say something?"

"No," Grim said, his eyes brimming with unshed tears. "I can't let him know how important cheese is to me." He sounded incredibly forlorn.

Damian pinched the bridge of his nose with his free hand to maintain equilibrium. "And why not?" He did his best to ask kindly.

"Because. It's my weakness." Grim's voice went quiet as if dying. "I can't let anyone know." The cat thumped his head on the floor dramatically.

"Oh my God, Grim," Damian began, to tell his cat to snap out of it, but then, both of them heard a tap against glass. Grim was up on all fours in an instant, head swiveling in the direction of the sound.

One of Damian's other mirrors was active—a thin, genteel oval mirror with an ornate frame. The fog inside it had cleared, and there was a familiar large red bird on the other side, delicate as an egret, pecking frantically on the glass.

"Lyka!" Grim said, excitedly naming the guardian on the other side.

"Ryana?" Damian whispered to himself, naming his half-sister, its owner, as he quickly moved to stand. The bird flared its wings out, flapping heavily against the mirror's boundary, throwing itself wildly against the glass.

"Can we let her through?" Grim asked with concern, running over to stare between him and the fluttering bird.

Damian reached for the mirror's glass without thinking, then hesitated. When he'd abdicated the throne twenty years ago, coming to earth to postpone the inevitable fate of turning into his dragon, he'd sworn to Ryana's mother, his stepmother, that he would never return nor interfere with the politics of the Realms in any way. Would letting Lyka through break that truce?

Why would Lyka have ever left Ryana behind?

"Little bird, where is your owner?" Damian wondered as Lyka threw herself against the mirror again, leaving a smear of blood behind on her side of the glass.

Damian's eyes widened, and he clapped his hands together. "I need to see," he commanded, sending out a wave of magical energy to all the mirrors on his wall. One by one, mirrors sought mirrors, and images from the Realms came into focus—a view from a parapet of distant smoke over rubble, a mirror over the ballroom showed courtiers and servants running wildly below, a mirror in the library showed books—his father's books, and the only treasure Damian ached over leaving behind—on fire, edges curling. Each mirror glass showed a new portion of destruction, some piece of his former home falling apart.

Grim made a strangled sound as Damian's hand slammed over onto the mirror, where Lyka struggled, opening the glass between them. The bird flew through, disappearing from sight only to reappear in the room with them, then soar up, making strange sounds along the way, scanning the mirrors that Damian had open, searching, and Damian knew for whom.

His sister.

He put both his hands to the glass in front of him. Though apart now for twenty years, he and Ryana had once been close—and he called on the link between them. Their childhood had pitted them against one another until they realized they were more alike than not, and well before Damian left, he considered Ryana his only true family—not his mother who'd forgotten him, not the stepmother who loathed him and saw him as an obstacle to her throne, not his father who had been overtaken by his dragon at long last.

Ryana was the only one who understood what it was like to grow up as a pawn, forced to play a game you didn't know all the rules to, one you didn't even want to win—but one you had to play, because if you lost you'd die.

He gathered his energies, all his thoughts of her and the history between them, and summoned a view of her.

The mirror in front of him erupted into a multifaceted gaze like he was seeing through a kaleidoscope of eyes, and overlapping pieces of her came into view. He was catching her reflections from fallen candlesticks, polished marble columns, the metal legs of chairs, anything nearby her that was even remotely reflective. She was face down on the ground, her face covered by her hair, her wings bent and torn behind her, with no mirrors big enough for transport nearby, and smoke making it harder to see her by the minute.

Grimalkin howled in worry while at the same time his dragon lunged up. *Who hurt her?* it bellowed inside him

"Ryana! Where the fuck are you!" Damian opened up the connections he could to shout at her, even though he couldn't fit through them. "Wake up!"

If he couldn't figure out where she was, he'd never find a nearby mirror big enough in time. The palace was so big it could take days to search. Lyka hovered in midair beside him—bleeding freely—then soared up to dive into a mirror high on the wall, before returning carrying a leather bladder. The bird then wedged itself into one of the facets Damian was shown, pulling itself through to appear in the scene on the other side, to beat about Ryana's face with its wings.

What's she doing? his dragon asked, pushing forward again.

I don't know, Damian admitted, feeling pained.

Lyka soared up and out of view with the bladder, then returned, hovering low enough that Damian could tell Ryana's guardian had changed, up to the size of a much larger bird now, perhaps an eagle, and he saw it tear the side of the bladder open. A metallic substance spilled to the ground, pouring out in a broad puddle not far from Ryana's quiet form, and he saw even more massive claws grab hold of Ryana's body and pull her forward to it. Just as he began to be able to see through the new reflective substance on her side with his magic-sight, he reached through the spreading reflection, feeling the cold and the hands of the void grab at him, as he made contact with Ryana on the far side. He heard Lyka shriek and Grim growl, and he pulled back as hard as he could, yanking Ryana through the between-space to fall through the mirror into his bedroom, into his arms. Lyka passed through the mirror just a second behind her, instantly transitioning from a bird the size of a vulture down to a tiny blood-red starling, to collapse atop Ryana's chest.

Damian carefully spun away from the glass and took her to his bed, laying her down as carefully as he could, considering the condition of her wings. The bag she clung to thumped down beside her. He stroked a lock of burned hair away from her neck to feel for a pulse. It thrummed beneath his fingers—slow and thready—and he looked over to Grim. "Get everybody here. Now." Grim disappeared to obey, and Damian took in the destruction of his sister's form.

The pine-needle green wings his sister had were the only trait of their shared father Ryana had, much to her stepmother's chagrin. She'd always wanted to fly, even as a little girl, but they were just for show, not muscular enough to pull her aloft without using egregious amounts of magic.

As contenders for the same throne, they should've been enemies, but the shared trauma of being raised royal in the Realms bonded them instead. When Damian left for earth, it seemed like the best of both possible worlds: he got to escape his past, and it cleared the path for Ryana to ascend safely. But what had happened?

"Ryana, wake up," he said, cupping her face in his hand. Her eyes were swelling now, bruises mottling her pale skin, all of her smelling of smoke. One of her legs had swung freely when he carried her in a way Damian knew was bad, one of her wings was shredded, and the other bent at a cruel angle.

Austin was the first to burst in. "Damian!" he shouted, surely scenting smoke, running for the bed as Damian looked back at him.

"Help her," he commanded his friend in a strangled voice.

Austin paused a second to take both of them in, his eyes

widening as he surveyed the broken-winged woman before him, then said, "Of course."

It didn't take long for two more of his crew to crowd into his bedroom. Mills ran for the bed first, her floor-length hair streaming behind her, while Max intuited what was going on in all his open mirrors the quickest and stood still before them as if struck by lightning.

"What the fuck is happening over there, Damian?" he growled, transfixed by the images reflected in the goggles that covered his eyes.

"I don't know yet," Damian admitted, as the bear-shifter shook himself free to rush up and peer out the nearest mirror. It showed the library, all of it on fire, clouds of ash twisting in whatever wind blew them—thousands of years of knowledge gone in the blink of an eye.

Grimalkin ran from mirror to mirror, like if he just kept looking, eventually, everything would go back the way it was, and Damian understood the inclination. As much as once upon a time he'd wanted to destroy everything of his former life—all the more so after meeting Andi—actually seeing it happen was like a knife twisting in his gut. He knew he should close all of them and not leave any trace of a magical connection between Earth and the Realms, but he felt like closing them would be turning his back on his home, a home he'd never get to see again—not like it was—and he found he couldn't look away.

"Is she okay?" He dragged his attention from the mirror back to the bed where Ryana lay, breathing shallowly.

"Hard to say," Austin said. The shaggy, brown-haired werewolf scooped up Lyka and handed her to Mills. "We need to move her to someplace with no mirrors for safekeeping and plenty of room for supplies. Can you have Grim change the library downstairs back to the way it was when Zach was hurt?"

Damian grunted. "Grim," he commanded.

"I heard!" The little cat stopped its pacing, yowled, and disappeared.

"It'll be done. What else?" Damian asked. Over in the Realms, a tower of rubble fell, shattering the mirror on the far side of one of his, so now it showed them only nothingness, like a jack-o'-lantern's empty eye. Max started making a keening sound.

"I know," Damian said. It was affecting him too. Mills came to his side.

"Damian, is this what I think it is?" she asked, proffering the bird she held up.

Mills was the most powerful witch he'd ever met. Of course, she knew. He nodded. "Her name's Lyka. And, yes, she's a guardian like Grimalkin."

"Then," Mills began, twisting back to the bed.

"That's Princess Ryana. Damian's sister," Max said, naming the comatose woman at last. He looked back at her. "What happened to her wings, Damian? Who could—how..." he began, and the goggles that hid the magically replaced eyes Mills had given him from the rest of the world weren't tight enough to hold back the tears Damian could see streaking down his face. His questions faded into an incoherent shout, and he swung back toward the mirrored wall to punch it to dust between two frames.

"I know," Damian repeated, putting a restraining hand on the bear-shifter's shoulder, watching another tower fall and another glass go black.

Inside of himself, his dragon seethed uncomfortably, full of the need to act but with nothing to actually do. Everything in him wanted to vow vengeance—but on whom, and for what? And...why? This was what he'd always wanted. To never be constrained by the machination of the Realms again—or any promises he'd made to his stepmother. To be free to fully be with Andi.

So, this—the echoing images of destruction in each of his mirrors—looked like freedom.

Was it?

"I'm sorry, Damian, but you need to close them," Mills said from beside him. "It's not good to have so many mirrors open at once. The energies in here are unsettling."

Grimalkin rematerialized at his feet and said, "Finished!" as Damian looked to Mills.

"If I close them, I may not be able to open them again," he said, voicing his deepest fear.

Mills gave him a sad smile. "That is true," she agreed. "And yet, it must be done."

Damian knew his witch wouldn't lie to him, both because she cared for him as a friend, and because she couldn't—she was cursed to always tell the truth. He took several steps back, so that he could see all the mirrors at once, and tried to memorize what was happening in each of them, taking one long, last look at the world that had stolen his mother and his father from him, where he'd been tormented and tortured, where he had killed others as they had tried to kill him.

His home.

Then he slammed his hands together in a clap and said, "All eyes closed," and one by one, each image of the Realms in his mirror frames winked out, replaced by darkness.

CHAPTER

TWO

Damian carried Ryana carefully downstairs to his library, closely followed by Max, Mills, and Grim, and tried to answer Austin's questions on the way.

"So, what kind of healing factor does she have?" The well-tanned werewolf was holding onto her lower leg so it wouldn't disconcertingly dangle as he walked backward down the stairs.

Damian thought back to their childhood. "I don't know."

Austin made a thoughtful noise. "What about vasculature? Or heart? Hearts?"

"Austin," Damian growled as they reached the landing.

"I'm just wondering! Like, am I supposed to pretend to be a vet here or what? She has freaking wings, Damian."

"Just...do what you always do."

"But I've never gotten to treat a dragon," Austin pointed out. "You're always fine—or too pissed off to touch."

Damian grunted, feeling rather pissed off now, as they turned into the room Grimalkin had appointed for his sister. His guardian cat had shifted the spatial layout of the castle so that his old library was now a bright and airy stone-floored room with long tall windows, one of which Max walked over to look through pensively, surely thinking of other recent views.

Grim had even put sheer green and pink silks on the wall, just like Ryana's had had back home—which was now covered under fifty feet of rubble. Damian tried not to think about that as he set Ryana carefully down on her new bed. The same medical equipment Grim had created for Zach, he'd replicated for Ryana, only this time in room complimenting shades. Austin fussed with her leg, hissing on her behalf as he brought it down even though she hadn't woken, and arranging her wings in the way that made the most sense so that none of the bones nor leather were working at odds. Then he tugged down her dress to start putting stickers on her for one of the many electronic things Damian didn't understand, and Damian fought down a warning growl. It pained him to see Austin be so familiar with Ryana, but he was comforted by the way the werewolf moved, with a mixture of clinical distance and awe, treating her with the utmost respect.

"Oh, nicely done, Grim," Mills complimented the cat on the room. "Now, what to do with her friend?" She knelt down and showed the little bird to Grim.

Grim looked over to Damian. "She needs cheese."

Damian squinted. "Does she, Grim?" He was in no mood for jokes.

Grimalkin swiped a nervous paw over his whiskers. "I don't know. I need cheese. This is awful. Cheese will help." Damian had never known his guardian to panic before. He knelt down, and Grim ran over to him to wind against him as Grim went on. "I just always thought we'd go back someday. I knew you didn't want to, but that didn't mean I wanted everything to be like that."

"I know," Damian said, rubbing underneath Grim's chin and smoothing his whiskers back into place. The cat let him, closing his eyes and leaning into Damian's fingers for several settling breaths before walking over to Lyka, still held in Mills's palms.

"Feather-butt," he said. "Feather-butt, wake up."

24

Damian bit his lips not to laugh because his cat seemed entirely earnest. Grim looked back at him. "Tell Mills to put her on the bed for me? Up in a corner?"

Damian did so, and Mills gently transported the bird to the bed's upper corner, as per his request. Grim jumped onto the bed, sniffed along Ryana's length, and let his hackles raise and settle at least three times, before kneading the sheets right in front of Lyka's face. "Feather-butt," Damian heard him whisper, before making a tiny sad sound as he wound himself around her, encircling the red bird nose to tail. "I'll keep an eye on both of them," Grim promised Damian, placing his head flat on his front paws.

"Thank you," Damian told him, then looked to Austin. "Anything you need, ask the cat."

"Can I get a half-dragon-half-human medical text?" Austin snarked, watching the numbers on the monitor nervously. "I don't even know what your normal blood pressure is, D—"

Damian grabbed his shoulder. "Just keep her in human ranges. She's not like me."

Austin looked down at her before meeting his gaze again. "Okay."

"You two," Damian said, turning to Max and Mills, "come with me."

DAMIAN PACED one wall of his narrow conference room, matched by Max, pacing the other side. Mills sat down at the head of the table, out of both of their ways, plaiting her hair back quickly.

"I'm sorry; I was at a board meeting, and I couldn't leave," Zach said, practically running in. Magic made him look like an older version of Damian so that he could pretend to be Damian Blackwood the Elder, billionaire industrialist, in lieu of Damian's younger 'Damian Black-wood the Third', who was also a dragon, who didn't age as fast as humans and who needed to be more available to fight Unearthly. Seeing Zach with magic on always shocked Damian a little because the older version of himself looked so much like his father, which felt especially poignant now as somewhere in the Realms, his father's legacy was burning. Then Zach slid his hands up his face and out, ripping Mills's magic off himself, showing himself to be a younger werewolf underneath, wintery where Austin was warm, with his own pale skin, black hair, and blue eyes, instead of Damian's golden ones. "What'd I miss?"

Max made a pained sound, and Damian inhaled but couldn't quite speak.

"Damian's sister is here now," Mills said, saving them both. "Injured, in the library, under Austin's care, just like you were not that long ago. And the Realms seem to be in chaos currently, although all mirrors are closed, and I think they need to stay like that," she said, looking pointedly at Damian.

"Agreed," he said. Looking at the Realms again would only be like pouring salt in a wound.

"But," Zach said, hesitating before sitting down, "does her visit count as interference?"

"Technically, her guardian brought her over here, not me," Damian said.

"Does your stepmother traffic in technicalities?" Zach asked, tilting his head, knowing the terms of Damian's arrangement.

"For all I know, she's dead." Damian stopped pacing and dropped himself into a leather chair.

"Is that good or bad?" Zach asked.

"I don't fucking know," Damian grunted.

"We just saw our home obliterated as far as the eye could see," Max growled at the wolf.

"Sorry, sorry," Zach said, holding up his hands. "Although...this does explain why they were trying to kill you, D."

Damian glanced in his direction.

"It's probably a coup," he went on.

Damian inhaled and exhaled. Zach not only pretended to be an older version of him for convenience's sake so that Damian himself could fly under the radar as a distant cousin, but he'd managed to learn a thing or two sitting in on all the cutthroat business meetings Damian got to dodge. "Probably," Damian granted. "Because the same silver stuff Stella knifed you with...that's how Ryana made it here. Her bird went and got a bladder full of it and poured it on the ground to make a reflection big enough to push her through so that I could catch her."

"And you still didn't get me a sample?" Jamison said, coming in last. He sat by Mills, catching one of her hands for a quick squeeze before releasing it. "I was running an experiment in the lab; I couldn't shut it off until it was through."

"What'd you hear?" Mills asked him.

"Enough," Jamison told her. "What do you think's going to happen?" he asked Damian.

Damian spread his hands on the table in front of him. "I'm not entirely sure. If The Snake is dead, the throne's up for anyone to take. Everyone in the Realms knows I've said I'll die before I go back, but that doesn't mean they all believe me. And they probably won't rest until they find Ryana's corpse, to prove the end of my father's line— which they won't because she's here."

"Hmmm," Mills said and pouted thoughtfully.

Jamison looked at her and beamed. "You're going to say something genius aren't you, baby?"

"I am," she agreed, eyes narrowing thoughtfully before turning to Damian. "I don't think it'll be all that hard to fake a corpse. Especially one that's all damaged. Burned, even?"

"Ooh, heavy, I like it," Jamison encouraged her.

"You can do that?" Zach asked.

"I can sure as fuck try," Mills said. "Jamison, can you buy me some tissue culture equipment and growth media? And," she turned to Damian, "I will need an actual sample from your sister so that it passes muster. But between my magic and a thin veneer of her own tissue, I don't see why it wouldn't work."

27

"And then when you're done, we'll just shove it through a mirror, eh?" Max said, hands clenched over a leather chair's back.

"Underneath some rocks. Looked like there were plenty of them falling. Why not?" Mills turned to Damian for permission.

"Yes. Absolutely. As fast as you can...money is no object." Not when it came to possibly curating Ryana's freedom.

"I know," Mills said, looking pleased. She stood and left the room to begin.

"And the rest of us?" Max asked, finally sitting down.

Damian looked around the room one by one. "Keep your guard up."

ANDI SHOWERED SEXILY for five minutes and then gave up because she really, really had to pee.

Only, she couldn't in her bathroom anymore, could she? Because any minute now, Damian would be waltzing back through with a Magic Cat Diner breakfast for her, and she really wished they'd come up with some rules on general privacy.

But that was a thing, she thought, as she furiously slathered herself down, that they could talk about when he got back. Over eggs benedict. Or steak and eggs. Or it would honestly be okay if he came back with scrambled eggs, as long as he also brought really crispy bacon.

She finished up her shower, wrapped a big towel around herself and trotted through her room and down the hall to Sammy's bathroom, to use it as quietly as she could. She set the lid down, flushed, washed her hands ever so softly, and then stepped back into the hall and into Sammy.

"Andi?" her roommate blearily asked, rubbing her face with a hand. "Why're you here?"

"Would you believe I ran out of toilet paper?" Andi asked.

"Completely. Weirdo," Sammy said, brushing past her to go into the bathroom herself. "There's more in the hall closet," she added as she shut the door. "Andi!" she said more loudly, gathering steam. "Oh my God, Andi, I've got to tell you about last night!"

"Can...it...wait?" Andi asked, feeling more like a jerk with each additional word.

"Do you have someplace to be?" Sammy asked, flushing the toilet and pulling the door back open. "Come on now," she chided, wiping at her face with a makeup-remover cloth. "I listened to your whole sex-in-a-Pagani escapade."

"I know, but..." Andi began, but she couldn't very well tell Sammy that things with Damian had sparked again. "Fine. Hit me."

"Okay, so, you're right. Tasha's brother is dumber than a bag of hammers. But...his friend," Sammy began, putting toothpaste on a toothbrush, "is fine as hell. And is getting a Ph.D. They're like friends from childhood because someone saved someone else's dog, I don't even know...but he's dreamy."

Andi hovered just outside the doorway listening to Sammy's story as politely as she could, well aware that her fantabulous breakfast, brought over by her exceedingly attractive new man, might be cooling in her bedroom even now. But Sammy was her friend before Damian was in the picture, and if anything should ever happen to Damian, Sammy would still be her friend after.

She didn't want to think like that, but she couldn't just assume things like Damian did like everything would be okay forever and ever amen. Despite the fact that he'd promised her the world at least three times the prior night. It was nice to think about being happy forever and all, and she was glad that he didn't seem to be bolting out the door, but she'd had twenty-seven years of rather brutal personal proof that bad things happened to good people. And there was still everything with her brother and her uncle to deal with. While amazing sex helped, it wasn't just going to make that shit disappear.

"And then," Sammy continued, "we were finally alone. He pulled out a cigarette, and I was all *you'd better smoke that fast.*"

Andi blinked back to attention. "He smokes? Ugh."

"Don't concentrate on that; concentrate on the fact that I was fucking suave as hell."

Andi grinned at her roommate, who had much the same hair as she had had pre-shower. "You're a dork. A suave-as-hell dork."

"I give up on you. Go back to your room," Sammy said, and shooed her off. Andi laughed and ran back down the hall. "Hey! I thought you were sick!" Sammy called after her.

"I got better!" Andi shouted back.

ANDI LEAPED INTO HER ROOM, hoping to eat, but Damian wasn't there yet. She flopped down on her bed and envied Sammy brushing her teeth. Also, deodorant. Andi sat back up and marched into her bathroom because it was her bathroom, and if he was going to catch her putting deodorant on, well, whatever, it was a thing people did and... nothing. She brushed her teeth in silence and decided to even floss because what the hell, and...still nothing.

"And here I thought breakfast was the most important meal of the day," she muttered to herself, but then, suddenly, she wasn't hungry anymore because there were too many other things to be worried about instead. Like what Damian was off doing and if he was safe. And a stupid niggling fear that he hadn't meant a single thing he'd said the prior night. That even now, he might be out with, oh, say, any one of the women she'd seen him with online before all this—before she'd ever taken the job at his house. The ones who had the hair and the clothes and who already knew what a Pagani was on sight.

Andi went back into her bedroom and was sitting down on her bed when she saw Damian's shoes on the ground. Yes, she'd been in his closet once. She knew he had like fourteen pairs of them, each more expensive than the last, and he could definitely—*definitely*—afford a kajillion more. But seeing them, she couldn't help but think he'd really been meaning to come back.

It was just hard to believe, was all.

Maybe even harder to believe than the fact that he was a dragon.

Or...that Danny was.

She stared up at her apartment's popcorn ceiling. How long did Danny know he was a dragon? Did it start when he disappeared three weeks ago, or before that? Why didn't he tell her? Why'd he run away last night? Was he hiding from her? Protecting her? Or just doing whatever the fuck he wanted to—like he always did?

Why wasn't he here to yell at when she needed him to be?

Andi swept her phone up and texted him quickly: *So, was, like, our entire childhood a lie or just most of it?*

To her surprise, she saw the message go 'read' and the hovering dots of someone about to text her in return: *Not all of it,* he messaged her back. She bit her lip and waited as the dots went on: *I mean, all the times I refused to eat salisbury steak at school—those were real.*

Andi clung to the phone like a life preserver as she was flooded with emotions. He was alive. And somehow now accessible. That made the betrayal of his recent absence sting even worse. She texted back: *What the fuck, Danny!*

I just figured if they were going to make a meatloaf-type thing, they could put it in between buns and call it a hamburger without the gross gravy, you know?

DANNY, Andi typed back, as he sent a laughing emoji over. *I'M GLAD YOU'RE ALIVE BUT I'M ALSO SO PISSED AT YOU RIGHT NOW.*

Yeah, I figured. Want to talk about it?

YES. Where?

The dots hovered again, and if Danny didn't message her back, if he was just playing her, she was going to figure out a way to strangle him with her mind—use-the-force style.

Mom's, he finished.

Andi bit her lips again, hating that she had to ask it, but needing to: *Is it safe?*

Of course, it is. Now?

Now, she agreed, dropping her phone to run for her closet.

ANDI TROTTED down the front stairs of her apartment fifteen minutes later with wet hair in the crisp autumn chill and still didn't make the bus. She watched it drive off with a groan and dove into the warmth of Eumie's bakery to wait for the next one.

"Andi?" Eumie said with surprise after clocking her arrival. "You're up...and it's daylight?" They stepped out from behind the counter to give her a hug. The nonbinary baker had become one of Andi's best friends after she and Sammy rented the apartment upstairs a few years back.

"I know...I thought the light would burn me too," Andi said, waving one of her hands at the outside world. "Can I get a tea to go? And some butter cookies?"

Eumie winced lightly. "Thinking about your brother?" They knew those were his favorite.

"Kind of...sort of," Andi partially confessed. "I'm going to see my mom. I figured since it's daytime, I should get some good daughter points in, and I've got fifteen minutes until the next bus." Andi slid herself and her bag into her normal spot and fidgeted with her phone as she watched Eumie go through the saloon doors into the back of the bakery where the magic happened. She wanted to text her brother and tell him she'd be late, but maybe it was okay for him to just wait on her for once in his entire life.

Plus, she was worried if he didn't respond, she'd think he'd abandoned her again. There were only so many times she was willing to put her heart through that particular wringer in one twenty-four-hour period.

"So, how was that furniture delivery?" Eumie shouted out to her from the back.

"What?" Andi shouted back, distractedly.

"You know! The one you got around four a.m. this morning!" Eumie shouted back with a wicked chuckle, and Andi groaned.

"Eumie!"

"It's not my fault the ceiling is thin...hang on, we're out of chamomile...how did that happen? I mean, maybe if the furniture you got delivered wasn't quite so heavy," Eumie went on with a snicker. Andi flushed, shaking her head, and saw someone familiar on the stairs outside, walking up to her apartment's level.

Elsa, her uncle's Nordic looking secretary. She'd recognize the ice-blonde hair and sneer of disdain anywhere.

Andi grabbed her bag and bolted into the back of the bakery, leaving the saloon doors swinging behind her.

"It's not an emergency...I found some!" Eumie announced at seeing her, holding a half-empty tea tin, before clocking the emotions on her face. "Wait, what's wrong?"

"Just...someone I don't want to see outside."

Eumie rose up in height, their dough-kneading slouch straightening, and it felt like they'd become a foot taller. They reached for a rolling pin. "Furniture man?"

"No. A friend of my uncle's."

"I thought you liked your uncle?"

"I did too. It's a story I don't have time for right now." Andi heard the woman above knock on her front door. She knew Sammy would never let Elsa in their apartment again; she'd call the cops first, for sure, and she hadn't told Sammy where she was going this morning, besides. "Can you let me out the back? And if that woman comes in —the tall, angry-looking blonde—tell her that you don't even know who I am?"

"Of course," Eumie said, pulling aside so that Andi could run through the corridor of supplies and down the hallway for the alley with Eumie on her heels, a bag of pastries in hand. "Hey," Eumie said, pressing the bag to her, catching her before she could bolt away. "You know you don't have to do everything alone, right?"

"I know," Andi said. "And, thank you," she added, before bouncing up on her toes to give Eumie a quick, fierce hug before running down the alley, shoving the paper bag of treats into her bag as she ran.

ANDI DARTED through the maze of alleys behind their buildings, lurking in the shadows on the farthest side as she summoned a ride with her phone, and then threw herself down in the back seat after it arrived.

Why was Elsa visiting her? Her uncle still had her phone number and clearly knew her address. He could apologize on his own.

But what could he really apologize for? For murdering other people? She wasn't going to listen to that—not from his mouth or his secretary's. If everything Damian had said about Hunters was true—if they were cruising her hospital looking for shifters to murder, to use their bones and skin for magic—*Jesus Christ!* There was no way she could forgive that. Not ever.

But why hadn't she known? Why couldn't she have guessed? She felt like every neighbor in a true crime show, ever. *Oh, he seemed so normal! He was so nice! I would've let him babysit my kids!* And to think, he'd tried to set her up with David. Andi had to bite her lips to not want to barf.

Her brother had better tell her straight. At least spotting Elsa at her apartment likely meant that her uncle didn't know she was meeting up with him, because if Danny tried to pull the three of them having a surprise family reunion graveside, Andi was going to explode.

She caught a glance of herself in the car's rearview and saw the unhappy way she was frowning. She wondered if somewhere Damian was looking at her, too, even though he'd promised not to. And if he was okay. Because there had to be a reason he hadn't gotten in touch with her yet. She dawdled her phone on her knee as the driver took the final turn in, and she directed him to the back of the cemetery.

From last night through this morning was a lot to juggle. And the longer she was away from Damian, the more everything had this crumbling sand feeling like she couldn't hold onto anything real, no matter how hard she tried.

The driver stopped where she told him to, in front of a series of gently rolling hills dotted with tombstones. "I'm so sorry for your loss."

"Thanks," she said, hopping out of the car with her bag. "Me too."

ANDI STRODE up the hill toward the plot Uncle Lee had picked out for her mother. This was the nicest cemetery in town—a beautiful, gently sloped park with neatly trimmed grass and large trickling fountains so that you heard the sound of falling water no matter where you went. One entire hill of it was dotted with tombstones primarily written in Chinese, which was where her mother was. Uncle Lee'd been the one to handle all of her mother's bills and affairs after she'd gotten sick. He was the only one who could afford to. And since her mother had never expressed any strong desire to be buried one place over another, Andi didn't see any point in fighting with him, especially as he'd picked a place with such nice feng shui and plenty of ghost-neighbors to play mahjong with her.

She knew where her mother's red marble tombstone was by heart. It had carved dragons around the edges and a sepia-toned portrait of her mother that Uncle Lee picked out to have displayed on it, enameled onto the cold dark stone. As Andi walked up the hill, she saw the wind catch and press a jacket against a slender man standing where she'd stood so many times herself, making his black hair spike and flutter. He was at least half a foot taller than she was, but she felt even shorter behind him, standing on the hill's slight slope.

"About time," he said, as she came to a stop.

Her heart jumped into her throat. "Sorry, missed the bus," she said, waiting for him to turn around—part of her afraid that he might be a ghost, too.

He slowly turned, and it was really Danny, flashing her the same grin she'd seen from him for as long as she could remember, the one that said, *Hey, I'm about to get into trouble, wanna help?* She flew at him without thinking, and he caught her in a hug, picking her up and spinning her around before setting her down again.

"I can't believe you still don't know how to drive."

"And I can't believe you can turn into a fucking dragon, so hey, we're even." She caught his head between her hands. "What the fuck, Danny!"

He laughed like it was nothing. "You really just want to jump in the deep end?"

"Yeah. Or we could back up to the ten thousand dollars of bail you owe me."

"Jesus, Andi," Danny said with an eye roll, bringing back every similar moment of his exasperation with her during their childhood.

"How the fuck did you think I would take this?" Andi stepped back to look him up and down. "First, I thought you ran out on me; then, I thought you were in trouble; then, I thought you were dead, and now.... I don't even know what I saw last night, Danny." She caught his hands in her own. "I need you to tell me everything from the beginning. Please."

His brown eyes searched hers. "I'm sorry. I didn't get a choice in how it went down. The timing was bad, they couldn't have me go to prison, and then I never should've called you. It was just a moment of weakness during one of my tests—"

"I don't understand any of that; back up and slow down," she pleaded.

He swallowed, looking down at her. "Andi, I'm not sure how much is safe to tell you, honestly."

"Does Uncle know you're here?"

"No. If he did, he'd murder me."

Andi frowned up at him. "Are you helping him?"

"He's...showing me things."

"What the fuck does he know?"

Danny gave her a soft smile. "A lot. You'd be surprised. More than all those bullshit stories he told us on holidays, that's for sure."

Andi felt like she was hovering on the edge of a knife, and the longer she waited, the sharper it got. "But did you know that he's killing people?"

Danny's jaw clenched, and he nodded slowly. "Not like a lot of people—"

Andi danced three steps back, coming perilously close to stepping on her mother's neighbor. "What?" she sputtered.

Her brother inhaled and exhaled slowly. "If you'd seen the things that I've seen now, Andi—they're these creatures from other worlds, and they don't belong here. They're not like us. And they'll kill all of us if we don't kill them first."

Andi stared at her brother, aghast. "Do you hear the words coming out of your mouth? You sound so evil right now. I don't know what to do with you. And...what's this 'like us' bullshit when I freaking saw *you* change?"

Danny stood up straighter. "That's different. I'm special. I'm one of the good guys." Andi just stared at him, stunned, as he continued. "I know it's hard for you to believe, but it's true!" He hit his chest with his hand.

"Danny," Andi began, waving him down. "I love you. No matter what. I do. But you were going to jail for stealing cars. I'm not saying I'm perfect; we used to go out and steal money from people playing pool together, remember? But like...you're a lot of things, and some of them are positive qualities, but *good* is stretching the truth a little, don't you think?"

"Oh, so only Andi-the-martyr gets to be the nurse out there saving lives, but when I want to be the good one, it's impossible for me to change?"

Andi crossed her arms. "Well, I did see you changing last night."

"Do you believe this?" Danny said, twisting to include their mother's portrait in their conversation. "I told you she'd be mad at me."

"Don't even," Andi said. "Mom would be mad at you, too, if she were here, Danny."

Danny wheeled back to face her, tilting his head. "Yeah, so, that's where you're wrong." He leaned over behind the tombstone and pulled out a plastic bag, handing it over to her. "I've gotta go."

Andi blinked. "Wait...what?"

"I still have to be careful. I'm not in control all the way yet. I shouldn't be alone very long—especially outdoors." He put his hands in his pockets and started down the hill.

"But I still have questions!" Andi shouted after him.

He shrugged. "There's no point in me answering them if you don't bother to listen."

"Danny!" Andi yelled, reprimanding him with his own name, and he looked back at her for a still moment, recreating every time she'd ever been disappointed in him in the past. She reached into her bag to grab Eumie's pastries and threw them at him, to land at his feet. "They're your favorite, dammit!"

He picked them up, then turned and kept walking.

THREE

Andi sagged onto her heels just off to the side of her mother's grave, holding the bag Danny'd given her across her lap, her whole body trembling.

After everything she'd been through—that he'd put her through!—how *dare* he. And fuck him in the neck for being right about her listening because she shouldn't have to listen to him when he was wrong in the first place!

Andi tightly grabbed the thing inside the plastic bag and went to tear into it as her phone buzzed. She yanked it out of her bag and swiped the screen open.

Where are you? It was Damian. She put a hand to her face. In her anger over her brother, she'd almost forgotten that she needed to be angry at him, too. For either ditching her or worrying her, take her pick.

At the Morganhoff Cemetery.

Are you okay? he asked her.

Andi stared at the phone in her lap, unsure how to answer. *Maybe,* and then she quickly added, *Are you?*

The dots on the screen danced for an exceptionally long time before she got the simple answer: *No.* Her heart sank into her stomach as he continued. *Can you give me twenty minutes to get there?*

His house in the Briars was at least a thirty-minute drive away. Andi looked around at the rolling greenery and fountains. Maybe he really was going to fly. *Sure,* she responded. *I'm in the back. Blue coat, in front of a red marble tombstone.*

I'll find you, don't worry. Wait for me.

Andi stared at her phone for a moment longer before putting it back into her pocket and returning her attention to the package in her lap. It was in a plastic grocery bag, and if Danny'd brought her something stupid like a stuffed bear in an attempt to get back on her good side—or candy.... She sighed, exhausted by the idea of being angry at him again.

She peeled the plastic bag open and found another bag inside, only this one was made of silk. Andi jammed the trash into her pocket and flipped the silk over. It was heavy, and there was a roped frog-knot lock on the other side. She undid the loop and let the object inside slide out.

It was a photo album—one she was sure she'd never seen before. She knew because when her mother died, it'd been her job to go through all of her mother's things. Danny had ditched her for most of that, too. The cover was coarsely grained leather, and inside were sheaves of photos placed in between cardboard pages and cellophane.

Andi sighed and flipped through them at random. A lot of old photos. What good would looking through them do? Make her miss her mom more? She already missed her enough. It was hard not to feel like if her mom had been around that nothing bad would've happened to Danny. Even if Uncle Lee had still been a murderous bastard, he could've kept that to himself, and they could've just been at a cordial arm's-length red-envelope status.

Andi looked instead at the sepia-toned woman on the tombstone in front of her. She didn't remember that photo either; she assumed it was just one Uncle Lee had laying around somewhere, seeing as he'd never asked her for one.

People used to tell her that she and her mother looked alike, but Andi never saw it. Her mother was always much more beautiful than she was. Her mother always cared more, for one. She never left the house without makeup on and always had her hair coiffed up just so. Andi could count on two hands the times she'd ever seen her mother's hair down, and most of those were at the end in the hospital when they both knew she wasn't going to make it out. She'd helped her mother braid it into one long plait. It was so strange for her mother to have kept her hair during chemo that every single nurse had to comment on it—so much so, that Andi was worried her mother was getting the wrong drugs, but by then, she was a nurse and could read the labels herself.

Not only that, but her mother had had a perfect birthmark— somewhere between a Cindy Crawford and a Madonna—just a dot over the corner of her smile. When it moved, you knew she was genuinely happy and not just smiling because it was expected of the "nice Chinese lady" or whatever hell else her neighbors and coworkers were calling her this week.

Andi reached out to touch her mother's portrait on the stone. "I wish you were here, Mom." Because if she were, she'd somehow make everything better.

"Andi," called a familiar voice from behind her.

She turned to look over her shoulder to find Damian there. He was in a suit as black as his hair, with a white shirt and a black tie, striding up the hill with ease. Something about seeing him again— and seeing him here, of all places—made her chest so tight it hurt, like her ribs didn't fit her anymore. She stood up to give herself room to breathe, tucking the album under one arm.

Damian was careful not to walk on any of the other graves as he made his way to her side, and then he stood beside her, making to catch her hand with his. She let him and felt the way his bigger, slightly rougher, hand held hers, their fingers intertwining naturally like he'd already been standing there the entire time.

"Damian, this is my mom," Andi said lightly. "Mom, this is Damian."

Damian surprised her by making a precise bow in the direction of her mother's tombstone, as though he'd done this sort of thing before. "I am honored to be in your presence," he said, sounding one hundred percent sincere, and Andi realized that maybe he was. Did dragons have ghosts? Souls? Religion? She would have to add all of those things onto her list of Things to Eventually Ask Him.

He turned to look down at her with his golden eyes. "I can see the resemblance. You're both very beautiful."

"My mom was prettier," Andi said. Damian inhaled to fight her, but she put a finger on his lips to stop him. "You can't argue with me here, or she'll hear you." His lips curved into a smile behind her touch as she took him in. "Why is your hair wet?"

"Because I didn't want to meet you—or your mother—without showering." There was a tightness in his shoulders that hadn't been there when he'd left her that morning. It made her want to knead it out of them, to turn him back into the person he'd been when he'd seemed like he was happy.

Andi took a small step back but didn't let go of his hand. "Why didn't you come back?"

He exhaled deeply, and the tension around him increased like the pressure change before a storm. "Duty called," he said, then his lips pressed together in a thoughtful line. "I messaged you as soon as I felt I safely could. I hope I didn't worry you."

She gave him a small frown. "No. I mean, I only partially thought you'd died. And then I was a little mad at you for not telling me that you died, I think."

"And so, you came here to head me off at the pass?" he teased, glancing around at their surroundings.

Might as well admit the truth. "No, I came here to see my brother."

Damian's attention whipped back to her. "Why didn't you tell me?"

Andi blinked. "Did you really just ask that?"

She watched his jaw grind as it clenched and unclenched. "I suppose that was unfair."

"Pretty much. I mean, if you're too busy to tell me what's going on with you, then," she said, looking out over the rolling hillsides, "I didn't want to distract you from...world saving or whatever it was with my small problems."

Damian abruptly focused all of his attention on her, and for the first time since he'd joined her, she felt like he was fully present in that way that was almost too much for her to handle. "Your problems *are* my problems, from here on out," he said, looking at her as though he was willing her to believe. Andi's heart beat in her throat. No, the rhythm took over her whole body, pounding so hard she could feel it down to her wrists and ankles as she pulled both her hands away from his. "What?" he asked her, confused.

She took a moment to gather herself, free of him. "You can't just say things like that, Damian," she explained, shaking her head, unwilling to meet his gaze. How could he not hear the words that came out of his mouth? How could he not know?

"Why not?" he asked, sounding pained.

Mother, I'm so sorry you're having to watch this, Andi thought, and made herself look at him again before saying aloud, "Do you really not understand?" His expression was so bewildered that she went on. "Have you ever said anything like that to a girl before?"

It was his turn to shake his head. "No."

Andi closed her eyes for a long moment before responding. "I googled you, Damian, so don't you dare lie to me, plus you swore—"

"No," he said again, more firmly.

"All those other women. All the photos, all the smiles? You were playing them all along?"

"Or they were trying to play me," he said, his voice low. "I've been told I'd be quite a catch, but I never once promised any of them anything, Andi." He licked his lips slowly as he seemed to search for the right words, staring at her with smoldering intent. "I've never done this before, but I want to...with you."

His eyes were hot on her, and she felt irradiated by his attention. It made the little hairs on her arms prick up, and a shiver crawled over her scalp in a rush. When it was done sparking over her, it settled in her hips like red-hot coals. "Want to...what?" Everything else in her life was so surreal at this point. If he really wanted something—wanted her—she needed to hear the words.

"Be in a relationship. With you."

Andi crossed her arms and swallowed, shielding her heart with the solid thump of the photo album. "You've never been in a relationship with a human?"

His head tilted as he tried to read her. "Not with anyone."

The wind picked up and pushed locks of her hair toward him like they were reaching out. "And what if I'm not ready for that?" she asked, then bit her lips. "I know what I said last night about you not leaving, and I meant that. I like having you around, but I've also known you less than two weeks." She was now looking anywhere but at his face, because she was scared of the earnestness she'd find there. It was too much, too soon—too insane, even for her—which was saying something.

"I know," he agreed slowly, then he stepped forward, closing the space between them. "But I know everything about you, Andi. Things that no one else does. And I don't want to say that you can't live without me because I know you're strong and you can. But I can tell from the way your pulse jumps at your throat when I'm nearby that you don't want to. Not yet."

She closed her eyes. He wasn't wrong. But that didn't make it right. "It doesn't matter; you still can't say things like that," she told him. *No matter how easy it is for you to read me and somehow know what I want before I do.*

"Why not? If I mean them?" he asked kindly.

"Because it's cruel." She bowed her head and breathed the musty scent of the photo album in deep. "Because if you've never been in a relationship before, statistically speaking, I'm just breaking you in for the next girl."

"Andi," he said, and she could hear the smile in it. "I'm a dragon. I'm not bound by statistics." His hands reached for her jaw and gently raised her head up to face his golden gaze. "Can I take you back to my place?"

Old cautious Andi would've fought him, but there was a chance that Elsa was still staking out her apartment, and who the fuck was she kidding, even if he said utterly ridiculous things and made promises he couldn't possibly keep, she didn't want to leave him just yet. She nodded slowly against his hands, and he smiled, releasing her, sliding one of his hands down her arm and back to her hand, leaving a fresh trail of fire in its wake. "Let's go," he said, pulling her to his side.

Damian gave her mother's grave another courtly bow and then led her confidently down the hill heading to another part of the cemetery, with his arm looped around her waist. She was walking fast to stay up with him, then he noticed, slowing down to her pace without her asking him to. His hand on her hip felt hot even through her coat, as it did where she leaned against him, all the places where they touched. She rested her cheek against him briefly and felt him pull her tight.

Then he took them up another hill, and she paused to crane back. She was intimately familiar with this cemetery; she'd been here often enough. "Where are you parked?"

"I didn't. I was in a rush," he said, like that explained things.

She stared up at him, doing origami in her mind, trying to imagine him transitioning to fly. Would she need to run half a block away to not get squished? "I'm not sure if I should ask where or how."

He chuckled. She felt it reverberate in him. "Michael's buried here. The cemetery's only open during the day. Sometimes I wanted to come at night, so I had to find another way in."

"Oh," Andi gasped. Michael was Damian's friend who'd died doing the exact same thing Damian did. Like whatever he'd bolted from her this morning to do. And even though he was still right here beside her, she felt worried for him all over again. Damian led her to the edge of a shallow pond, bounded by cement pavers, and stopped. "I'm sorry for your loss," she said, knowing it was never enough, because how many people had told her that exact same thing before?

"I promise you, there's nothing for you to be sorry for." He moved to stand in front of her, on the large stones surrounding the pool. He reached a hand out, and she took it without hesitation. "I'd like to tell you about him sometime."

"I'd like that too."

He smiled down at her, easy, earnest, disarming. "Can I pick you up?"

Andi blinked and looked around herself quickly. "Why?"

"Just say yes again," he counseled.

"Yes?" she guessed. He swooped her up against his chest like she weighed nothing, her bag swinging as she clutched the photo album to her chest. She remembered the time he'd run through his house with her to throw her in a pool, then realized there was quite a large body of water behind him. "No...no, no, no...it's too cold for that, Damian—"

"I'll keep you warm." He pressed her tightly to his chest. "Hold your breath. Trust me," he said and stepped forward into the water.

EVERYTHING WENT BLACK. She expected water to rush up and leave her sputtering—or for Damian to be standing in half a foot of mud—but what happened was that she couldn't see anything around her, and she didn't even have a sense of how big the darkness was. It could've stretched on for miles in all directions.

But what she did know was that it wanted her. It was hungry, thirsty, lonely, all the "y" words that meant that you wanted something you would never get to have—that made you angry with its lack. Freezing hands reached out to grab her, and she screamed as Damian pulled her close against the radiating heat of his chest, and then they were somehow through, stepping out into a room she recognized at his house.

The one with the green velvet walls and black leather furniture—not all of which was designed for comfort. Functional benches with what looked like tie-downs, ornate couches with swooping scrolled backs, and off to one side a made bed that looked loosely caged by metal.

"What the fuck...and how?" Andi gasped, looking around as Damian set her down. She was still clutching the photo album to her chest.

"If you're strong enough magically, you can jump through any reflection that will fit you. The pond was reflective enough for me, especially coming back home."

Andi took a step, appreciating the solidity of the ground and the warmth of the room, then looked around again and back at the mirror, reflecting them both behind her. "And out of all the mirrors in your house, you picked here?" she asked. She supposed that walking into his sexy times dungeon wasn't any worse than walking into his bedroom, which she knew had mirrors lining one entire wall, but still.

Damian looked around and snorted. "I didn't think of that. I just didn't want to be in my bedroom right now. Too many mirrors there...too many memories."

"So that's too many, but this one is just right?" she questioned, gesturing at the huge rectangular one they'd arrived through.

He walked over to it, grabbed a corner of its frame and flipped it around, revealing a massive plush leather-covered X on the other side, with bolts up and down the margins to chain someone down. She blanched, and he laughed. "It's a safety measure. No one wants to get hit by broken glass."

"I don't think I want to get hit by anything," she said, looking around the room. If this was who he was and what he needed, this was not her. She was adventurous, yes, but if this was some kind of lifetime compatibility commitment thing, all the more reason to keep him at arm's length.

Except for all the times when she wanted him a lot...a lot closer.

"I would never do anything to you that you didn't want me to, princess," he said, watching her like he always did.

Andi went over to what might as well have been a weapons rack and lifted something that looked very much like a bullwhip up in horror. "Good, because this shit is off the table."

Damian chuckled, taking the implement from her and setting it back down. "The only thing I want on a table right now is food of some sort if you're still hungry."

"Please," she agreed. Between this morning and the cemetery, she was running on adrenaline and fumes. And she was still carrying the photo album. Uncle Lee had to've given it to Danny. Danny wasn't nearly responsible enough to keep something so old around. He'd have forgotten it three moves ago—or at an ex-girl-friend's.

How could someone so irresponsible, and with such a long rap sheet, think that they were the hero now? Was her brother truly so unaware?

"I'll be right back," Damian said, walking for a door that matched the wall behind it.

"You mean it this time?" she called after him.

"Absolutely," he promised, disappearing.

Andi watched him go and looked around. "Just what've you gotten yourself into?" she asked herself before gingerly sitting on a bench as though it was spring-loaded and might trap her.

Damian ducked into the hall outside, heading for the stairway, pleased in a way he couldn't express to be in Andi's presence again. It just felt right—reverberatingly, meaningfully, right.

Mates, his dragon said with a pleased sigh. *Assuming your appetites don't scare her off.*

They're yours, too. Don't lie, Damian thought back at the beast. *And she's braver than you give her credit for.* He went into the library and found Austin still at Ryana's bedside, Grimalkin still wound about the bird. The cat's eyes opened briefly at his arrival, then fell back closed again with a loud purr.

"Any change?" he asked the werewolf keeping watch.

"No."

"Is that good or bad?"

"Hard to say," Austin said, shaking his head deeply. "I'll be happier when she wakes up."

"Me too," Damian agreed. His sister was the only one who could tell them what'd happened running up to the final moments of his old palace's destruction, what forces had been at play, and if his stepmother, The Snake, was still alive.

"You smell like the nurse," Austin said, without recrimination.

He wondered, for the first time, if the wolf scented her like he did —her apples, caramel, and the sea. "Her brother reached out to her this morning. I brought her here for her own safety," Damian told him.

Austin smirked. "Is that what they're calling it these days?" Damian groaned as Austin went on. "I'm just blowing off steam. After what we saw in the mirrors, you deserve to be happy. No matter how fleeting."

Damian put a hand on Austin's shoulder and squeezed. "I appreciate that."

The werewolf reached up to clap his hand and then waved him away. "Go. Have fun. I'll tell Grim to get you if I need you."

"Thanks. And...anything happens here—good or bad—you let me know."

"Will do," Austin said, and Damian went into the kitchen.

WHILE HE COULDN'T COOK PERSONALLY, that didn't mean that others couldn't. Jamison enjoyed cooking the most out of all of them, and he usually made sure the kitchen was stocked, via Grim, and his own electronic connection to all sorts of delivery services. Damian ran through the cupboard and fridge and created a tray full of food-like items that he thought Andi might like or at least would tide her over until he could get her something that she really did. He brought it back upstairs, pushing the door behind him open with his back.

"Hold this, please," he asked her, and she took it from him, so he could go down the hall and liberate a non-leather-covered coffee table from another room, bringing it back for them to use. He placed it in front of her and sat down on the ground. She set the tray down on it before joining him with a laugh.

"Peanut butter and jelly sandwiches? In here?" she asked, glancing around again.

"Unorthodox, I know. But there's fruit, too. I wasn't kidding earlier about not being able to cook. The magic cat is indisposed," Damian said, pushing the tray at her. "Eat something, please."

She tore into an orange, her nimble fingers piercing the skin and tearing pieces off expertly, and he had never wanted to be a piece of fruit so badly before. And then he noted the leather-bound book that she'd been carrying. She'd placed it between them when she'd sat down. "What is that?"

Andi sighed. "My brother gave it to me this morning. It's an old photo album of my mother's." He reached for it, and she put her hand on it to stop him. "Can we not?" she asked him earnestly, the same as he had not long ago in his car, regarding Michael. Emotions he couldn't read streaked across her face, culminating in a pervasive sense of sorrow, and the edge of the salt water he'd scented on her last night. "It's just going to make me sad."

After the morning he'd had grappling with his past, he understood. "Of course," he told her.

"Thank you," she said, pulling herself back together again, hiding the album beneath the table. "So, how was your morning?" she asked him brightly instead, clearly forcing the conversation forward.

If only he hadn't promised to always tell her the truth. "Also sad," he admitted.

Her eyes widened, and she reached for his hand in sympathy. She did it so quickly that he was tempted to feel special until he remembered that as a nurse holding people's hands was probably part of her job. "What happened?"

"I watched my old home being torn apart." He knew places couldn't die, but that's what it felt like, watching the towers of his youth turned to rubble, and he felt his throat start to choke. "I opened a mirror and basically saw my childhood being destroyed."

She looked at him with the same confusion he felt. "Why?"

"I'm still unsure, although war's the best guess. In the Realms, if you live in war, you die in war. One of the many reasons why I left." He concentrated on the way her hand felt in his—small, smooth, and cool, in comparison—and marveled that she was here. He moved to hold her hand in both of his so that she couldn't leave him—not now, nor ever. "I knew I was never going back, but still."

She nodded in response. "Yeah. I know. Not one hundred percent the same, but you expect the past to be how you remembered it, and when it moves on you, it's disconcerting." Her lips twisted to one side in thought. "It's like you're climbing up a staircase your whole life, and one day you turn around, and it's not there behind you."

He knew she wasn't just talking about his problems. "An apt analogy."

"Was anyone hurt?" she asked tentatively.

"My sister."

"Damian," Andi gasped, pulling herself up to her knees. "Is she okay?"

He thought of Ryana, ensconced in his library. At least she wasn't in the Realms anymore. "For right now, yes."

She sank back a little, still eyeing him, wary on his behalf, and he wondered if this was what her patients felt like at the hospital—cared for, protected—and it moved him in an unfamiliar way. "Are you all right?" she gently asked.

That was such a good question. "I don't know yet, really." He squeezed her hand in his own and stroked a thumb across her wrist. "But I'm better now that you're here...if that's not too mean to say."

She smiled softly at him. "I think that's just the right amount of mean." Then she dramatically looked around the room before pointedly returning her attention to him. "And probably the least mean thing in this place," she said with a snort. "Do people really want all this?"

He knew what she was really after. "By which you mean, do I?" Damian let go of her hand and rocked back to consider her fully. She was biting her lower lip in the way that tormented him. Her dark eyes were wide, and her pulse picked up as she waited for his response, just as fearful that he'd scare her as if he wouldn't. He purposefully leaned forward with slow intent to brush an eyelash off her cheek and felt her shiver at his touch. "I don't need all of it all the time, no. But I do like to be in control. It's how I'm wired. Which is why I need you to give me a safeword now. Even if we never use any of this. I need you to know you have an out with me...always."

Andi went from hovering attentively to laughter. "Oh my God, you're just like Sammy."

He grinned. "Well, I haven't serial killed you yet, have I? So maybe your roommate has some good ideas."

She swept another glance around the room. "Okay. Fine. Same one then, so I won't forget it. Rambunctious."

"Three syllables? You're sure?" His eyebrows rose. "I mean, I do intend on rendering you speechless as often as I can, so that's a lot."

She flushed and laughed again. "I'm sure, and trust me, once you get to know me better, you'll have a hard time shutting me up." She knelt beside him, her hands in her lap, her head tilted up, breasts subtly forward. He was busy making the mistake of thinking she was tamer than she knew when she asked, "So, what's yours?"

He paused. "My what?"

"Safeword."

Damian chuckled. "Why on earth would I need one?"

She pouted impudently. "Because I want you to know that you have an out with me, too."

He watched her and found her utterly serious. "That's not how this works, Andi."

"Says the man who's never been in a relationship before?" she asked archly, but he knew she was teasing from the expression on her face. Then she stood, eyeing him through downcast eyes, and there was something regal in her expression—the angle where her neck met her jaw and the straight sweep of her hair. The way she came into her own as if living in her space more fully, just by standing over him, and deep inside, he felt his dragon begin to stir.

"Give me one, or I'll make you give me one," she demanded, like a queen.

Damian rocked back, bemused and unsure where this was going, but entirely willing to play along. "I would like to see you try, princess."

"All right, then," she said. "Stand up."

He contemplated fighting her, then wondered if that was what it was like to be her, all the time.

It's hardly a fight when she's so tiny, his dragon said, watching their exchange through him.

True, Damian agreed, but said, "Your wish is my command," as he stood for her.

"You're a dragon, not a genie," she said, then grabbed his arm, pulling him over to a bench with latches on either side of its back. "Sit down," she directed him, then went to rummage around behind him, returning later with chained leather handcuffs.

It was hard not to ask her why she was doing what she was

doing, and he wondered if this was something that she liked, or that she'd read in books or seen on TV, as he let her buckle his wrists to the bench behind him.

"Do you feel safer with me tied up?" he asked her honestly.

"No. Because it's not about safety with us, remember?" She stood up, surveyed her handiwork, and then began taking off her shirt. Damian's breath hitched as he watched the fabric trail up her stomach, exposing warm brown skin and more than a few marks from the night before. She was so fucking edible, dammit. His cock thumped inside his suit slacks, and he leaned forward without thinking only to feel the buckles around his wrists stop him.

"I'm not even done yet," she taunted, dropping her shirt to the floor and then unclasped her bra. "I'm sorry there's no sexy dance. I do like dancing; it's just that I'm nervous right now."

"Don't be," he murmured, watching her slide the bra's straps down her arms, revealing the small raindrop shaped breasts it'd hidden, each dotted with nipples the size of his thumbprint, tipping up at being exposed to air, and he bit back a groan.

She grinned at him impishly, then went down to her knees in front of him, and started working at his belt buckle. His cock reacted each time she brushed it, bobbing for her as it filled with ache, and he watched her work, feeling tortured until her fingers unbuttoned his slacks, and she unzipped him and reached inside the elastic of his boxer briefs.

"Andi," he whispered, feeling her take him in her hand, bowing his head down over hers.

She pushed the fabric down enough to see him, so they could both watch her holding him there. He saw his cock turn dusky red with need, and as she started to stroke, he moaned, feeling himself flex against her hand as if he could draw her closer, faster.

She kept one hand working him as the rest of her rose up, pulling roughly at his shirt so that she could send her other hand searching underneath it, running her fingers along his skin, before kissing down his stomach until he knew where she'd end up and she looked wickedly up at him.

"Say it," she taunted him.

Damian chuckled deeply. "Never."

She pouted, then swiped her thumb over the precum pearling on his tip, swirling it in a gentle circle over his head, and he hissed in desire. "Not even if I do this?" she asked.

"No," he told her flatly while smiling.

"Hmmm, then what about this?" she asked, keeping eye contact with him as she pulled his cock out toward her, parting her perfect lips to take just the head of him in her mouth so she could follow the path her thumb had just taken with her tongue.

I like this game very much, his dragon told him. He didn't respond to it, but he gave Andi the reward of a ragged breath and watched her smile mischievously around him, as she started to suck his cock in earnest, her head framed neatly by the crisp lines ironed into his black slacks. Her mouth was so warm and soft, and as she took him deeper, he filled it and could feel himself rubbing at the back of her throat like she was fit to swallow him, as her hand kept working at his shaft, and another sank lower to cup his balls.

"Andi...goddamn," he got out, and she stopped everything, slurping off of him and looking up expectantly, kneeling between his legs with her pert breasts between his knees that he was torturously not allowed to touch.

"Your safeword is a curse word?" she asked. "I don't know a lot about these sorts of things, but that seems like an odd choice."

He made a sound between a growl and a groan. "No, my safe-word is not a curse word."

She gave him the same look she'd given Rax before she'd rooked him for a two-million-dollar car. "I'd better suck harder then," she said breathlessly, and Damian knew he was in trouble.

Good trouble. The best possible kind.

She took him back into her mouth and bobbed her head down as she stroked him, and her fingertips teased against the seam of his sack, and his hips pulsed up to meet her of their own accord. He was panting, ready to come like a date in the back of a car on prom night, but that didn't matter because she made him endlessly hard. He would always want to fuck her, to want her, like this, or any other way she'd let him.

"Andi...I'm going to cum," he warned her in guttural tones, and then she moaned. He felt it reverberate around him, and that's what set him off—the thought of her pleased to please him, wanting to take what he had to give. He made an anguished sound and pulsed, hard, feeling himself jet inside her, wave after wave of pleasure reeling through him and out into her waiting throat, all the while her purring around him. She didn't stop until he was finished. Her one hand released his balls gently while the other held his shaft still as she pulled off of it, not losing a single drop. She sank back onto her heels, her lips slightly swollen from the effort of taking him, and gave him a cat-that-ate-the-canary smile before speaking again.

"So, what you're saying is that cum is your safeword? I guess I respect your non-traditional ways," she said, and he leaned forward, breaking the chains behind him easily.

"That's it," he said, as she squealed at his freedom. He swept forward and picked her up. "I have a cage in here somewhere, I'm going to put you in it."

She laughed and fought against him. "Damian!"

"You have a safeword now. Use it if you want to," he said, putting her over his shoulder and biting at her hip through her jeans on the way to the bed in the back. When he got there, he tossed her into it and watched her bounce. "Jeans. Off. Now. Underwear too. I can't be destroying all your clothes."

"Less laundry, though?" she laughed, working at the button of her denim. She got it vaguely loose as he pulled her shoes off for her, casting them aside, then grabbed the cuffs of her jeans to yank. She squirmed free as he did so, breathing heavily, and then she was fully naked on the bed ahead of him. He took a moment to coolly appreciate her perfection—the pout of her lips, the way her dark eyes watched everything, taking all of him in, the way her breasts slightly pulled to the side because she was on her back—waiting. His cock was already throbbing again, and he reached into his slacks to give it a stroke as his eyes slid down the slight rise of her belly to between her legs where her heat began. The air around him was thick with her delectably heady scent, and he wanted to breathe in more.

He mounted the bed, kicking off his own shoes as he did so. "Grab hold of the bars over your head."

"Are you going to cuff me to them?" she asked, her voice rising in alarm.

"No, princess, but you're going to want to hold on," he said, and came for her, freeing his erection.

CHAPTER

FOUR

S he couldn't blame him for anything after the way she'd tortured him. She did let go of the bars to grab his head and bring his mouth to hers as she spread her legs to take him. He kissed her hot and heavy as she felt the rasp of fine wool rasp against her inner thighs and the hot head of his cock pushing up as she arched her hips to match him.

He was right. He slid into her, and the whole bed shook with it. She grabbed ahold of the bars behind her to withstand the onslaught —his mouth on hers, at her ear, neck, and shoulder—as he thrust relentlessly in, making her gasp with each pumping stroke.

Then he growled at her throat before reaching down to grab and pull her hips to him. He leaned back, kneeling, pulling her ass up over his thighs, and she groaned at this new angle in her, giving herself over to the sensation. He was a sight to see, still in his worsted wool suit—his tie askew, his shirt hanging free, his slacks only down enough to keep his cock in her. The whole scene was so decadently different from her normal life—them together, which she still wasn't used to and couldn't quite believe—in this room of all the rooms of his house. It felt like she was watching someone else experience all this, like a very elaborate dream, until he thrust again and took her breath away. He reached down to grab her breast and bent over to kiss her, and she was sliding her hand between them to rub her clit when—

Klaxons rang out. She stiffened, as did he, and then he said, "Fuuuuuuck," slowly thumping his head against her chest as he stopped thrusting.

"What is it?"

"Rift warning. If this is a drill, though, I will be shooting Jamison later." He moaned and pulled out of her. "I cannot believe the timing. I've got to go...I'm sorry...."

Andi moved to sitting as he made his way to the edge of the bed and dismounted. "If there's anything a nurse understands, it's an overly strong sense of duty. And hey, at least you still have most of your clothes on?"

"True." He set his hard-on into his pants and refastened them, tucking his shirt in and latching his belt back on. As she watched him work, she felt she could see his responsibilities settle onto him like a mantle, in the way he set his shoulders, bracing for whatever would come next. So, she wasn't surprised when he gave her a cold look shortly thereafter; it was how he had to be for the outside world. Then the corners of his lips ticked up, chipping away at the ice and warming her. "I like the look of you in my bed, Andi."

She felt herself flush. "Thank you," she said shyly and hopped off the side of the bed to retrieve her jeans.

Damian had his belt buckled and was pulling on his shoes. "There's a hidden door on that wall to my bedroom," he gestured with his chin. "You've been there before. Help yourself to the bar or bathroom. Take a bath or shower; I've got extra robes there if you'd like. You can even swim in my dragon's bathing pool if you want. Just don't touch any of the mirrors." He fixed her with a stare. "I mean that. They're magical objects. It's not safe."

By then, she had her jeans on. "Wait...can't I come with you?"

He snapped a hand through his hair, whipping it back into place before straightening his tie. He looked almost pulled together, with the exception of all the new wrinkles on his previously crisp suit. But the ice had returned all the way now. "Absolutely not. I can't be fighting monsters and be worried about your safety."

Andi gawked. "So, it's okay for me to be worried about yours, here? Can your magic cat make me a fainting couch?" The klaxon went off again, and she jumped.

He put his hand on her shoulders. "This is a fight we will have to have later," he informed her, and she was tempted to say *rambunctious* just so that he would take her seriously because this was kind of bullshit. Then his expression softened, and he lifted her chin. "I don't need a safeword with you, Andi. But when I call you princess, know that I mean it."

She squinted up at him. "We'll talk when you get back."

"Among other things, princess," he promised, then let her go and turned on his heel to walk out the door.

Andi watched him leave with a pout, then wandered the room, collecting the rest of her clothing. She didn't bother to put it on, just scooped it to her chest as she walked over to the wall he'd pointed at to find the door. She traced her hand along the green velvet wallpaper until her fingertips felt a small gap and then pressed, sending a well-balanced door swinging open. She passed through and watched it twirl shut behind her, finding herself just past the wall of mirrors on the other side, in Damian's barely familiar bedroom—and everything smelled like smoke.

Not cigarette or cigars, but campfire smoke, and worse—like burning hair. She put a hand to her mouth to cover it before running across the room to the window and found it barred by metal shutters.

"And what was that about serial killers?" she muttered, looking back the way she'd come. All the mirrors on the wall were black, like doorways into deep caves, and that was far creepier than the fog she remembered from last time. She realized belatedly she'd left the photo album and her coat behind in the green room, but she couldn't see the edge of that particular door anymore against the mirrored wall, and Damian's warning not to touch any of them was only amplified by the scent of recent fire. Andi chewed on her lip. Without him in the room, all the black frames looked like so many empty eye sockets.

She trailed along the far wall, opening doors until she found the bathroom and let herself inside. She'd had every intention of just cleaning herself up a little until she looked around.

Damian's bathroom was larger than her and Sammy's entire apartment. There was a massive claw-foot tub on a dais off to her right, a shower that could've fit ten people at once with the kind of sprayer bars that blasted you from all sides on her left, and in front of her, over a wide granite counter with the kind of sink basins that cost more than her annual salary, was a massive mirror that didn't currently look angry. Everything was in a gorgeous red stone, and she was one hundred percent going to take a bath in that tub.

"You are not going to believe this, Sammy," she said, wedging herself into a corner so she wouldn't show in the mirror. She pulled out her phone to take photos to share and saw that she'd already missed a series of frantic texts from her roommate.

Where are you?

That crazy lady is here again!

She's still outside!

Elsa, her uncle's secretary. Andi groaned and felt like an asshole, she should've warned Sammy. *I'm so sorry!* she texted back quickly. *I went out this morning, and I dodged her. I should've told you.*

Are you all right? What the hell, Andi!

I'm super, super sorry, S! Did she go away?

No! She's in the parking lot like a stalker! Sammy sent her a string of frowning emojis after that. *Like why can't she call you? Jesus.*

Probably because she knows I wouldn't pick up.

Where are you? Are you safe?

Andi's fingers twitched to share everything and send Sammy her recent photos, but she held back. *I'm totally safe.*

Good, her roommate texted back. *I'm still a little pissed, though. I mean, if you were going to get up this early, you could've gone out to brunch with me and listened to more about my date.*

Andi smiled at her phone, knowing all was forgiven. *I'll be back later, all right? Just don't tell Evil Elsa that.*

Now that I know you're alive, your secret is safe with me, Sammy sent back, with an emoji sticking its tongue out and then a kiss. Andi smiled at the phone then set it down on the counter, pulling off her jeans to advance on the bath.

DAMIAN'S PLUMBING WAS FANTASTIC—IN more ways than one—but the bath really didn't help things. Andi sat up to her armpits in exquisitely scented bubbles that smelled like some combination of lavender and snow. She should be indulgently relaxing, but her brain just wouldn't stop.

What was he off doing? Was he safe? Would anyone else die? Would he? Hell, for all she knew, could he?

Andi bunned her hair up to keep it dry and save the blue streak in it from fading, then sank in the hot water down to her chin. She didn't want to be one of those women who just thought about a man, but knowing he was out there putting himself in danger, it was awfully hard not to be thinking about him. How did people with spouses or children in the military survive?

She gave up on the tub and got out to dry herself off—his towels put any towel she'd ever touched before in her life to shame—and found his robes made of the exact same stuff. She cozied into one, folded her clothes up nicely, and tried to decide what to do.

She didn't want to lounge in here forever...she wasn't a mermaid. Did Damian know mermaids? Were they really a thing? But she also didn't want to hang out in his smoke-scented bedroom, which left making her way through the rest of the house.

She had been here before, technically, and while she knew the rooms could move on you without warning, she had a feeling she belonged here now. Maybe. So, she darted through the bedroom, holding her breath against the acrid smell until she reached the door.

The hallway she remembered—no green dragon blood on it this time, though, so that was good—and she went down the front stairs.

"Hello?" she asked aloud as she reached their bottom. Was she truly alone? Maybe she could find the kitchen and make herself another sandwich. "Is anyone home?"

Andi wound her way through the mansion, which was substantially less maze-like than when she'd last been here, and accidentally walked to where she'd had a patient last. She knew that Zach was better now since she'd officially met him as a human last night—which was why she was surprised to see another patient in the hospital bed, Grimalkin curled up at their feet. Austin was sitting, apparently half-awake, in a chair nearby.

He turned to see her, taking her robed state in with a wolfish grin. "Well, hello again."

"Hi." She gave him a small wave. "I, uh...."

"I know," he said, turning back to the bed behind him.

She could've minded her own business and walked away, but when had that ever stopped her? Andi snorted at herself and walked up to the bed like she belonged there and gasped.

The woman lying peacefully on the bed appeared to have wings. Actual wings. They'd been splinted and bandaged, but there was no mistaking the struts on the linen or the way their dark green leather splayed out from each shoulder.

"She has—" Andi gasped, and Austin cut in.

"Wings. Yeah." Andi couldn't help but stare. Beneath the sheets, Andi could see the outline of generous curves. The woman's face looked like she'd been beaten up. Her eyes were swollen shut and dark, and her hair was cut raggedly short, and the same worrisome smell she'd scented up in Damian's room was here. She knew Austin had done the best he could cleaning her,

64

but she also knew from her own time at work that there was no getting rid of certain funks, not without a real bath. "Princess Ryana, meet Nurse Andi," he said. "Nurse Andi, meet Princess Ryana."

Andi wavered, once more experiencing the increasingly familiar feeling of being blindsided. She clenched her hands into nervous fists in the robe's pockets. "She's a princess? A real one?"

"Well, yeah," Austin said. "She's Damian's sister."

"Oh." Andi definitively put two and two together. "Which means...he's a...."

"Prince. Of the Realms. Although we're currently uncertain what's going on back at the ol' homestead." Austin scrunched his face thoughtfully and rubbed the golden shadow of a beard on his chin. "Do titles follow you forever? I can't remember if those British people gave them up or had to turn them in. I mean, would they still be royalty if Britain didn't exist?"

Andi fought a rising tide of panic, swallowing it down. "So, uh, what does being a prince—or princess—of the Realms typically entail?"

"Fuck if I know. Damian hated it there," Austin said and shrugged, then looked intently at the woman on the bed. His voice turned low and menacing. "And if they treated someone like her like this, it can fucking stay burned, for all I care."

Andi stared at the woman and bit her lips. So, the man-dragon who wanted to date her was also a prince. This was all intensely normal!

Not.

She inhaled and exhaled and pulled her nursing persona on. "So...what's her neuro status?"

"She doesn't wake up, but she withdraws to pain."

"Can you even check her pupils like that?" Andi asked, leaning in. A small red bird popped out from in between Grimalkin's front paws and chittered a warning at her.

"I'd step back if I were you," Austin advised. "And, no, not really.

She could have orbital fractures for all I know. I don't really want to get in there."

Andi put her hands on her hips. "What about taking her to a real hospital for a CT scan?"

"Oh, you mean the same hospital where we found Hunters? That one?" he said. "Fuck, no."

"Austin—"

"She has *freaking* wings."

"So? Don't y'all have *freaking* magic?"

"Even if we could hide those things with magic, we can't just wedge her into a CT machine. It would hurt them even worse, and what would we do with the data besides? Who're we gonna show her scan to who'd believe it? On what planet would it make sense? And then we give her over to someone else to do surgery on? Hell no."

Andi crossed her arms and frowned, scanning the numbers on the screen over the bed. They were normal, for a human, for now. But that didn't mean the woman didn't have fractures or a slow, oozing bleed.

Austin reached out to stroke a charred lock of hair away from the woman's face, and Andi saw the red bird eyeing him closely. She got the impression that if he moved wrong, it'd attack, and at the thought of a cardinal haranguing a werewolf, she snorted. "I'm not happy about this."

"Neither am I," Austin agreed. "But she's got some dragon in her, just like Damian. They're tough motherfuckers, if you hadn't noticed."

She glanced at the monitor screen again and noticed the time in the corner; it was late afternoon now. How long had Damian been gone? "How tough?" she asked Austin.

He turned toward her, clearly ready to wisecrack, she could see it in his eyes, but he caught himself in time. Instead, he gave her a compassionate nod. "Very. And he's got Zach and the others with him besides."

"Aren't you worried?"

"Always. But my brother can handle himself. So can D."

Andi sighed and leaned against one of the bookcases on the wall. "How do you deal with the not knowing?"

Austin contemplated this, then shrugged. "Same way you do with patients, I suppose."

She rolled her eyes. "I'm not attached to them."

"Like hell. I saw you take on Damian to save my brother, which, thank you, by the way."

"You're welcome...but it's not the same." The truth was, caring about patients sucked in an entirely different way. Sometimes you worked your shift and went home and came back in a few days, and the person you'd poured hours of your life into saving was gone. Dead, discharged or transported to another floor. Being a nurse was like reading random chapters in a novel or only watching a third of any movie. Sure, you got some in a report, you could read some notes, and listen in to gossip and hearsay, but unless you were with that patient from beginning to end—almost an utter impossibility—it felt like you never knew the whole story.

Whereas with Damian, she might actually get to read the entire book.

Which was also, apparently, a fucking fairy tale. Andi stared at his sleeping princess sister and thought, *are you kidding me?*

"Help me turn her, will you?" Austin asked. "I'm trying to logroll her in case her spine's injured, but the wings make it hard."

Andi moved over to the side of the bed. "You should have your magic cat install a ceiling lift," she said, and one of the cat's ears perked up.

Austin snorted. "The magic cat doesn't like me very much," he said, reaching over to use the sheets beneath Ryana to pull her gently on her side. Andi took pillows and shoved them carefully, evenly, beneath her, and Austin set her back down. "Thanks." Then his phone chirped, and he pulled it out quickly, reading a message with a smile, before flashing her his screen. "They're on their way back already. Told you."

Andi's hands went into the robe's pockets again and found her own phone, which while on, hadn't beeped or buzzed. "Thanks for telling me." *Unlike some people.* "Let me know if there's anything else I can do to help."

"Will do," Austin said, sitting down and kicking his feet up onto the end of the bed to tip his chair back in repose.

ANDI WOUND her way back up to Damian's bedroom. The metal shutters in the window had come up sometime during her adventure downstairs, so she opened it up and squinted at the road outside. She thought if his car drove up right now, and he saw her staring out the window in a robe forlornly, like some kind of Asian Rapunzel, she might die.

This was not her.

She was not a girl who *waited.*

She turned and went back into the bathroom to quickly pull her clothes on, rescuing her phone from the robe's pocket before she put it back on its hook. Definitely no calls. She shoved her feet into her shoes and stomped back into his bedroom. The windy weather outside hadn't died down, so the smoky scent was quickly dissipating—except for where it wasn't.

Andi walked as close as she was comfortable to the mirrors, rounding the bed, and saw a leather bag on the floor. That was where part of the smell was coming from, and she realized it wasn't like a bag you could get at the mall. It was more like if someone did their shopping at the renaissance fair. She walked over to it, nudged it with her toe, then squatted down, grabbing part of the nearby sheets so she wouldn't be touching it with her own hands when she opened it up.

Inside was an imposing stone box about the size of a hardback Stephen King novel. She shimmied the bag off of it so that it sat flat on the room's low pile carpet. There were intricate designs carved on the sides, inlaid with opalescent metals. She'd seen enough horror movies to know that you should never, ever, open strange boxes.

And yet.

Andi reached for the edge of the box with a fabric-covered finger, and to her surprise, it opened.

"This had better be a legitimate emergency," Damian announced as he reached the bottom of the stairs. He felt flustered, flushed, and fucking alive. Andi, his Andi, was here with him, upstairs, like it was meant to be. God, how good was it going to be to go out and wrestle down some Unearthly monster and then come back here to fuck her in triumph?

Careful. You sound like me, his dragon warned him with a sharp laugh.

You were there too, Damian said, walking out of his castle toward the lightly armored SUV, full of weaponry inside, that they jokingly called the tour bus. *You know what she's like.*

I do, his dragon said, making a satisfied sound.

For all that his dragon was nearby now, he hadn't felt the beast riding him earlier. Not like he usually did—especially during sex. Damian wondered if his dragon was still granting him the space he'd claimed to be giving him last night, but not enough to question it. If the dragon wanted to fade away entirely and leave all of Andi to him, that would be fine by him.

But how would you wrestle monsters without me? his dragon told him, slowly uncoiling to take up more space, readying for the fight.

I would find a way, Damian promised the monster inside himself and headed out the door.

· · ·

DAMIAN HOPPED into the tour bus and found himself joined by Max and Zach up front and Jamison with his tech gear in the back.

"No Mills?" he asked, taking a spot in the back beside Jamison. Jamison was already running his one metal hand over the equipment, a stark contrast with the dark skin of his other hand, triangulating the latest rift between Realms.

"Turns out faking your sister's death is a little bit harder than we thought," Jamison said without looking up. "The coordinates are on your dash, Max."

"Got it," the bear-shifter said, putting the tour bus into drive.

"How so?" Damian asked Jamison.

"Magic reasons. We took a sample from her wings, but now, Mills is pretty convinced that it won't work."

He bet Lyka loved the sample taking process. Damian had a mental image of Grim holding the red bird back. "Why?"

"For the same reasons you can heal yourself, but we can't heal you. *You* can make more of *you*, but apparently, *we* can't. For anything more detailed than that, though, you'd have to ask her," Jamison said.

"Makes sense," Zach chimed in from the front seat. "I mean, if you could just culture out magical cells, couldn't you create magical meats? Like those Impossible Burgers, only from us?" Zach pondered this for a second. "I mean, if you could, you could figure out a way to have ethical magical ingestion."

Max recoiled. "That's still disgusting."

Damian gave Zach a bemused look. "Since when did you become a scientist-slash-philosopher?"

The werewolf laughed. "I do occasionally *do* things at the board meetings you skip out on. Like researching what to invest your money in."

"Heh," Damian said, relaxing back. "Well, back to the here and now...what's the stat on the rift we're heading toward?"

Jamison made portions of his screen larger, and Damian watched his expression darken. "Fuck me.... It's the Clearcreek Mall." That meant a ton of space to cover—and far too many people to protect. Damian felt the tour bus pick up speed.

"Size?" Max asked.

Jamison pulled his head away from his screens to give a grim look. "At least a meter."

"Goddammit," Zach hissed from the front seat, and Damian knew why. A lot of things could wedge themselves through a meter-sized rift. And, conversely, you should shove a lot of things back into a meter-sized rift to save to eat later.

"I'll know more once we're closer," Jamison promised. "Maybe it's only in a janitorial closet."

"One can hope," Damian muttered.

"Spheres," Jamison said, as Max double-parked the van. He handed out one of the magical objects to each of them. They turned them on, blinking out of sight one by one as the magical barrier the spheres provided showed whoever was watching on the other side just what they wanted to see—which, presumably, wasn't four muscular, well-armed men running for the entrance of a mall with guns out.

If Damian hadn't known what they were there for, it would've been a nice day. The wind from earlier had died down, the sun was out, there were birds chirping, and a janitor in a navy jacket was sweeping a metal detector across a patch of grass out front.

They entered and jogged down a broad tiled hallway between storefronts, dodging groups of people—mothers pushing strollers, teenagers with swaying bags. Damian did his best to avoid places like this; there was something about the way they were constructed that made him feel trapped, and he didn't particularly like meeting strangers. For all that he had money, this wasn't the kind of place he liked to spend it when he bothered to.

"Fuck," he muttered, dodging a gaggle of preteens sharing a soda. They reached an atrium with wide stairs leading up, and beside them, someone was shilling face creams from a cart. "Jamison?"

"Overlaying blueprints...second floor!" Jamison said and started up the stairs. Damian overtook him, dodging people too busy with their phones to pay attention. The sooner this was over with, the sooner he could get back to Andi.

"And now?" Damian asked from the top, looking around. But he didn't need Jamison's tech to see it.

"Shit," Max said, pulling to heel at his side.

Halfway down the next stretch of tiled hallway, equidistant between a women's clothing store and a store full of candy and dolls, a rift fluttered.

A flexible triangle hovered like the entrance to a teepee, beginning at knee height and ending at the floor. Its edges flared through colors Damian's eyes could only barely retain—a bright portal in comparison to the otherworldly darkness it held inside.

And out of it burped a small furry creature. It had white and tan splotches, was about the size of Damian's fist, and it started zigzagging down the hall toward them on six legs.

"Start shooting; I'll be right back," Jamison announced, racing back down the stairs the way they'd come.

Max whipped out his gun and aimed it as Zach stepped up. "Whoa, whoa, whoa!" Zach said. "Why do they look like hamsters?"

"All the better to infiltrate a place like this?" Damian guessed, picking the creature up so that it was hidden inside his sphere with him. With it suspended, he could see a chitinous underbelly and that all six of the legs ended in claws. It was all too easy to imagine a kid taking it home with them to post on the internet, if nothing else. "We've got to get everyone out of here."

Zach looked wildly around, then apparently spotted something familiar on a wall. He ran to it, hit it, and a siren started wailing.

"What on earth did you do?" Max complained.

"Fire drill," Zach said, grinning. "I have *always* wanted to do that."

Everyone else in the mall paused for a moment taking a collective breath, and then they flipped out. People started screaming and running for the exits. Damian moved to the side, watching the tide of humanity rush by, before chucking the hamster-like creature back into the rift like a football. A second one leaped out—or perhaps the same one Damian threw, racing back—this time heading for the stairs like it was following the people.

Max pulled out his pistol and shot it, sending its components splattering against the red tile and the glass wall that held the railing for the balcony.

"Disgusting," Damian said, shaking a glob of creature off his dress shoe.

"Yo, peeps," Jamison spoke up in their earpieces. "Good news, bad news time. The good news is that the bottom of this rift is inside a storage closet that I evacuated and locked. The bad news is that there's like two hundred of those creatures already inside it."

Zach groaned. "I am not going to feel good about killing hamsters, guys. I don't care how Unearthly they are."

And as the werewolf was complaining, the pieces of the hamster Max had shot—including the lump of flesh Damian had kicked away—beaded and rolled back together. All three of the men watched the creature reform. Damian picked it up; it was whole again, impossibly.

"Oh, shit, I take that back," Zach whispered.

"I'm gonna bomb them so I can seal the rift," Jamison went on. "One sec—"

Damian grabbed his earpiece. "No!" he shouted, but it was too late. The floor beneath them shook as he ran for the stairs, carrying the reanimated hamster with him.

DAMIAN RACED DOWNSTAIRS and found Jamison walking out of a men's clothing store, smoke billowing out from a closed door behind him.

"What?" Jamison asked.

"They can reform," Damian said, holding the hamster-looking thing up so that Jamison could see its stomach. Its six legs strained out for him, waving in the air as it chittered.

"Oh, God, it's like a furry roly-poly," Jamison said with revulsion. "I hate those things."

"Not that...this," Damian said, twisting the creature violently into two halves—with mysteriously little dripping blood. Then he put the two pieces back together, and both the men watched them reseal—like a magic trick.

"Oh, fuck," Jamison muttered, then winced as ominous rustling and thumping sounds began in the storage room he'd bombed.

"I don't think you killed any of them," Damian said, "so much as you made them mad."

"How do you kill something that can't die?" Jamison asked as a mad scrabbling started on the wall behind them.

"With dragon fire," Damian growled. A wall full of drywall fell forward, and a tan and white furry creature the size of a VW Bug scurried out and into the store, on hundreds of tiny legs, each one of their claws scratching gouges into the tile. Both the men dove sideways out of its way and watched in bizarre fascination as it trampled over racks of clothing to go out into the mall. "Seal the rift," he commanded Jamison, tossing his sphere to the man, racing after the thing to change.

His dragon had been waiting for just this moment.

It was hard to explain the changes that overtook him when his dragon was revealed. There was a moment of intense pain, yes, but he was never fully sure if it was physical or emotional, the sensation of his body changing into something utterly *other*, gaining in mass and expanding in scale, or the knowledge that each time he did so, it was like he was ripping himself in two and being left with a little less of himself each time. The process was slower now that he was on earth, but the sensation was the same.

Freedom, his dragon growled and reveled in it. *Except,* it complained, gnashing its teeth as its wings were trapped by walls.

It is what it is...burn that thing, Damian said, and the beast snaked after it. His claws caught on the tile now, his dragon dragging itself down the now-narrow hallway, propelling itself off the ground and walls around them, sending carts and benches scattering to each side, gaining speed. They reached an intersection and wheeled themselves around it, experiencing a moment of freedom in an atrium, before diving back into another hallway, hot on the creature's tail.

The furry thing appeared to bumble to a stop, reaching the wall at the end of the hallway, bouncing against it like a blind mole.

Damian's dragon inhaled and then exhaled with intent, catching its breath on fire, releasing a torrent of flame at the furry thing. The scent of burning hair was instantly in the air, just as it'd been this morning. Then the shield of fluff burned through, revealing the insectile creature beneath, and it started to scream and...broke in two.

No...thirds. One third of it was dead, Damian knew, from all his dragon's senses. The fire had killed it, but the other two had abandoned ship and were now reforming into discreet entities, racing away on different paths. One scurried up into the ceiling; the other raced at him, finding speed, diving between him and the wall.

As his dragon was hardly smaller than the hallway, he roared and then took out the storefronts of the establishments on either side of itself, so that it had more room to turn, chasing after the third of the creature that was still visible to him. He howled fire after it and clipped it, right before it ran down another hall.

Faster! Damian urged.

Yes! his dragon laughed because, Damian realized, it was having fun. For the first time in weeks, his dragon didn't also want to run to Andi, knowing she was safe back home, and it wasn't fighting him, as they both wanted the same thing. It was in its element hunting here, even in this strange environment, and for the first time in a long time, Damian almost felt a part of it. The same sensation of ability and glee, the knowledge that there was nothing he couldn't do as a dragon, the way that they were working as one.

There! he shouted as his dragon spotted it with their eyes, circling behind a bench. In the atrium again, his dragon pounced on the thing. *Don't shred it!* he warned.

You're no fun, his dragon complained, and then let loose a burst of fire at it, close enough to feel the heat himself and bask in it—this revelation of his power.

When it was done, Damian prompted, *And the third?*

His dragon pulsed out with his senses. *There!* it crowed, spotting the last piece of the creature frantically climbing the ceiling over the atrium, trying to get to the glass at the top and the presumable freedom of outside.

Damian's dragon bunched and leaped for the creature, knocking it down, and every instinct flooding through him wanted to play with it, to rip it apart with teeth and claws.

Fire only! he reminded his beast.

Fine, his dragon complained as it dropped to the ground with the creature, holding it clasped between its paws, crashing down the stairs. It rolled as it landed, folding its wings in the small space, holding the creature up and letting out a gout of flame as the creature writhed and clawed, trying to escape. It chittered pathetically as the dragon crisped it, and then they were done—the cause that'd brought them together finished.

Damian waited until his dragon had righted itself before demanding, *Change back.*

And what would you do if I said no? his dragon asked him.

Then we would fight. Again. Damian braced himself. Before he'd met Andi, it felt like all he ever did was fight. He hadn't expected the knowledge that there was another way to be to leave him so exhausted with his former reality. *Do you really want that?*

There was a long internal pause as his dragon contemplated things. *No,* it said, *not right now.* Damian felt himself fold back.

Changing always cost him his clothing. He jogged back up the stairs to find his men, his bare feet slapping on the cold tile.

He saw Max first, casting the light of the Forgetting Fire he'd brought about to undo magically caused structural problems and erase them from any cameras. Jamison was inside the now reset and restocked clothing store, the wall behind him solid again, as he rewound the end of his rift closing detonation cord, which Damian knew was warded strands of Mills's long hair. And he heard the static blast of a flamethrower, spotting Zach torching a few remaining hamsters down the hall.

"I'd forgotten we had this in the bus!" Zach announced at seeing him.

"Yes, but it's not magic...those stains'll stay," Damian said, looking at the scorch marks Zach was leaving on the ground.

"Well, we did pull the fire alarm," Zach said matter-of-factly. "At least *something* should really be on fire."

"Pyro," Damian snorted, as Jamison tossed another sphere at him. He caught it and switched it on.

AFTER A GROUP of firefighters burst in, it was all hands on deck to help Max spot and erase the last of the Unearthly physical damages with the Forgetting Fire before they clocked it. But when they were through, and after Damian had swiped a pair of red gym shorts from an athletic store, making Zach give him a twenty-dollar bill to leave behind, they descended the front stairs triumphantly—at least in their own minds.

Because none of the kids, mothers, or employees who'd stuck around to gawk could see them. Even the same janitor who Damian'd seen earlier had stayed to stare, casually leaning on the metal detector he'd been waving, probably wondering just how much work they were leaving behind for him. Damian would have to give the mall an anonymous donation to make up for the damage Zach's flamethrower had caused. He brushed by the janitor, bringing up the rear, and heard the metal detector the man had clicking louder.

So did the janitor, who suddenly stood upright.

But instead of looking at the ground, where one would think you would be able to find dropped coins and jewelry with a metal detector, he started looking around him.

Damian paused as the rest of his crew loaded into the tour bus and watched the janitor raise the detector up. The thing clicked more loudly as the man pushed it in his direction, but the janitor couldn't see him because of the sphere's magic, although he definitely was looking at something. Damian turned and saw what the man had focused on. A small brunette girl with a pixie cut. Not even in high school, surely, she was riding a girl's bike with tassels off the handle—she was probably from the elementary school down the street.

And the janitor was absolutely looking at her with intent.

Damian backed up, shielding the girl with his body, assuming the worst and feeling murderous. Did this man even belong here? Was this his gimmick, his way to get close enough to kids?

Damian sidestepped, ready to yank the man into the sphere with him, punch him out, and grab his wallet to figure out who he was and how to prosecute him when the janitor's attention waved because the metal detector was still going after Damian. The janitor turned, swinging it his direction, and Damian realized it wasn't a metal detector after all.

The janitor was a Hunter. They'd just affixed a handle to the tool he'd seen the Hunters running around with at Andi's hospital.

And if Damian hadn't been there, he'd have been scanning the mall to find people with just a bit of shifter blood in their background, maybe so little that they didn't even know it was there.

Hunting them.

Kill him! his dragon demanded, rushing forward so hard that Damian swayed.

No! Damian shouted him down inside.

Kill him now, his dragon hissed, seething, clawing, and Damian tensed.

Don't you think I want to? Damian asked, biting back a groan. The thought of this man preying on kids—at least the Unearthly were carnivores from other Realms, they had an excuse—but this man was human, and he knew what he was doing.

The Hunters they'd encountered recently had been better equipped and better hidden than those in the past. He needed to know more about them, and this was an opportunity to not just torture someone—who might prove strong or a liar—but to spy.

His dragon roiled, and it felt like the beast was biting chunks off his flesh and rending them with its teeth.

Fucking...stop, Damian gritted out, stumbling over to where the tour bus was.

"Damian?" Jamison asked from the safety of the interior.

"Tracking device. Now," Damian spit out, holding his hand up. Jamison jumped to rummage through a tethered bag and pulled out a chip the size of a dime.

"It's on," he said, flicking it with a thumbnail. "But who—"

"Janitor," Damian said, grabbing hold of the tour bus's side.

"Are you okay?" Jamison asked.

His dragon was unrelenting. *Why are you letting him live? If I were in control—*

But you're not!

Damian pushed the tag back to Jamison. There was no way for him to do it, to get close enough without enveloping the janitor inside his sphere and giving himself away or appearing as a naked man except for gym shorts. That, plus the fact that he would definitely set the detector off. "Tag the janitor. Now."

"Okay," Jamison said, snapping to. He set his sphere down and stripped off half his gear in the darkness of the tour bus quickly, thinking along the same lines as Damian.

The dark-skinned man bounced out of the tour bus in black slacks and a black long-sleeved shirt and didn't look entirely out of

79

place on a chilly day—especially since both of his hands were covered in gloves. He wandered over to the group of people watching the firemen and expressed some interest before walking on, right by the janitor—who was now inspecting his device, probably trying to figure out why it'd registered so strongly just a moment ago—and bumped him, seemingly on accident. Jamison patted the man's shoulder in apparent apology, and Damian knew he'd slid the tracker into the man's pocket.

It was done. The tracker would at least lead them to his home, which they could stake out and work back from.

Jamison walked on naturally, and the tour bus circled the block to pick him up. Damian tried to relax, but his dragon wouldn't let him. It was slamming against his flesh like his body was a cage; he felt bruises blossoming from the inside out.

It's over...stop! Damian commanded, but the beast wouldn't. It was as though a switch had been flipped inside. *You've got to—*

I don't have to do anything! the dragon snarled.

What is wrong with you? he demanded.

The same thing that has always been wrong! I am chained!

I know. Damian breathed deeply, trying to regain control. *I'm sorry.*

At that, the dragon suddenly stilled, but Damian didn't know if he could trust it—if he could relax too—or if that only meant that he should brace for what was coming next.

Your regret means nothing to me, his dragon said, but it stopped fighting. Damian had the sense of it receding inside him, to wherever it hid.

"D, are you okay?" Jamison asked quietly, from where he was sitting beside him.

"That's a matter of opinion," Damian muttered, then more loudly, said, "I don't want to talk about it. Let's just get home."

. . .

THE OTHER THREE men let him off the hook and began talking about other things—how ignoble it was to kill hamsters, even if they were half-zombie, half-insect on the inside, and how no one would believe any of this shit if it were ever in a TV show, a perennial complaint. But at least they weren't suffering alone and had each other to talk to and laugh with. Damian listened to their jibes and bragging and envied them.

There were days when he wanted to be like them, when he wished his world was simpler. But he couldn't let go of the fact that he was different, and his differences kept him alone.

Except that now, he had Andi.

He sank back into his seat and closed his eyes and thought of her until Max put the van in park.

"I've got that tracker on a trace, okay?" Jamison said as he opened his eyes.

"Good. I'll check in with you later. I want to know everywhere it goes."

"Why?" his tech master asked.

"Because that wasn't a metal detector in his hand. It was a Hunter's tool," Damian said with a sigh.

The mood in the van changed instantly.

"Are you fucking kidding me?" Jamison responded, his voice rising in disbelief.

"Why'd we let him live?" Max growled.

"Because," Damian said, unbuckling his seat belt and getting out of the tour bus, indicating that they should do the same. "We need to know where he lives, where he goes. We need to figure out what the Hunters are up to. Whatever they're doing now, it's far more organized than last time. For all we know that man really is a janitor there—under cover—or maybe doesn't know shit, and he's just getting paid fifty bucks a week by them to report back. I'm not going to yank someone up to torture them if I'm not sure they don't have something to tell me when—and if—they flip."

"Fuck, D," Zach said, with a head shake.

"I know. It's awful. And I hate having to think like that. But now we'll know where he sleeps at night if nothing else. We can stake that out, get a name, have you do your electronic thing," he said, looking at Jamison, "and track him down. Put traces on his car and credit cards, see who pays him, how and when. If we're lucky, he leads us someplace good. If we're not, then we can grab him in a few days and beat what he knows out of him."

"I don't like this," Jamison said, frowning deeply.

"I don't either. But we need to know more. We're breaking up a well-funded gang now; they're not just loose groups of cannibalistic yahoos anymore," Damian said, and Max grunted. Being from the Realms, he understood the necessity of acceptable casualties more than most.

"I understand, but I'm still pissed," Zach said, his face curdled by disgust.

"And you have every right to be," Damian agreed. "Can you contact Stella and find out what information she got the other night?"

"Sure," Zach said. "I won't tell her about this, though. She'd hunt that guy down and kill him herself."

"I'm not asking for long," Damian said.

"And how long will it take him to murder someone?" Jamison pressed.

"These are the kind of choices you had to make in the Realms," Max said, coming up behind him. "Which is why Damian's making it. Not you or me. A situation where both choices are shitty, and neither one lets you sleep well at night."

"I'm telling Austin," Zach said.

"I didn't expect you not to," Damian granted.

Zach made a small growl and shook his whole body like he was shaking off a fly, a visceral response to Damian's decision, but he stayed tight-lipped as he turned for the castle.

"Mills is not going to be happy about this either," Jamison added with a sigh. "But, I'll restock the bus before I tell her."

"Thank you," Damian said, clapping his shoulder, following Zach's path back in with Max at his side.

"Are you all right?" the bear-shifter asked once they were out of earshot.

Damian shrugged, then realized who he was talking to. "I'm the one who should be checking in with you." Max was his old weapons master, and he'd come over from the Realms horribly injured a few years after Damian.

"No, I wrote that place off as solidly as you did." Max snorted ruefully. "What with the whole being blinded and left for dead."

Damian nodded. If he were a weaker man, he'd still have nightmares about the condition Maximillian was in when he'd come crawling through the mirror. "As long as Ryana's okay, I don't really give a flying fuck what happens back there."

"I just hope the Realms feels the same way about you, brother," Max said, as they mounted the mansion's front stairs.

DAMIAN PAUSED ONCE he was indoors, though Max's words reverberated around him.

His house smelled like Andi. And it felt like if he could just be around her again, everything would be better. He would know he'd made the right decision, and his dragon would behave. He trotted up the stairs quickly, hoping to catch her napping in his bed, because how glorious it would be to crawl under the sheets beside her and pull her close, breathe in her hair, and sleep—or not...depending.

He opened up the door to his bedroom quietly and found her awake and waiting, sitting clothed and cross-legged on his bed, playing with her phone. She seemed startled to see him and emotions he couldn't quantify played across her face until she took in what he was wearing.

"Were you out jogging?" she asked, arms crossed. There was a strange box sitting on the bed beside her.

"It's a long story."

Her eyebrows went high, and then she shook her head helplessly. "I was going to be mad at you, but now I'm just going to laugh."

He grinned at her. He'd been right; everything *was* going to be better now that she was here. "Do I normally keep extra clothes in the tour bus? Yes. Do I restock them as often as I ought to? No."

"So, where did those fetching red gym shorts come from?"

"The mall. I grabbed them on our way out the door. We were in a rush...I didn't get to try them on."

"No wonder they're tight on you then." The corners of her lips quirked into a knowing smile.

"I don't know, I thought you might like it," he said, advancing with a leer.

Andi laughed and pulled back slightly. "No. First off, I've seen you fighting monsters before. You're gonna have to shower before you touch me. Secondly, I'm still mad at you."

He paused a good three feet away from the bedside and dragged up a chair. "Okay. Why?"

"Because. You raced off again. And I get that's what you do, and the world needs you, but I don't like being the girl who waits behind. That's not me."

Damian sighed. "I can't have you out there on the field of battle, Andi. I just can't. If anything happened to you, I wouldn't be able to control myself."

Andi frowned thoughtfully. "And everyone else here has some kind of superpower?"

"Pretty much."

"Well...how can I get one?"

Damian blinked. "What?"

"My brother got one. Why can't I?"

Damian stared at her. "Because you're not a Hunter, Andi."

Her frown deepened. "So, there's no possible other way?"

"As far as I know, no. I've never smelled magic on you or in you, Andi." And Rax had confirmed as much last night, aloud. "I can't

84

claim to fully know what they did to your brother, but whatever *is* happening to him, I wouldn't wish that on you." Damian watched her sigh and sink in on herself. He could almost see the wheels turning in her head as she cycled through other options, and he hoped that one of them wasn't leaving him. She did have pride, and Damian suspected it was hard going from always feeling capable to helpless. It was part of what he liked about her, the way she was brashly willing to do what needed to be done—regardless of the personal expense.

Maybe he could talk to Mills. See if there wasn't some object of power she could give her. Or some facet of operations here he could give her control of. Maybe she could help Austin with Ryana. He opened his mouth to say as much, then saw her hand idly play with the lid of the box beside her. It looked familiar.

Like a nightmare he'd tried to banish long ago.

Suddenly, his dragon surged forward, eager to see through his eyes, waiting with bated breath.

Is that what I think it is? it asked him, roiling around in anticipation.

"Where did you get that?" he asked sharply, standing up.

"What?" she asked, looking up at him, then over at the box beside her. "I found it a little bit ago, in a bag. The bag was making everything smell smoky; I put it by the window."

Damian swallowed slowly. "Andi, please come over here away from that."

Andi blinked and then did as she was told for once, to her credit, bolting to his side. "Why?" she breathed.

"Stay right here," he commanded, walking to the bed.

It is, it is, his dragon whispered. *It is!*

Damian stared at the ornately decorated box, haunted by memories of his childhood. *It could be empty.*

His dragon laughed cruelly. *We both know it's not.*

"And...you opened it?" he asked her, looking back.

She winced. "Just once. I saw what was inside. But then I remembered what you told me about the mirrors, and I knew I shouldn't mess with it without asking you."

Damian picked up the box and turned toward her. He didn't dare open it up, but if Andi had, that explained his dragon's outburst when he'd been at the mall when it'd tried to tear him up from the inside to be free. "What did you see?" he asked her.

Andi swallowed. "It...it looked like a heart made out of crystal. Like a real heart—not a Valentine's one—and it was beating."

Damian inhaled and exhaled deeply. The Heart of the Dragon—the same as his father had shown him once, right after his first change—the object that bound his linage to dragon-kind. The object that granted him obscene amounts of power as a dragon, but stole his soul till he became one.

And the same object he'd come to Earth to get away from, brought here by his incapacitated sister.

Inside him, his dragon's laughter doubled in triumph.

"Damian?" Andi came up to him. "Are you all right?"

He set the box down behind him on the bed and walked over to her and roughly pulled her against him.

CHAPTER

FIVE

ndi let Damian hold her tightly. Something was clearly wrong. She didn't know if she'd done it, or if whatever was in that box had, but he was hurting. She could see it in his face. She could feel it in his arms and in the ragged way he breathed against her. She buried herself against him, holding him tight.

After a long time when they hadn't moved, and she wasn't sure what to do, she asked, "What's wrong?" He pulled himself away from her, and she looked up. His expression was so dark, so clouded, so serious—far worse than she'd ever seen before. "Damian, talk to me," she pleaded.

She watched him pull himself from the haunted place he'd been with force, returning his attention to her. "You make me human. You keep me human." He looked at her with a sorrow so deep that it almost broke her. "I just want to be with you."

"You are with me." She grabbed both of his hands, to prove her reality to him. "I'm right here, aren't I?" But she could almost see the despair lapping at his heels and felt him fading away from her like he was walking backward into a cave. "Damian...please." She let go of his hands to catch his face. His golden eyes were so dark, and she didn't know what they were seeing, but it wasn't her, and the worry she felt for him was worse than when she'd been sitting on his bed just minutes ago. "You're scaring me." She pulled his face down to hers and leaned up on her toes to kiss him softly. "Come back," she whispered, and then pressed her face against his, like a cat, trying to warm him, trying to bring him home, and when that didn't work, she looked wildly around the room, trying to figure out a way to ground him. She spotted the bathroom door.

"Come on," she said and tugged him toward it.

He followed her inside, walking like if she weren't pulling him he wouldn't know how, and she felt like she was daring losing him just letting go of one of his hands to open the door. She pulled him in and kicked the door closed behind them, hoping that more distance between him and whatever had just happened would help, and then she grabbed the waistband of the silly red shorts he was wearing and yanked them down. "Step out," she commanded, when they were on the ground around his feet, and he did as he was told—no more, no less.

She let go of the hand she still held reluctantly. "Stay right there, okay?" she commanded and quickly shimmied out of all the clothing she'd just put back on, standing in front of him as naked as he was. But his eyes didn't search her hungrily and his breath didn't catch and his cock didn't rise.

"Come on, come on," she said, taking his hand again, pulling him into his enormous shower.

She closed the door behind him and then worked the overly complicated mechanism to make the water spray blindly, cycling through settings until she found one that stopped the wall sprayers and opened up some lever in the ceiling, to let hot water drip down on both of them like soft rain from the sky. She positioned Damian directly under the spray and watched him close his eyes.

"It's going to be okay," she promised him, reaching up to stroke his dark hair off his face. It was the same promise she made a thousand times at work, sometimes a thousand times a day. And each time she made it, she meant it, she was going to try the hardest she could to do whatever needed to happen to make her promise good. "Everything's going to be all right."

She darted out into the bathroom again and grabbed a towel, bringing it in, folding it over and over on itself until it was just a small rectangle, and she set it on the ground. "Kneel," she commanded, pulling down on his arms.

It seemed to take forever until he did so, his knees on the soaking towel, and then he was the very image of a penitent man, his head bowed before her as the water came down. She hit the button of some soapy substance trapped in glass along the wall and took a squirt of it that smelled like lime and vanilla, and it didn't matter what it was—shampoo or conditioner or body wash—just as long as she could touch him with it.

"You're okay," she repeated, the water over them both streaming down. She stroked her hands through his hair, sudsing it, scratching her nails against his scalp so he would feel her. "You're here. You're real." She played her hands down his broad shoulders, kneading them along the way. She caught his chin and pulled it up, making him look at her. "Damian...do you hear me?" She pushed his hair back from his forehead with one hand. "If you hear me, I need to know."

He didn't respond to her for a long while, and then he blinked. Heavy beads of water rolled off his eyelashes, and for the first time since they'd gotten into the shower, Andi felt like he could see her. He didn't say anything after that. He just rose to wind both of his arms around her waist, pulling her close, putting his cheek on her stomach. She could feel his hot breath on her as the water ran over both of them.

"It's all going to be okay," she soothed him, running her hands through his hair and down his back over and over again, petting him, just feeling him breathe. His arms tightened, and his head turned toward her, still bowed, pressing his forehead against the slight rise of her belly. Andi took this as a good sign and traced the outline of his ears with gentle care. "See? I'm really here," she told him, and then he kissed her, just below her navel.

Andi froze. She hadn't been expecting that, and she wasn't sure if it was a good thing as he kissed her again. She trembled. If something was wrong, maybe he needed time to think and recover. Maybe this wasn't wholesome. "Damian," she breathed as his mouth moved lower. "I'm good. I just want you to be okay." He sank back onto his heels in front of her, as his hands moved to cup her ass and bring her closer to him. "You don't have to," she protested, pushing gently back on his shoulders.

He paused to look up at her. His expression was still haunted, but at least he had words now. "No, Andi. I do," he said and started kissing lower.

Each of his kisses held the promise of another until he was pushing his chin against the place where her thighs met, nudging them apart for his mouth. Andi squeezed them together and had one last moment to think that maybe this wasn't right or good for him, but his mouth was insistent, and his tongue slid between her legs, trying to taste whatever she would give him, and she shuddered and parted for him all at once.

Damian made a rumbling sound beneath her, like thunder for the rainstorm they were in, and positioned himself below the inverted V of her thighs, kissing up, and when his lips met on her clit, she swayed. He grabbed her ass to hold her there, as she wound her hands down into his hair, making a soft sound as he kissed her there again. He rose slightly higher, pressing his face into her so that she could feel the stubble of his chin press into her heat, and she could ride it, the same as she could ride his mouth and tongue. She started whining without meaning to, unable to stop herself, making small helpless sounds as he kept pressing her, kept kissing her, kept drinking her down.

"Please, yes, please," she breathed, turning her face up to the water above, feeling it beat on her skin, sliding over her body like another set of hands. His hands on her ass were insistent. She could feel the pressure of each fingertip, keeping her close as she began to grind. His tongue pushed under her hood, his lips sucked her clit in, and the roughness of his chin—she wound up on her tiptoes, hips arched, only barely upright and hanging on. Her hands in his hair went tight, and she squirmed, her hips rocking of their own accord, taking what she needed from his mouth and tongue, moaning as he held her there, letting her use him to wind herself tightly, and she realized this was what he wanted, what he needed, to feel like he was *here* again. If salvation of a sort lay between her legs, then she was going to fucking give it to him.

She looked down at him and saw his eyes were closed, like in letting him eat her out, she was granting him communion. "Look at me, Damian," she panted out. "I want you to see what you do to me." His golden eyes slowly opened, and while they were still wary, they weren't as haunted as they had been. His hands on her ass tightened as he sucked harder at her eager clit. "Oh my God," she whispered, teetering above him, barely able to stand or stand it any longer, feeling everything he was giving her coil inside her like a snake waiting to strike. "Oh my God, Damian," she hissed, curling forward until it was too late, and she was hit by the first crashing wave. "Oh my God...fuck...yes!" she howled, pounding her hips against him, giving each wave his name. "Damian...fuck...Damian!" The thrashing sounds of her coming reverberated off the shower's glass and back on them until she moaned and trembled, the last of her orgasm flowing out of her.

He took his time releasing her, pulling carefully away, and she swayed, coming slowly back into her body. How was she supposed to protect him and make sure everything really would be okay when she could barely stand? Then he was standing too, again, and he wasn't the same despondent man she'd dragged into the shower with her. He wasn't back to the version of himself he'd been earlier, but a portion of him had returned to her...and to him. Water poured down his shoulders, rippling down his abs and laying the fine hair of his stomach down in a dark trail to where his cock was now arching up, a dark lightning bolt looking for somewhere to land.

His breath was heavy. His eyes were on her, and Andi pushed her hair out of her face. "Damian?"

"Yes, princess," he said, his voice low.

"Are you all right?" she asked him, well aware that she didn't even begin to have a way to quantify that when she didn't even know what was wrong in the first place.

"No. But I will be," he said. She watched him swallow, taking all of her in, and then he leaned down to kiss her.

When she let his tongue in, it felt like he was taking all of her, as his hands swam up her body, sending sheets of water cascading in their wake, until his fingers were in her hair, same as hers had been in his just seconds ago, and he pulled her closer, kissing her mouth just like he'd eaten her, with presses and sucks and licks that left her lost and breathless.

Her hands started wandering his body, feeling the slope of his shoulders again, tracing down the front of him, letting the definition of his muscles lead her down, down, down, until his hips rocked for her, begging her to touch him, to take him, and so she did, wrapping a hand around the base of his cock and lifting up slowly, feeling him moan into her mouth at the same time as he arched up. He stopped kissing her and looked down, watching her hand move over him with dark eyes, then said, "I need you."

"I'm here," she whispered, and he pressed in.

He spun her quickly before she could even register it and pushed her against the shower's glass. She gasped at the sudden chill, feeling her nipples turn to diamonds, whirling her head to look behind her where he was grabbing her ass with one hand, using the other to leverage his cock down and slide it between her legs again.

This time, there was no teasing, no subtlety. She felt the wide head of him notch against her and then press up, stretching her to fit him, making her take him in a tight slide as he growled her name. She leaned forward, bracing her forearms against the glass to tilt her hips up to fit all of him, feeling the sharp chill of the glass against her cheek as he pulled out and then thrust again. She marveled at how the cold of the glass made the heat of the still falling water and the place where they met that much hotter, and she made a willing high-pitched sound.

He grabbed her hips to his and found a rhythm, pulling her high enough to meet him, her rocking on tight calves and pointed toes, dragging the entire length of his cock almost out before plunging in again, landing in her with a grunt that said that she was his, that this is where he had to be. She started crying out with each thrust, unable to stop herself, wild sounds of being taken like she was some animal being mounted in the woods. He growled more at that, then ran both his hands up alongside her, reaching down to cup her small breasts in his hands and pinch and pull, using them for leverage to ram himself even more deeply. Then he moved past them, winding up her body and arms to find her own hands, clenched to fists against the glass as she tried to withstand his onslaught. His hands encircled her wrists there, keeping her trapped beneath him. It was like he was holding her there, but it was also like he was helping her to stand—helping her almost to fly—because he stepped closer, so close that each thrust was only a small rough jolt of pleasure as the head of his cock rubbed the back of her, far inside, and he bent over her, biting her shoulder as he plowed her deep. There was no way she wasn't going to come again, she was going to give him every-thing—"Damian!" she cried out, merciless shudders running through her body, as he kept her pinned by his cock against the glass. She felt him start to twitch and pull her inside as her pussy grabbed him, and he groaned.

"Andi...fuck...Andi," he whispered in her ear in a guttural tone, and everything was primal and right. They rocked against one another tight and grinding, each of her waves wrapping him, her channel sore and swollen and insatiable and his spasming cock wanting nothing more than to give, give, give until she was filled up and couldn't take anymore.

Damian pressed one of his hands flat against the glass and caught her with the other, holding her up as he finished—three more final thrusts like he couldn't give her up, before pulling himself free with a hiss.

"Oh, God, Andi," he said, lifting her to him and spinning her around to hold her to his chest, the water falling over them, his cum dripping from between her legs. "Princess, what was that?" he murmured.

She had no words. She swayed again and let him hold her. Each time they fucked, whatever common sense part of her that told her that this was impossible and such a bad idea that there was no point in chasing dreams, much less a dragon, became smaller and smaller, and if she kept doing this with him—kept letting him do this to her —then it would go away, and there would be nothing stopping her from getting hurt at all.

Him fucking her until she was sore was one thing. She could not —would not—let him fuck over her heart.

But his hands were at her chin, pulling her up to drift a kiss across her lips, and she couldn't tell him no. Fuck, she could barely stand, and when he turned both of them so that she faced the shower bench and put a hand on her back so that she would bend down and hold onto it with both hands, she thought he'd seen the dazed look she surely had, like a woman trying not to pass out.

Then he moved beside her, his hands expertly controlling the shower, pulling a sprayer off the wall to give to her on a gushing setting, where all the water welled out of the center like a fountain. She took it, breathing, trying to find herself again after giving so much up and saw him settle himself to kneel on the towel that she'd folded for him earlier, behind her.

"Damian?" she asked him.

"Use that on your clit," he told her.

"What? Why?" she asked, her mind still fuzzy as he put a hand on each of her ass cheeks and pulled her open for him, forcing her to show him her most intimate part. "Oh my God...no!" she gasped, snapping alert and dancing forward.

"Why not?" he asked her. He wasn't prying anymore, but she could distinctly feel the outline of where his hands lay, almost as if she'd been spanked.

"Because!" she protested. "It's...it's—"

He chuckled behind her. "Princess, nothing about you is dirty." He slid his thumb down and he touched her there and she felt a quick spasm of attention roll through her entire body. "And everything about you is mine."

"We'll see," she panted, hesitating and unsure, as he left his thumb on that spot, gently rubbing, not pushing in in the least, just holding space, touching her soft wet skin. She let out a ragged sigh and leaned back into him, offering more of herself, and heard him rumble in response. "But Damian, you can't go in there just yet, okay?"

"I would never. Not without a lot of lube and patience and permission. It would be a thing we would do together—not in the heat of the moment, but planned, because we both wanted to try it." He leaned forward, and she felt him kiss the apple of her ass at its highest point. "That said," he went on, still rubbing the rim of her asshole with his thumb. "You've already done so much for me today, Andi. Just let me do this for you."

She swallowed, as one of his hands reached forward and brought hers into position, so that the water from the sprayer was lapping at her clit, and then both of his hands were on her ass again, pulling her completely open for him. She felt him lean forward, and then his mouth was where his thumb had just been, kissing her tight hole, and she fought not to jump.

This was wrong. It felt so dirty. How could he want her there? A cacophony of reasons why she shouldn't be bent over in front of him circled in her mind, but as he kept kissing her, she couldn't help but respond to him, leaning back, letting his tongue dance in delicate circles around her edges, fearlessly flickering against her tightest point, and she felt something in her—impossibly, it seemed—wind again. She took better control of the spraying water now, making sure it was gushing up underneath her hood, and her hips bobbed, unsure if they should rock into the water to satisfy her clit, or stay angled high to be played by his tongue until she moaned.

Damian moaned, too, in response to her. Between her legs, she could see where he was already hard again, his lonely cock straining up, until she bent over farther, and as if sensing her motive, he let go of her with one hand and sent it down to stroke himself.

That...was hot as fuck. And it proved he wasn't working her over with his mouth just to prove himself a good lover or out of some sense of obligation. Doing what he was doing to her now turned him on. So much so that he needed to touch himself.

Realizing that, Andi gave herself over to the experience, breathing harder as she used the water, trapped between its stream and Damian's relentless tongue, listening to the slick wet sounds of him pulling his thick cock faster and faster. New nerves sang, and everything felt *wrong* until it started feeling *good*, until the goodness outweighed anything she could possibly be afraid of, and she knew that there *would* come a time when she *would* trust him to let him put his tongue or fingers or anything else inside her there, as long as it kept feeling just like this. Her hips got that full-tight feeling, like something combustible inside her was going to explode, and she started writhing faster, rubbing herself against his tongue, playing herself with the water, listening to him moan as he brought himself up to the edge alongside her, and somehow, everything felt right. He was making her feel good and she was making him feel good and they were like one of those eternal world-circling snakes that bit its own tail in Nordic mythology, in some endless cycle of pleasure until she reached one hand forward to hold the bench in front of her again so that she had something to brace on and cried out in wordless passion.

Damian growled and rose to his knees, his mouth following her through until she started to buckle, dropping the sprayer, and she turned over her shoulder in time to see him finish himself off, his hot cum spurting into the air and rolling like candle wax down his hand.

"You came again," she said, breathless, collapsing against the bench behind her.

"Of course," he said simply, looking up at her with a dark smile. "Do you know how many times I jerked off just thinking of you last week? There's no way I'm not going to come around you now that I can, anytime I can."

Andi flushed, even in the heat of the shower, then guessed, "Eleven?"

Damian laughed. "More than eleven. Less than forty. Probably."

She grinned and sank down to be at his level on the shower's stone floor, and crawled into his lap, where she tucked herself against his chest and underneath his chin and pressed herself to him. His heartbeat was slow and steady, and she took great comfort in it.

"Are you better now?" she asked him.

He rumbled thoughtfully against her. "I will be. I'll figure out something."

"You mean we'll figure out something," she corrected him.

He ran his thumb down her arm that he held. "I thought saying things like that was mean."

"Don't overthink it," she warned, thumping her head against him. "But also, don't make assumptions."

"Oh, I would never, princess," he said with a soft snort, though he pulled her closer against him. "Although I think you should know it is killing me to not make some kind of assumption, ass-ump-tion joke."

She groaned. "If I had known eating my ass would allow you to make shitty puns, I never would've let you."

"Shitty puns, you say?" he teased, and she lightly punched him.

"Ugh. Just...no. Don't even." She shuddered. "Make sure you go use mouthwash."

"Of course. I'm a dragon, not a monster." He pinched her bottom gently. "Let's get up and get clean for real and somehow not fuck again for at least twenty minutes, or until I've dealt with some things."

"Do we have to?" she asked, teasing on purpose, but she saw the look in his eyes. If she snapped her fingers, he'd follow her into the bedroom, and everything would start all over again. Hell, they might not even make it that far. She closed her eyes and drew on strength from somewhere deep within, before standing to take a real shower.

ANDI HAD NEVER HAD a man bathe her before. She'd done sexy things in the shower with men, but none of them had ever decided that she needed to be doted on afterward. There was no point in not washing her hair again, seeing as it was all wet and probably tangled, so when his hands went for it with more of that lime and vanilla stuff, she relented, just to see what he would do. His hand traced through her hair and softly scratched her scalp and then tilted her chin and brought the sprayer over to rinse it all back. She felt rather like a horse being groomed—or a race car being detailed—and it was incredibly sexy and also just incredibly good. Sweet. Wholesome, considering everything else they'd just done.

His hands wound around her body holding soap, cupping and massaging the muscles they'd used so strenuously earlier, until she reached that phase of being awkward, feeling silly for being spoiled, and she moved to do something similar to him when he shushed her.

"You've done enough already, I promise you," he told her, but it was hard to believe.

Then again, all of this was unbelievable—her...him...here—so it wasn't worth questioning, really. When he was done washing her, he made her get out and get a robe as he washed himself, and she watched his hands trace over his perfect body through the fogged glass, and it did terrible things to her deep inside. It made her want him again, somehow, which was insane at this point. If they fucked anymore, he'd break her, and she realized she just liked seeing him. Even without the nudity. Just seeing him made her happy.

Goddammit.

She brought her hands to her face to remind herself what an absolutely terrible idea falling for someone who was an otherworldly creature, plus who'd never been in a relationship before, was when he called out to her. "There're extra toothbrushes in a drawer, princess," and she resolutely turned to attend to her dental hygiene and put her clothes back on.

WATCHING him brush his teeth was too couple-y, so she ditched the bathroom entirely as he got out of the shower and then found herself in his bedroom with the Mysterious Box. At least it didn't smell like smoke anymore. But the black mirrors were still creepy, and she wasn't prepared to watch a crystalline beating heart again if she could help it. Human organs were difficult enough. She had not volunteered to take care of any magic ones.

Damian followed her out of the bathroom not long after, with a low-slung towel around his hips and wetly spiked black hair. He smiled at seeing her, and then let loose a low wolf whistle—not at her, she realized, when the magic cat appeared, yowling.

"Yes, it's important," Damian said in response. The cat—which had just somehow *poofed* in out of nowhere—complained in Siamese, then looked at *her* and said something else. "No," he answered. "But the box on my bed...I need you to move it to the room with the Forgetting Fire and erase the door."

The cat grumbled, doing a feline imitation of a teenager being told to clean their room, before hopping up on the bed and spying the box in question, and springing backward three feet, levitation-style.

"That's why I need you to erase the door," Damian repeated. He hadn't gotten any closer to his bed in the meantime, and Andi had a feeling he was staying away from the box on purpose.

The cat had some additional choice words about the situation and the box—Andi may not have spoken "cat," but years at the hospital had made her very intuitive about inflection and fabulous at charades—then up-sized itself to a Siamese the size of a miniature horse, taking the box carefully into its mouth and walking out the door.

Andi watched the whole thing unfold, feeling like she was trapped in some kind of old fairy tale where absurd things happened one by one and no one stopped them. She turned to him. "I cannot believe I'm about to say this sentence, but what did your cat say about me?"

Damian inhaled deeply, calmer now that the box was gone. "He wanted to know if you had any cheese."

"Why?"

He held his towel around his hips with one hand and went into his closet, leaving the door open behind himself. "I can't say. He just really likes cheese is all. Don't tell anyone, though; he's very secretive about it."

"Of course. Why wouldn't your magic cat be?" Andi muttered to herself, sitting down in one of the leather chairs. "So, what was in the box?"

She heard Damian pause in pulling on clothing. "A dragon heart."

"From, like, an actual dragon?" she quipped, rolling her eyes and snorting.

"Pretty much," he said, emerging. He was wearing a dark T-shirt that fit him snugly across his chest and jeans that clung to his thighs. She was embarrassed by how much she noticed that sort of thing now. He made his way over to her and sat down on the ground in front of her, cross-legged. "I have a confession to make," he said solemnly.

She braced. *Here it comes.* The moment she'd been waiting for. When everything between them got flushed down the drain. She stared down into his golden eyes and fought not to cross her arms. "Okay."

"You may have noticed that I'm magical," he said, looking up at her with a tight smile. "Even without the dragon thing, I probably would be—something like on the level of Mills, who you met the other night." Andi nodded as he went on. "So...a long time ago, a great-great-great-grandfather of mine, who was also magical, needed help to stop an epically dangerous world-destroying beast. Something with too many heads, tails, mouths; the painters had a hard time capturing it back then, and everyone who wrote about it sounded like they'd lost their mind. Just know that it was bad, okay?"

"Okay," Andi agreed, hesitantly.

Damian nodded. "So, to save his people, he met with a dragon—an actual dragon, who was never a person, and always his own creature—as equals, and they decided to combine their powers to defeat the creature."

He took a deep inhale and rocked back before continuing. "Well, my distant relative was somewhat of an asshole—also, possibly, another family trait—and when he was working with the dragon to defeat the Beast that Eats Worlds, he learned how to overcome the dragon too. So, when they finished the great battle that ended things, my grandfather killed the dragon and took his heart."

"Why?" she asked and bit her lips.

"Because he didn't want to give the power he'd gained from the dragon back."

Everything about him was serious: his tone, his stance, his expression. "So now you have a magic beating heart as a family heirloom. And here I thought photo albums were rough," she teased, then realized he didn't find it funny. "There's more, isn't there?"

"Yes," he nodded. "Because of the magic involved, and because of the underhanded way my grandfather did things, the heart—and the power it grants my family—comes with a curse."

"Which is?" she prompted after he went quiet.

"Eventually, you become your dragon. Permanently."

"The dragon that you change into? Like, instead of being a prince-frog you become a frog-prince?"

"No. The dragon...it takes over. But it isn't you, really. Not anymore."

Andi felt her jaw drop like it belonged to another person. Here she was, finally on the verge of caring about someone, letting him in after everyone else in her life had seemingly ditched her, and he was cursed. Of course.

God forbid Andi Ngo should ever catch a break.

She put her face into her hands and seriously thought about putting her head between her knees.

"This is a lot, I know," he said, sounding pained. "I tried to get away from it. It's why I came to Earth, to stop it from happening as fast to me."

"Then why is it here?" she asked from inside her hands.

"Near as I can tell, my sister brought it with her."

Which was a whole other thing she'd forgotten to be pissed about. Andi flushed with remembered embarrassment, letting her hands drop. "You mean your sister-the-princess?" she asked. "Like the actual fucking princess and not whatever it is that you call me?"

"Andi," Damian began like she was being unfair.

"No, Damian." She cut him off and crossed her arms. "You didn't tell me you were a freaking prince someplace else. When was that going to come up? I mean, I guess I get that's not first date material, but it's not like we've gone on many dates, have we? And like...and now, you're telling me you're cursed? Like an actual magic curse?" she said. She knew her voice was rising, but no matter how good the sex was, she'd been letting the insanity build for too long to hold back now. "What the *fuck* were you *thinking* trying to get involved with me?" She gave him a pause for an answer, and when he didn't, she went on. "No wonder you haven't been in any relationships before because...Jesus Christ!"

Her words rang out, and for a moment, everything was empty silence.

She watched his jaw grind before asking sharply, "Are you done?"

"No," she said back, just as sharp.

He inhaled and exhaled deeply again, clearly gathering his control. "No," he said, turning the question back on her. "I mean, are you actually done? Because I'm not going to try to apologize to someone who is walking out the door."

She let her head roll back. Just last night, she'd wanted him to promise that he wouldn't try to leave her because she couldn't handle being abandoned again. And here he was now, worried that she would leave him.

Would she have made him promise her a single thing if she'd known all of this ahead of time?

Andi stared at the ceiling. She didn't want to look at him. This was too confusing, and it made her both mad and sad in turns. But when she was quiet, she remembered the way his hands had felt on her...and how warm just looking at him had made her feel. At peace. Despite everything. She sighed, returning her attention to him at last. "I'm not done yet, Damian," she said more quietly. "But shit like this makes it really hard to stay here."

"I know," he said quietly.

"I already had to watch my mother die of cancer." And if her feelings for him kept multiplying like spring clover, she didn't know if she was strong enough to watch him die of a curse. "Surely, you get that it's hard."

"I do," he granted, looking at her with infinite compassion. "I'm sorry there's not an optimal path to follow, Andi."

"An optimal path to find out that the person who wants to be in a relationship with you is secretly royalty and magic and also cursed," she snarked. "Yeah. I can imagine that'd be a lot to try to work into a tinder profile." Andi gave up and let herself sink down, resting her head on her fists on her knees.

He brought the crown of his head to gently rest against hers.

"You do have a safeword you can use if you'd like me to stop talking. They can be multipurpose."

She shook her head, still hunched over, feeling her head rock against his. From this close, she could breathe him in. No matter that they'd just showered, he had a faint manly scent that was intoxicating to her. It calmed her down and riled her up both at once, made her want to sleep in his arms and rip all his clothes off at the same time.

To be with him quietly forever and *right the hell now.*

"Fuck it," she sighed. "Tell me about the dragon. Is he an alternate dimension you? Is he like your twin brother you absorbed in the womb?"

"What?" He pulled back, laughing, sounding confused. "No, of course not. Wherever would you get that idea?"

"Stephen King," she said from the vicinity of her knees, without looking up. "And because getting taken over sounds kind of horrible."

"It is."

Which was why he'd gone almost catatonic not that long ago. Andi took several large breaths and pushed herself back up a little. "So, what changed between you seeing the box here earlier and now?"

"You did," he said. They were on the same level now, and she wanted to crawl off the chair and into his arms again, and however it was he did that to her, it was *not fair.* "I realized you're here. And now that the Heart is here, maybe we—my people and me—can figure out a way to stop it. I was just surprised was all. And deeply disappointed."

She bit her lips. "So, the time that I saw your dragon—when it saved me from that monster-thing in your courtyard—that wasn't you?"

"Not entirely, no. I'm there, but I'm like a rider. And while I guess you could say I hold the reins, I'm not always in control."

"Is the reverse true, now? Can he make you—human you—do

things?"

"In general, no. It frequently has suggestions, though," he said with a soft snort.

"Like what?" she asked.

"I plead the fifth," he said, shaking his head.

"No. You promised to tell me the truth, Damian. And you wanted to be in the deep end...well, here we are."

He rocked back, putting his arms behind him to lean on. "It's a dragon. What do you think it wants to do?"

"Dragon stuff," Andi said sarcastically, then guessed, "Fly?"

"Yes, that," he reluctantly agreed.

She thought back to every silly story she'd ever read or heard. "Burn things with fire?"

"Which I never give it the chance to," he said dryly. "Except for sometimes when we're fighting."

She thought harder and remembered the time when the dragon had saved her from the teleporting-demon thing right outside his castle. "And...kill stuff?"

"It enjoys that the most, yes. Although I am there inside it, so I suppose you could argue we both do." She watched his arm muscles bunch and relax as he talked. "We're good at it."

"Uh-huh." She was trying not to ask the next logical question but also unable to help herself. "Is he around when we..." she began, and then let the words drift because in a conversation full of awkward questions there were still some things she couldn't bring herself to say out loud.

Damian closed his eyes guiltily. "He pays attention. Yes."

"And...just what does he think of that?"

"Andi," Damian groaned. "I should've given you a safeword when I had the chance."

She snorted, remembering that that was just this morning. How had a day with Damian already felt like a week? "It wasn't my fault," she teased. "I tried to help you—"

"And I enjoyed it," he confessed suddenly, cutting her off. She watched a wash of color sweep over his pale complexion. "We both enjoyed it." His gaze trapped hers, daring her to consider what that meant. "All right?"

"Oh," Andi said, biting her lips shut again. "Well...then."

"Yeah." He blew air through pursed lips and looked pained before he raised a hand to push hair out of his face. "I want you to know I've never talked like this—about these things—with anyone before."

"I can't imagine why," she quipped. "This is all quality first date material, Damian. No reason why you couldn't have ordered the lobster and then jumped in. But don't worry, I'll help you set up your dating profile for the next girl after me: 'Hi, my name is Damian, I like to run marathons, drink craft beers, and burn things.'"

One of his dark eyebrows arched. "I only drink whiskey," he corrected her, as his eyes narrowed. "And I am seriously considering spanking you."

"Like I'd let you."

"Like I'd let you stop me," he challenged her, giving her a wicked smile that made parts of her throb with ache. "Safeword aside, of course," he allowed after they both knew slightly too much time had passed.

The way he was looking at her now was decidedly unsafe, and, God, she liked it so much it almost felt shameful. Heat rose inside her unbidden, as the chemical-electrical thing it seemed they shared between them sparked, like a battery being charged. But Andi knew better than to let lust drag her off track. They needed to talk. And there were things that she needed to know if she was somehow going to really let herself do this, to knowingly run toward the spinning knives for this man.

As he leaned forward with intent, she scooted the chair away. "Have you always had it inside you?"

She could almost watch him downshift to idle like he was in a car. "No. It came out for the first time when I was ten."

"Why?" she asked, imagining Damian losing a game to his sister and going dragon to protest it in the way of little boys.

"Because someone tried to kill me," he said simply with a shrug.

"Really?"

"Yes, really. Things like that happened where I'm from. It's not very nice there."

Andi tried to remember what she was like at ten. What it would've been like to discover that she had a monster inside of her. And here she'd thought puberty was bad.... "What was it like?"

"Horrible? Frightening? Awesome? In the literal, not colloquial, sense." His arms and shoulders bunched up again like he was remembering.

"Does it hurt to change?"

"Yes." He nodded slightly. "Always."

She bit her lips again. "Does it hurt the dragon?"

Damian's brow furrowed and his eyes glazed over as though he were communing with something inside himself, and Andi knew he was. "All the time," he said quietly. "It feels...chained."

Andi pushed the chair behind herself back and got on her knees on the floor so that her face was even with his. His gaze was on her again, and she looked deep into his golden eyes, trying to see the beast and wondering if it, too, was looking out at her. "Can I talk to it?"

"No, princess. It cannot speak. We've tried." His gaze softened. "I can tell you what it's thinking, though if it tells me."

"Does he like me?"

She didn't like the way her voice sounded when she asked, all little-girl and hesitant. But she needed to know. If Damian's dragon hated her or was indifferent, then there was no way the plan coalescing in her mind could work.

She watched Damian think inside himself, and at the same time, saw everything that was "together" about him fall away, as though he were dropping pieces of unseen armor right in front of her until he finally gave her the completely open look he'd had so often after sex.

"Oh, yes, princess," he said softly. "Very much."

CHAPTER
SIX

Damian watched Andi gulp for air after his confession.

"Even though I'm human?" she pressed.

"I don't know what to tell you. My mother was human, too. It happens."

But "it" didn't happen. *Mates* happened. He wished so badly he could tell her without scaring her, but if she couldn't even acknowledge she wanted to be in a relationship with him—despite the way that her scent changed whenever he came around, the way he watched the heat that flushed her core—there was no way for him to safely push her forward.

And as it was right now, he needed to be ready to pull his dragon back. It'd never paid so much attention to a human conversation before. Damian could feel it lying right underneath his skin, watching, waiting, listening so closely that it was a wonder that Andi couldn't see it. The carnivore in him calculated the myriad of changes flowing over her as they spoke. The way her pupils dilated, how often she licked her lips, the rise and fall of her pulse at her throat. He wasn't sure if his dragon wanted to eat her or fuck her or if there was all that much difference between the two in the end.

Tell her I like the way she smells, his dragon commanded in the lull.

Damian blinked. *No.*

Why not?

Because it's creepy.

Why? his dragon pressed like a human child.

Internally, Damian sighed, then supposed at least if he told her that, maybe she'd believe it because it wasn't the kind of thing *he* would say as a human. "He'd like me to share with you that he likes the way you smell."

Her eyes widened in what he was afraid was horror. "What do I smell like?"

Everything I've ever wanted, Damian thought but didn't say aloud. "Apples, caramel, and the sea."

She blushed and then tentatively brought the back of her hand up to sniff it. "You're joking, right?" she said as she squirmed.

"Not at all."

Andi was quiet so long after that that he thought he'd said the wrong thing. His dragon kept ticking away seconds patiently, reporting on Andi's physiology like she was a weather front, an increase of pressure here, rising heat there—when what his human-self needed were her words.

Her full lips finally parted to rescue him. "Does he care about me?" she asked so quietly that if he hadn't been part-dragon, he wouldn't have heard.

Yes, his dragon answered for him, without hesitation.

Damian froze. How would any human react to finding out a dragon cared for it? What reaction could there be but horror?

Tell her, his dragon pressed.

If I do, she'll run.

His dragon didn't deny this. *You swore to never lie to her,* it countered.

There's lying, and then, there's elaborately dodging the truth, he told the beast inside. It roiled inside him. He'd let it get so close to the

110

surface while it was listening that the sudden motion hurt him. He had to fight to not let it show.

She wasn't asking you. She was asking me.

He braced himself to shove the beast back, to pretend that his dragon never thought of her like that, like he hadn't spent the past week of his life tortured by how badly it wanted to see her, how much it yearned to just be by her side. It couldn't have her like he could, couldn't take her like he could, but it was content to just be in her presence with him. How could he ever explain to her that the horrific thing inside him that killed other monsters and men without thinking twice longed for nothing more than to lay its head down at her feet?

Damian knew that was all too much for right now. But he couldn't lie to her either. He'd already watched the outcome of a relationship built on lies in his parents, close up. If she ran off screaming, could he blame her?

No matter how much it hurt him, mightn't it also be for the best?

Damian closed his eyes because he didn't want to watch Andi recoil. "He says to tell you yes."

After that, he listened. He heard the beating of her heart and the beating of his own and a slight rustle of fabric, which he assumed would proceed her running out the door. Then a soft hand touched his cheek, and he blinked his eyes open to find her staring at him. "Tell him if that's true, and if he truly does care for me, then he's not allowed to have you."

Damian could feel his dragon staring out at her, thinking hard, the creature as heavy inside him as molten lead. As for himself, he could hardly dare to breathe.

Tell her...that I will try, his dragon rumbled, and for a moment Damian thought he might be free—had the answer always been so easy?—before the beast continued. *But even love cannot break a curse.*

His dragon's words hit him like an anchor dropped on glass.

"He says to tell you he will try," he said softly, staring into her beautiful brown eyes, shining at him in hope.

"That's good, right?" she asked with a smile.

"It is," he said, catching her hand in his and turning his face to place a kiss against her palm.

ANDI FOLLOWED Damian out of the bedroom and into the rest of the house. He'd called his magic cat to convene a meeting in some conference room. She hadn't asked if she could come along; she would assume so until he told her otherwise. But every step there made her a little more anxious than the one before because she'd only met his people...twice? Kind-of-sort-of? And here she and Damian were, both coming down from his room, with similarly wet hair—it wouldn't take a genius to figure out what they'd been up to. She knew Sammy was sex-positive, but she had no idea what Damian's roommates?—*Castle-mates*?—thought about things.

He opened a door and gestured her through. She walked in without thinking, found everyone else already inside looking deadly serious, and she felt even more out of place.

Andi named them again in her mind: Mills, the witch who could only tell the truth; Max, the very pale man with paler hair and strange goggles; Zach, the werewolf whose life she'd saved at her own hospital; and Jamison, a dark-skinned man with one arm made of metal. She assumed Austin was still watching the princess in the library, and she had no idea what'd become of the magic cat.

"Um, hi, again," Andi said, waving nervously. Damian strode around her and pulled a seat out for her, entirely ignorant of the room's tone. She sat down lightly, trying to figure out how much of a fuss she was prepared to make if someone told her she needed to go.

"Everyone, Andi. Andi, everyone," Damian said, sitting down roughly beside her. His mood had darkened on their way here, despite the fact that his knee touched hers—very much on purpose, she was sure—underneath the table.

Zach cleared his throat and started speaking. "This is a little unorthodox, Damian," the werewolf began, and she felt Damian tense.

"Whatever you have to tell me, you can say in front of Andi."

She looked around the table at them and noted that they weren't looking at her at all, only at Damian. *Oh, shit.* Andi knew exactly what this was from having watched them before on TV—an intervention.

"No...not her," Jamison said. "We've been talking and—"

"*They've* been talking," Max corrected, crossing his arms. "I still agree with you."

"Well, we—minus Max, apparently—think you made the wrong call," Mills said. "With the janitor. You should've brought him in."

"Why?" Damian leaned forward. "What've you found while tracking him?"

"He's gone home for the evening. I've got his TV listening in on him now."

"And are there screams of children being murdered in the background?" Damian asked flippantly, and Andi turned to stare at him in horror.

"That's not funny, Damian," Zach said.

"I didn't mean it to be," Damian said, turning toward him. "If there are, we'll fucking swoop in. But until then—"

"Until then, we just wait for the murdering?" Jamison pressed.

Damian sighed. "Mills...you of all people should understand. Do we have any other leads on the Hunters currently?"

"Nothing...except for the fact that Andi's uncle's home was rented through the same shell corporation as the van full of Hunter paraphernalia we need to slag. But, it's a wall." The woman frowned.

"And did you try to hack it, Jamison?" he asked.

"Everything but brute force, as per your request," the metal-armed man said, also frowning. "But I'd rather do that and out ourselves than wait here, like this."

Andi raised her hand politely. One by one, they all stopped and stared. "Excuse me, but what the fuck? Murdered children?"

"Only metaphorically," Max took Damian's side.

"Thank you," Damian told him.

"So far," Zach corrected both of them.

Andi made a time-out symbol with her hands. "Okay. I hate to be annoying, but could you please back up? I'm clearly missing info."

"Sure thing," Zach said, putting his elbows on the table and talking fast before Damian could cut him off. "Damian here decided to let a Hunter go free earlier today—one who was hunting at a mall."

She looked at Damian and could see the muscles clench in his angular jaw. "Why?"

He gave her a look that distinctly said, 'Not You, Too.' "Because, Andi, we're not set up for prisoners, torture isn't always reliable, and he could just be some schmuck getting paid to wave a wand around. We don't know a thing about your uncle's operation. He could be our only connection to it. If we can follow him back—if he says the wrong thing, makes a phone call, goes to their location—we'll know more."

Andi pulled out her phone and put it on the table with a flourish. "Did it occur to you that you could just ask me to call him?" She reached for it again, and Damian caught her hand, pressing it down.

"No," he said in a tone of voice that was used to being listened too.

She ignored it. "His secretary's been stalking me all day, according to my roommate. I dodged her this morning before I went to the cemetery."

Everyone else around the table looked at one another with a pregnant pause.

"We could...." Mills said slowly and began walking her fingers out on the table.

"No," Damian repeated, even more final than before.

"I'm just saying," Mills went on.

"Don't you dare," he clipped.

"Okay, fine, Damian, leave the room so I can hear what they want to say," Andi told him. He looked at her, eyes wide in some combination of denial and anger, and Max started laughing hysterically.

"Oh, you are well-matched!" The pale man clutched his stomach, shuddering. "Your father would've been so proud."

Damian exhaled in a rush. "Not now, Max."

"Yes, now. She's got fire. Let her spend it," Max said, grinning at her.

"I'll keep an eye on her, Damian," Jamison said.

"And we'll be following her in the tour bus," Zach promised.

Damian looked around the table, aghast. "She doesn't even know what she's offering—she's human!"

Andi stiffened and yanked her hand out from under his. "And is that not good enough for you?"

He rounded on her and spoke through gritted teeth. "That is absolutely not fair, and you know it."

"Oh? So, it's okay for you to go off and have adventures and me to wait at home, not knowing, but you can't handle the reverse for just one evening?" Her eyes panned over him, waiting for him to trust her enough to back down, and when he didn't, she came on twice as hard. "I told you I was not a wait-at-home woman. I want to do this."

He made a strangled sound and spoke like he was talking to a child. "Andi, if something happens to you, I will not be able to control my dragon. It will destroy half this city until it gets revenge."

Jamison cleared his throat.

"What, Jamison," Damian growled, while still staring her down.

"That's kind of why we have that one gun, isn't it?" he said. "For...just in case?"

Andi watched Damian glower as she looked between the men, then saw Mills subtly nod for her to go on. "Damian, I'd rather put myself in a tiny bit of danger than have you roll the dice on someone's death."

"And I would rather not be having this discussion," Damian said, his voice like grinding gravel, "but here we fucking are."

"He's not going to kill me." She put her hand back on top of his and much nearer her phone. "He won't do anything bad to me."

"Famous last words," Damian said like a swear.

"How do you know, Andi?" Mills pressed.

"Because," Andi said, looking around the table briefly. "My brother would never forgive him if he did. And I feel for sure he needs my brother, for whatever the hell it is he's planning."

Damian stared at her, and when she didn't fold, he turned to see the others all watching him. "I. Hate. This," he said, making the three words separate sentences. "And, if anything happens to her, I will never forgive any one of you."

"Well then," Mills said brightly. "We'd better do our best."

THE REST of the meeting was spent in logistics, and Andi was well aware of Damian seething beside her, listening to their conversation go on without him. The plan was for them to drop her off at the bus stop and for her to go home, where Elsa was still waiting —according to a fresh text from Sammy—and then for her to knock on Elsa's window and ask why she was there, in the hopes that she only wanted to coordinate a meeting and not a kidnapping.

But, if the kidnapping happened, their "tour bus" would be waiting nearby and would follow Elsa's car and wait in reserve, listening in via a tracking device that they gave her, running in for a rescue the moment she needed one. It felt like a sound plan to Andi, Damian's nonparticipation aside.

At the end, once details were finalized, the group stood to go out. Mills stopped by the door, turning back suddenly. "Damian, why did you call us here?"

"We'll discuss it later. I'm talked out," he said, despite not having talked for the past forty-five minutes.

Mills inhaled to fight him, then shrugged, and Andi had to fight not to grin because she precisely recognized that feeling. "Okay.

Everyone know what to do?" Mills asked instead and got a roomful of grunts and nods. "And...you feel prepared, Andi?"

"Yeah, thank you." She now had separate tracking devices in her bra, jeans pocket, and shoe, which felt like overkill to her, but hey... and then followed the rest of them outside to get loaded into Damian's Pagani for the short drive to the bus stop.

He opened the gull-wing door and sullenly watched her get in before closing it, his hands in his jeans pockets as he walked around the car for his own side. Once there, he buckled his seat belt and silently turned the car on.

"Are you just not going to talk to me?" she asked him as they passed through the first gate out of his compound.

"I don't want to yell. So not talking is safer," he said, swinging through a turn without looking over.

Andi curled up in the seat of the car and sighed. "When are you going to tell them about the dragon heart?"

He was quiet long enough she thought he might not answer. "Once I'm sure I'm not going to Godzilla out on the city later on this evening."

"You're being dramatic, Damian," she complained.

"I prefer overprotective. It's more manly." He finally glanced over at her. "You drive me crazy, you know that?"

"Clearly." She rolled her eyes.

"No. I mean it," he said, whipping the car over to the side of the road, rolling it onto a wide grassy berm. He hit the steering wheel, easily denting it.

"Damian!" she gasped. If the car was two million, how much was just that?

He growled, popped it back into a rough circle with his hands, and then turned on her. "What if this is the last time I see you alive?"

"It won't be," she said firmly.

"You don't know that, Andi." His golden eyes searched hers, and the tension radiating off of him was like the thrum of a high-voltage wire in humidity. "What if it is? I don't know what this is like for you or how many other people you've cared about before. But you are it for me. The only one. And if you die, a part of me dies too." His words echoed in the sports car, and Andi didn't know what to say. His hands wrung the steering wheel as he went on more quietly. "Maybe all of me, Andi. I feel that. Don't you?"

When he said it like that, she wanted to. She wanted to give in and just let herself feel with abandon, to never worry about not feeling again, or how she'd survive if the spigot were suddenly turned off. "Damian," she whispered quietly, ready to tell him as much when he whirled on her again.

"Don't you dare say that I'm being mean when you're trying to throw your life away to prove a foolish point," he snapped.

She bit her lips and swallowed. "Fine. Then I won't."

He closed his eyes, and she wondered if she'd driven him to counting, which was a thing that her ex Josh used to do, to make a show of just how infuriating she could be, and then his eyes reopened. "I can't imagine life without you."

Which was what he'd been trying to do with his pause, she realized. Not counting. Just trying to picture a life without her in it. She hadn't scared him away by being her most real self, and he was still fully present with her.

How on earth could all this feel so real so fast?

Maybe because he wasn't *from* earth at all.

But neither his feelings nor her response to them changed what needed to be done—although Andi had a sudden sympathy for moths drawn to burning flames. "I'm sorry, Damian. But I'm still my own person. I get to make my own decisions, and this decision feels right."

"What if it is not, though?"

She sighed sympathetically. "If there's one thing working at the hospital has taught me, it's that there are no guarantees. Not ever. If it's not this plan, then it could be some morning my bus gets hit by a semi. Or a patient chokes me out. Or I trip down the stairs on my way out the door." She reached over and put her hand atop his on the steering wheel. "I can't live my life being scared of a maybe."

He shook his head in denial. "But there are ways to control risks, Andi—"

"You mean like being followed by the best magical crew on the planet and having a man and dragon who are..." she began, and then caught herself before she put words like 'in love with me' in his mouth, even though that was surely what this was—which was why he hurt so bad and didn't know what to do about it. The thought made her heart leap into her own throat in some combination of fear and delight, and she knew she'd never be able to untangle the two. "Intimately concerned with my well-being," she finished quickly.

"Intimately concerned with you not being foolish, *princess*," he corrected her.

Her eyes narrowed. "There's a fine line between overprotective and infantilizing, *dragon*, and you're riding it."

He made a wordless sound of frustration, put the car in drive, and yanked it back on the road.

DAMIAN PULLED the car to a stop just inside the Briar's gates, completely unsure what to do. Everything in him told him that he needed to stop her, to protect her at all costs, her opinion of him be damned, but then he realized that it was a slippery slope from there to what had happened to his mother. Sure, he could use the Forgetting Fire on Andi and wipe even the idea of this from her mind, but who would she be without her fierce though foolish passion and seemingly endless strength?

"I still hate this," he muttered, but he hit the button that opened her door for her.

Andi turned toward him, lit by the dashboard lights. "I will be as safe as I possibly can, I promise."

"I don't believe you, but apparently you don't care," he said. She looked wounded, and he realized he didn't even begin to want those to be his last words to her. "I...take that back," he said, swallowing down all the bile in his throat at the thought of losing her. "I do believe you." He inhaled deeply. "I just need you to try your hardest."

"I will," she said hesitating.

And then what now? Kiss her like he might never see her again? If he touched her, there was no possible way he would ever let her go. He faced the steering column, holding it tight. "Good luck on your mission."

She waited, seemingly for something else, and then when he didn't give it, she leaned forward and brushed his cheek with a kiss before getting out. He watched her walk to the bus stop, cradling a hand to his cheek as if her kiss were a living thing that he could keep there.

If anything happens to her, his dragon began, then didn't finish; it just assaulted him with images of pain, destruction, and death. If someone hurt her, then the dragon would take out all of its rage on the city—the world, in turn—take out every moment of pain it'd ever had at being trapped in human form, revenge for every day Damian had kept it from the sky.

Yes, Damian agreed as the bus arrived, and Andi got on board. Because without Andi in his life, absolutely nothing else mattered. He wouldn't be able to—*wouldn't want to*—stop his dragon. Jamison would have to shoot him down; it would be their end, no doubt. *If anything happens to her,* he told it, *I will let you.*

He watched the bus pull away and whipped his car around, driving back up to his castle at top speed.

"I'VE GOT HER," Jamison announced the second he'd parked his car. Everyone else was already loaded up, and Damian took a seat in the back, between Max and Zach, most likely so that if they heard anything dangerous, they could stop him from throwing himself out the door. Jamison and Mills were in the front, and Austin was still on nurse duty.

Mills was driving, so from his spot, he could see the computer perched on Jamison's lap, with its not-comforting-enough beacon on Andi, and his thoughts were interrupted by the squealing sound of brakes and the warning chime that preceded a bus's stop.

"It's one-way only," Jamison said. "Although she knows that we can hear her."

"Can I sit there?" someone asked her, and his stomach lurched. What if it was a Hunter closing in?

"Of course!" Andi said too brightly, and Damian felt entirely hamstrung, just listening for any sounds of danger.

"She's going to be okay, Damian," Zach said.

"For at least the first fifteen minutes here anyways," Mills added. "That's the length of the bus ride."

"Not helping," Damian muttered aloud and folded in on himself.

THEY MADE it to their destination just before the bus did as planned, pulling in to parallel park far enough away to not be seen, but close enough to be able to use binoculars to see Andi's apartment's entire parking lot. As Andi walked off of the bus, a tall blonde woman got out of a waiting car and strode over to her. The woman definitely looked like an Elsa, and he momentarily wished that Andi hadn't told them about the claw she wore on a leather thong around her neck.

"Running plates," Jamison announced. "Leased to Bright Star Corporation again...same goddamned wall."

"Andrea," the blonde must've announced because no one else would've used Andi's full name for her.

"Elsa. Again," Andi said, crossing her arms and sounding perturbed. "What the hell are you doing here? Sammy said you'd been here all day."

"Waiting for you, obviously." The blonde's voice was husky, and

Damian wondered when the last time she'd eaten any meat/drank any blood.

"Why?" Andi asked.

"Your uncle would like to talk to you."

"I bet he would," Andi said, with just the right amount of snark. It wouldn't do for her to seem too eager, as they'd priorly discussed. "What makes him think I want to talk to him?"

"She's good," murmured Max.

"Agreed," said Mills.

Elsa took an inhale deep enough to come through over the wire and then sounded like she was talking through gritted teeth. "He would like the chance to talk to you. In person."

"So, why are you here and not him?" Andi asked her sharply.

"That was not part of the plan," Damian growled.

Mills looked back at him. "Her pain's genuine. Let it flow."

"Your uncle is a very important man," the strange woman went on.

"Yeah, fuck that," Andi said, and Damian winced as she went on, worried for her. "My whole life, I've been hearing about how Uncle Lee's sooooo important, but he's also a fucking liar. So, fuck him and go fuck yourself too." Damian watched Andi turn on her heel and walk toward her apartment with purpose.

Zach made a thoughtful sound. "Is she blowing this?"

Damian grunted. "I'm not getting my hopes up."

They heard the sound of heels trotting on concrete through the wire as the woman ran after her. "He wants to apologize to you. For keeping you in the dark all these years. He never meant to hurt you, Andrea, and frankly, all of this would sound better coming from him, not me. I never apologize."

Andi stopped three stairs up to make a rueful sound. "I believe you. You're shit at this."

The woman sighed again. "So, let him talk to you. Indulge an old man."

"A man who kidnapped my brother, let me think he might be dead, and then somehow turned him into a dragon?"

"One and the same," she said.

Andi put her hands over her face and rubbed her temples. "I can't believe I'm even beginning to consider this."

"You want answers, don't you? If nothing else?" the woman pressed.

Andi waited for what seemed like a long time even to Damian and then exhaled in a rush. "Yes. Fine. Fuck."

The woman chuckled, and walked back toward her car, opening up the rear door. "Get in."

DAMIAN'S STOMACH twisted in knots as Andi rode quietly in the back of the woman's car. Jamison endlessly triangulated possible destinations, laying odds on them with Mills, but Andi's signal was the only sign of life he had from her. He belatedly realized the trackers weren't attuned to her health. What if she was already dead inside the car they followed? If Hunters had jumped her with chloroform and knives the instant she'd gotten in? Surely, if that'd happened, he would've felt it somehow, through their inexplicable yet growing bond, but.... His muscles bunched, turning rock hard, as the dragon inside him readied to fight.

"Damian, don't," Max warned, bringing him down.

He regathered control of himself. He and his dragon had been so likeminded, he hadn't even realized he'd been losing it, and he nodded at the other man. "For now."

"They're at the ports," Jamison said, as Mills slowed the tour bus down to take a turn. His electronics put in a code that allowed them access not long after Andi's car had passed, but they had to fall even farther back—there were no other active cars here and even fewer places to hide. Mills hit the button to take the SUV into electric mode so it could coast silently and traced their way to the water's edge where the car that had held Andi was tightly parked in between two shipping containers, with no way to see the other side of any of them.

Damian's dragon growled low at the same time as Damian announced, "Fuck this." He tore his seat belt and lunged over Zach before the werewolf could react, throwing himself out of the moving vehicle to run for the water's edge. He jumped for the edge of a shipping container, caught the top of it easily, and hauled himself up to see what was happening to Andi on the other side...just in time to see her at the end of a pier, getting into a boat.

He grabbed hold of the metal beneath him, ready to tear it off and take it into the sky with him as he shifted, gasping out the word, "Boat," first for his earpiece, so the others would understand, and then, Max and Zach were there tackling him.

He shouted in incoherent rage and shoved them off, standing now to watch the boat as it raced away.

Chase after her! his dragon roared, surging inside of him.

"Jamison still has her!" Zach shouted while Max took the more direct route of punching him across his jaw. Damian's head snapped with the impact of the bear-shifter's hit, and he instinctively wheeled on the man.

Max fell to an obedient knee. "Control yourself, prince."

Damian panted, hands clenching into fists at his side. "Where is she?" he growled.

"I'll be able to tell you in a second here," Jamison said from where the SUV was parked below. Damian flung himself down to the ground beside it, as Jamison opened up a box and said, "Fly, my pretties!" Half a dozen drones the size of dinner plates swarmed out, soaring into the air and heading the direction Andi'd gone. Once they were aloft, Jamison glanced at Damian with that half-trance look in his eye he sometimes got when he was communing with his tech. "I can't keep an eye on them and be thinking about shooting you, too, so, behave."

Damian growled again, and then Mills was there, taking his hand in hers. He looked to her and knew she couldn't tell him any bullshit like that 'it was going to be all right.' Instead, she told him the truth. "She's smart, and she's tough."

Damian inhaled deeply, regaining himself, despite his tormented dragon's howls, pushing the beast back. "Where are they going, Jamison? And why isn't she talking?" He tried not to sound panicked about that—and failed.

Then as one, they all heard the tracking devices on her check-in, as a man's voice said, "Andrea!" at top volume.

CHAPTER

SEVEN

Andi had not been expecting the boat—more of a small yacht, really—but she could hardly back out now, plus surely Damian's people would think of some contingency. And she'd meant what she'd said earlier to Elsa. She did want answers, and it seemed like her uncle was the only one who had them. So, she followed Elsa to a nicely appointed room below deck, with a desk and a bed. She knew it was her uncle's because of two things: it smelled like his pipe smoke, and it had another elephant foot trash can by his desk. She prayed to God that he only had four of them and that all of them were from the same elephant.

The trash can wasn't the only thing that gave it away. There were other trinkets too: a jade pipe holder on his desk, with a matching ashtray. A sea turtle shell was mounted behind the desk's chair, and above that was a framed strip of snakeskin, at least ten feet long, before it tapered on both ends.

Andi sat in front of the desk like she assumed she ought to, and shortly thereafter heard a familiar voice boom, "Andrea!"

Andi slowly turned. It was her uncle, the same as always. Short in stature, in a navy-blue silk smoking jacket, beard and mustache impeccably groomed, with a pipe in one hand. "Lee," she said simply.

"Oh, so now I'm not even an uncle?" he teased as he rounded the room and sat down at the desk in front of her.

"I don't know who you are, really." Andi hunched down into herself. It was the truth. So much of her childhood had apparently been built on lies. "I just want to know what happened to Danny and how I can undo it."

"Andrea...I don't think that's possible. Nor do I think that your brother wants to be 'undone.'" He tapped the plug of his pipe out onto the ashtray on his desk and rummaged in a drawer before lifting out a pouch of Balkan pipe tobacco to send it scooping in. "What do you know of the true nature of the world, Andrea?"

Andi looked up at him. "What do you mean?"

"I mean, how much do you know? Or rather, do you think you know?"

"I...don't know. I know there's science...and apparently, there's magic. Or whatever the hell you did to Danny that I saw last night." Just last night. It hadn't even been that long ago. She bit her lips and wished she'd spent her time on the drive over trying to anticipate questions instead of just burning with righteous indignation. She'd foolishly assumed she'd be the one leading the charge. With a life-time's worth of experience dealing with her overbearing uncle, she should've known better.

"And just what were you there for?" Lee asked sharply. "At the club?"

"Trying to hunt down Danny like it's my job because, for my entire life, it has been," she said, crossing her arms. "His stupid friend Julian told his boss there I wanted to know things, and his boss invited me over. I thought I was helping you out...until I saw Danny and David fighting and realized things were fucked."

Her uncle made a thoughtful noise. "I'm sorry you had to see that. And sorrier still that David tried to involve you. He always was a bit hotheaded. I don't think Danny wanted to kill him, but after that, David gave him no choice. Dragons are nothing without their pride, you see." He struck a match and held it to his pipe, sucking down the flame until he billowed smoke, and Andi coughed. "And Danny's still discovering himself and his limits. Such a shame we lost the skin, though."

Andi let her eyes rove over the room at all his trophies before speaking again. "Skin? Whose skin?"

Her uncle gave his pipe another contemplative pull. "Danny's."

"You...skinned him? You skinned my brother?" Her hands clenched onto the armrests of her chair till her knuckles went white.

"Only a little bit," her uncle said, like that made it any better. "And it was freely offered. Don't worry about him; now that he's magical, it'll regrow."

"I think I'm going to throw up," Andi muttered, as acid zinged across her tongue.

"Don't. I mean, you can if you want, but there's no need, Andrea. Danny knew exactly what he was getting into."

"In and out of stolen cars. Back and forth to jail," Andi said. Everyone knew that Danny was a troublemaker since day one. The boy that everyone wanted, who got tacit permission to fuck every-thing up. "So how long did you wait after my mother died to embroil him in your plans?"

Her uncle took a great inhale and carefully set his pipe down. "Andrea, dear...your mother helped."

Andi didn't hear whatever he said next. She could see his lips moving, but she only heard static in her ears, and the acid at the back of her tongue increased like she was chewing on foil. She grabbed hold of the edge of the desk to stay upright.

Uncle Lee finally stopped talking and looked concerned. "Andrea?" he asked.

"You...you're lying," she whispered hoarsely, as her stomach churned. "You're wrong...and you're lying."

"Oh, my favorite niece, I am so, so sorry." He reached out for her.

"Don't touch me!" she shouted, and he pulled back in alarm.

129

Childhood memories assaulted her. She suddenly remembered every mysterious and strange meal she'd had at his place for the Moon Cake Holiday as a child, all the things she didn't want to eat...and all the things she'd gone ahead and eaten.

How one time, when she was six or seven, he'd made them all a vat of soup to share, and when she'd asked what was in it, he'd said shark fin, along with shavings of unicorn liver. Everyone had laughed like it was some kind of joke, but she'd been in a horse phase and was worried he was serious.

"Did you really catch a unicorn, Uncle Lee?" she'd asked him with the kind of lisp kids had when they were missing teeth.

She remembered his response like it was yesterday, him with his beard trimmed in the exact same style, his crinkled eyes pleased with himself, and the same self-satisfied smile, as he laid his hand solemnly on her small shoulder: *"Andrea, you can catch anything if you're patient enough."*

Andi could feel her heartbeat everywhere in her body—in her stomach, in her face, in her throat.

"Andrea...I am sorry. This is not how we, your mother and I, had planned to tell you. But we both made that decision, and I suppose it is now my burden to bear."

"I'm going to—" she warned him, just a second before she flew out of her chair and ran for the elephant foot trash can, wrapping her arms around it right before she threw up.

"Oh, my darling Andrea," her uncle crooned sympathetically, moving to stand behind her.

Andi's stomach lurched again, and she tried to tell herself that it was seasickness—the boat was still running full throttle, hull slapping the waves, although it did feel like it was slightly turning now —and not the knowledge that every single person who'd ever been in her life had betrayed her. She threw up again and again, down until there was only green bile left. She clutched her uncle's heinous hunting trinket, hating herself for it, trying not to weep, as he moved about the room.

Her mother...knew. And kept it from her? It couldn't possibly be true!

And yet—seeing as everyone else in her family had walked out on her—it made a certain amount of sick sense. Why not her mother too?

Andi pulled her hair back at her neck and tried to not let fresh tears squeeze from her eyes.

"Drink, Andrea," her uncle said, offering a full glass of ice water to her before returning to his seat.

Andi took it from him and swished and spit into the trash can, to clear the sick out of her mouth. "Thanks," she muttered.

"That's better," he said, sounding kindly. Just like the uncle she'd known her whole life. Why did he have to go and be an entirely different man? Tears were pressing, and she swallowed them down, roughly wiping her face with her sleeve. She went to take another sip when she realized she shouldn't trust him.

She shouldn't trust anyone.

Except for maybe Damian...so far.

She stared disconsolately at the wastebasket, feeling wrung out, and reached up to touch her heart where it was pounding...and fished the tracker out of her bra while she seemed to waver, pretending to be tempted to throw up again before she shoved the device in between the elephant's thick toes.

"You should drink more," her uncle said, as she got back up on unsteady feet and thumped into her chair.

"Is it poisoned?"

He rolled his eyes. "You might find it hard to believe, but I have better things to do than to poison my favorite niece."

"Only niece," Andi whispered out of long habit, setting the glass down on his desk, untouched. She looked over the desk at him—the sea turtle shell positioned behind his head gave him a malevolent halo. "Why?"

"Why what?"

"Why everything."

Her uncle steepled his fingertips in front of him. "You believe in the science of the world, yes?" he asked. "And now you believe magical things are also possible?"

"I guess," she said flatly.

"Andrea, what if I told you that magic wants to take this world over?"

"I would say, 'here, magic...take the world, it sucks.'"

"Andrea," he tsked. "I know you are hurting now, but there are actual lives at stake."

She fiercely rubbed the back of her hand across her eyes. She knew she couldn't let on everything she knew, and she still needed to play along to figure out his plan—for Damian and his crew. "If I believe you...a big if...how? And why?"

"There are other worlds than these, Andrea. We are in a war that you can't even begin to comprehend." He leaned back in his chair and opened up a desk drawer, pulling out paper and pen. "What I think is best for you now, Andrea, is that you accept your fate." He began to scribble quickly.

"And what's that?" she asked him as he switched pieces of paper. A quiet part of her supposed that sounded ominous, and she ought to be concerned, but the rest of her felt so distant and depressed that she couldn't be bothered.

"I want you to take this check here and cash it. Consider it a part of your inheritance—from your mother...not from me." He handed the paper over to her, but it was just that—a piece of paper, not a check—and on it, he'd written in his precise cursive:

My dear, *do you not think I know what dragon smells like?*

Andi read it, and her heart flew into her throat, finding sudden life. By coming here, had she put Damian's life in danger?

"No?" he went on loudly. "Such foolish, foolish pride," he said, handing her another piece of paper as he loudly tore the first in two. "Andrea! Don't be so stubborn!" he protested genuinely enough to earn an Oscar as she read his second note.

You deserve answers, *but I need to talk to you alone.*
  I'll send a ride two nights from now.

She stared at the note in her hand. Her uncle knew she was being followed and was wired even, which was why he was writing notes. And he knew there was another dragon in her life. Did he know who? She bit her lips. Her heart called out for Damian, even if she didn't dare say his name.

She had to fight to stop her hand from shaking.

"Well," her uncle continued, sounding contrite. "We're almost back to shore. But if I could counsel you, you should rest for a few days and consider what you've seen." His voice was congenial, but his eyes were narrowed and his shoulders set, as he leaned over the desk to stare at her. "Not everyone has an inheritance as rich as yours, Andrea. The least you could say is thank you to your uncle."

Her mouth was dry as she breathed, "Thank you."

CHAPTER

EIGHT

Andi struggled to stay steady as the small yacht her Uncle Lee had semi-kidnapped her in rocked to a stop. She heard the voice of men outside calling to one another, coordinating the tying of the boat to the pier, and she couldn't stop reading the note on his desk, the word "alone" echoing in her mind.

"Think about what I've said, Andrea," her uncle said, pointing to the piece of paper.

Could she keep her uncle's offer a secret from Damian? She did need answers—she longed for them. There had to be some way to make sense of things, to understand why her brother was a dragon now and how come her mother had betrayed her. But there was no way Damian would ever let her risk her life like this again if he knew.

Andi swallowed. "I will," she told her uncle. He gave her a silent nod.

After that, Elsa, her uncle's very blonde, very unhappy secretary swooped in and grabbed her arm, practically hauling her off the boat. The brusque woman loaded her into a car waiting at the dock, and they drove off at top speed, to Andi didn't know where—until she saw a horizon full of familiar towers, with the Blackwood Industries skyscraper dominating the rest of the skyline.

Andi realized she hadn't talked for at least five minutes and could only imagine how worried Damian was for her.

"How far are we away from my apartment?" she asked aloud for his sake.

"Just ten minutes now," Elsa said, after glancing at her phone. Did she know she was being listened to as well? Or was only her uncle privy to that information?

Damian claimed she smelled like apples, caramel, and the sea. She'd never thought to ask him how many other people in the world could scent dragons.

"So, what does henchwomaning pay these days?" Andi asked, reaching down to adjust her shoe as though she were uncomfortable. In reality, she was pulling the tracker Jamison had placed there out and tossing it underneath the passenger seat of the car.

Elsa snorted and rolled her eyes. She was wearing all black again, only this time a turtleneck and pants rather than a dress. She still had the same mysterious claw on a leather thong around her neck, though, like she was a goddamned hippie instead of a murderer.

"It's a serious question," Andi protested, righting herself at last.

The much taller blonde shrugged. "Top pick of trophies, first round of meat."

And no matter that she'd just thrown up, Andi clutched her hand to her stomach again. "Don't tell me that."

"You asked," Elsa taunted. "I can't believe that you and your brother share the same seed."

"Yeah, well, maybe he absorbed all the evil bits out of me in the womb, did you ever think about that?" Andi muttered. Elsa stared at her blankly. "Jesus Christ, does no one else read Stephen King?" and then she laughed to herself because if she didn't, she would sob.

The car pulled up in front of her apartment complex shortly thereafter, and Andi got out. Before she closed the door, Andi said, "Nothing...no...*everything* personal, but I hope I never see you again."

"I feel the same," Elsa said, leaning over to lock the door the second it was closed.

ANDI STUMBLED up the stairs to her apartment and then waited for a moment, wondering if Damian's car would come flying around the corner. When it didn't, she let herself inside.

She tossed her keys onto the portion of counter that she and Sammy used for such things and checked her phone. No notes from Damian, no "hey, glad you're not dead, sorry about the puking," and then she wondered if she needed to send *him* one. "Sorry you all had to listen to me puke."

"Sammy? Sammmmmmmy?" she said like she was calling a cat. No response. She opened up her phone and shot her roommate a text.

Home. Might be going out again. Or might not. Just thought you should know.

Not home, definitely getting laid again. Just thought you should know! her roommate texted quickly back.

Andi snorted, then made her way back to her bedroom, shedding all her clothes before heading into her bathroom to turn the water on.

THIS WAS GOING to be her third shower of the day. Hell, her thick hair wasn't even fully dry from the last one at Damian's, and all this hot water would strip the blue streak out of her hair like whoa. But if she didn't take it, the smoke from her uncle's pipe would haunt her in her sleep, and she couldn't cope with that. She brushed her teeth while the water heated, gargled mouthwash, and tried to erase the sourness of being nauseous from everywhere else that she could... because she couldn't quite clean her memory.

Her mother had known...about everything? All along? How was that even possible? How...and why?!...would she have lied?

And if she'd chosen a child to confide in about the truth of things, why the fuck had she picked Danny?

Andi splashed her face with water so cold it made her gasp, then jumped into the shower.

She stood beneath the hot water replaying every interaction with her uncle in her mind. It was all suspect, seeing as he knew she'd been followed, which was why he'd hardly told her anything.

He was right, though. She deserved answers. She needed someone to help her make sense of her entire goddamned childhood. Why could Danny turn into a dragon now? And why couldn't she? Damian...and Rax!...both thought she was normal. She looked at her skin in the mirror, willing it to change or willing her twin brother to come back and be normal with her. So that everything could go back to being the way it was again, like when she didn't have to entertain the thought that her own beloved mother was evil. When that didn't work, just like she knew it wouldn't, she stared down into the drain and let her thoughts swirl with the water.

A tapping at the shower's glass door made her jump. Damian was standing on the other side, holding a massive duffle bag. He'd apparently teleported from his castle to her bathroom through one of his many mirrors.

She slid the shower door open quickly, sending it rattling in its track and letting water spill on the floor. "You're supposed to ask permission!"

"Next time," he promised, before sweeping into her bedroom with his bag in tow, closing the door behind himself, keeping the heat in for her.

Andi raced through the end of her shower, worried about Damian left to his own devices in her room, and when she turned the water off, the bathroom door opened again.

"Damian," she protested, hiding behind a towel only to find him waiting on the other side of the door with a much larger, fluffier one —one of the towels somehow spun from clouds that he had on his side of the mirror in his much nicer bathroom. He stepped in and tsked, taking her towel away from her, giving her an appreciative glance, and then swaddled her in the newer, bigger, softer one, sweeping her up into his arms.

"You're ridiculous," she said. She wanted to be mad at him, but it was hard.

"And you're alive," he said, squeezing her tight as he navigated them through the door and into her bedroom where somehow he'd changed all of her penguin sheets out for fresh teal and white striped ones. A tea course sat on a tray atop her bed, where something spicy was brewing in a French press. He set her carefully down at the head of her bed, towel and all, and sat across from her after kicking off his shoes.

"What the hell?" she asked lightly, more than a little mystified.

"Okay, so, let's agree those penguins saw things their little furry virgin eyes were never meant to, eh? And then, I know things were rough for you, so," he said, gesturing to the tea set. She'd known he'd heard everything via the tracker she'd had on her—except for her uncle's note, of course—so he'd heard about her mother's betrayal and her subsequent throwing up. "I asked Austin what to get you for your stomach, and he said ginger tea." Then he reached into his duffle and pulled out a set of teal and white striped pajamas that matched the sheets. "For later if you want. Mills helped. She said nothing sexy right now." He gave her a look with a hint of a leer. "Let me know if she's wrong, though, and I'll go right back. And technically, Grim helped with everything, of course."

Andi put her hand to her mouth. "Am I dating you, or all of them?"

"Happy dragon...happy wagon?" he guessed with a grin, and Andi gave up and grinned back. He really did have feelings for her. And despite never having been in a relationship before, he was trying. Hard. He'd gone from being carved of ice to being...a pizza stone. Or a sauna stone. Some kind of fancy stone thing that had cheekbones you could slice butter with, but that was also hot.

For her.

And she'd just gone and possibly put him on her uncle's radar. She bit her lips. "Damian, my uncle...he really is a Hunter—"

"I heard," Damian said softly, his voice kind.

"No, like...he's dangerous, Damian."

Damian caught her chin in one hand. "And I'm a dragon."

Andi fought not to sway. Damian would never let her meet her uncle again if he knew what she now knew. But meeting her uncle alone would be the only way to get answers, not just for her life, but about what her uncle was planning. To keep Damian and his crew safe.

Because she knew—oh, she knew—that her uncle was a dangerously patient man.

"Are you okay?" Damian asked.

Not telling him about her uncle's note would be the hardest thing she'd ever done. She gave him a tight smile. "Not really."

Damian inhaled and exhaled deeply, taking his hand back. "I'm sorry, Andi. For all of it."

"Thanks," she said.

"No...thank *you*. After we realized you tagged your uncle's boat and car with the extra trackers we'd put on you, Jamison seriously considered proposing."

But if her uncle knew she was wired, how long would it be before he scanned everything she sat in, near, or touched, to make sure she hadn't tried to wire him? She shook her head. "My uncle's a smart man. I don't know how long they'll work."

"It doesn't matter. For right now, it's a win." He carefully poured her a glass of tea into a large teal mug. She took it from him and blew on it before taking a sip, and it did help. Looking around her room, she realized everything helped. Especially him. She watched him take a straight swig of hot tea and guessed that dragons didn't have to wait for things to cool...then saw he'd put her *Fast and the Furious* poster back up.

"Oh, my God."

He straightened, and followed her gaze, then grinned. "Come on

140

now. You know Vin and the Rock have seen some shit. They're gonna be okay."

Andi set her mug down on the table between them and then laughed full throatily. Maybe just a hint manic. Because just an hour ago she'd been throwing up into an elephant-footed travesty and now here she was sitting across from Damian, who'd casually redecorated half her room, brought her tea—and now as she noticed, tiny cookies—and was defending The Rock's sexual honor. "You're insane, Damian."

"No, princess...you are," he said seriously. "When I go do dumb shit, I know I'm still a fucking dragon. Where the hell do you get off being so brave when all you've got is skin?"

The second note her uncle had shown her hovered in her mind. *Come alone.* She hugged herself. "It's all I've ever known." He made a sound that shared what he thought of that. "Hey, though, it wasn't so bad, was it? You made it through on your side waiting?" She forced herself to sound chipper.

Damian set his now empty mug of tea down and rubbed at his chin. "Max punched me, and Jamison threatened to shoot me, so, yeah, I toughed it out." Andi snickered. "And now I know, being the person left behind sucks."

She took a careful sip of her tea then set it down. "Did you...hear everything?" she asked, her voice going high. Damian reluctantly nodded. "I'd like to say the interlude of me throwing up was just a clever ruse to get to tag his trash can, but...."

She watched his expression go dark on her behalf, brooding for her instead of because of her for once. "Andi, I was surrounded by traitors my whole life. I didn't know there was any other way to be until I came here. But the surprise of finding out...your whole family." Andi started nodding to agree and didn't stop, putting her hand back over her mouth now in horror, and he picked up the tea tray and set it on the ground. "Come here," he suggested afterward, offering his arms out, and she did so, flowing over the small distance between them, to curl up against his chest, still wrapped inside the towel. He pressed her head to himself and stroked her hair. "You can talk as much or as little as you'd like. And whatever else we do tonight...it's your call. I can take you out; we can stay here; we can go back to my place—"

"I don't want to go through a mirror again," she said quickly.

"They have this thing called Uber. You might've heard of them," he teased, then kissed the crown of her head. "You just tell me. Anything you want, consider it done. And you don't need to tell me anything else about what happened."

Andi clung to him, suddenly relieved of the need to tell him about her uncle's note. It was a technicality to not tell him, yes, but she wasn't even really lying to him until two nights from now, and so there was no harm in being good to herself in the meantime...as long as they didn't leave her place where anyone could see. She sighed into him and then spotted the pajamas Mills had sent over.

"Can we just have a simple night?" she asked, pulling back.

"Of course." He smiled down at her, his golden eyes glowing.

"Good." She extricated herself from his arms. "First, I'm going to go put these on," she said, picking up the pajamas that were perfectly soft and fuzzy like they were already broken in, "and then we're going to go sit on the couch and watch Netflix and order delivery."

"Is this what people call 'Netflix and chill'?" he asked her, sounding amused.

"Pretty much," she said, picking the pajamas up and heading for the bathroom.

"I just want the record to show that I'm not asking you to change in here. Just pointing out that I know I shouldn't ask," he said, as she made her way to the bathroom. She leaned out the door and stuck her tongue out at him.

"I'm changing in here so I can steal your towel. Even if we break up, it's mine," she called out, flinging the wet towel over her shower door.

"Duly noted. Not that I'm going to let you break up with me, though," he called in as she pulled on the pajamas, as soft as kitten bellies.

She walked into her bedroom, petting herself. "These are amazing."

"I'll tell Mills," he said, dismounting the bed to hold out his hand.

"We're just walking down the hall," she laughed, taking it.

"What? I've never seen the rest of your place. I might get lost," he said, whirling her around the bed to lead him.

"No, you're thinking of your weird magic cat fun house. There's no possible way that can happen here." She smiled and pulled him down the hall, nonetheless.

CHAPTER
NINE

Thirty minutes later, they were snuggled together on the couch, watching a documentary about a serial killer with half of a sushi restaurant's delivery menu incoming. Andi was leaning into him, feeling the comforting rise and fall of his chest as he breathed, the way her hair caught a little on the shadow of a beard on his chin, and one of his arms was wound about her body to hold her hand. He was intently watching the TV while she was watching him.

"Oh...no...don't *do* that," Damian said, as a woman's abduction was reenacted on the screen. He looked down at Andi. "Why did she do that? He was clearly lying!"

Andi bit her lips not to snicker.

"Is this really what you watch for fun?" he asked, sounding concerned.

"Yeah," she said with a laugh.

"Why?"

"Uhhhh...I don't know, really. They're interesting? And I'm morbid? And...not everyone dies. If you watch one of these to the end, usually the guy gets caught."

"Not if the police don't listen to that one woman who escaped," Damian muttered.

"It's a two-hour show," Andi chuckled. "They've got like ninety minutes left."

"Wait...then how many more people does he murder?" His eyes widened in horror. "I have to admit, Andi, I thought earth was a lot safer than this—"

"Oh my God, now you're not going to let me go outside—"

"I can think of so many more things worth doing inside, it's true," he said, leaning meaningfully toward her, as they both heard feet upon the stairs.

"Dinner!" Andi cheerfully laughed as keys slid into the lock, and Sammy let herself in.

Sammy stumbled into the hall, kicking off her shoes, and shouting, "Andi!" out of habit before spotting both of them. "Oh...um...hi?" she guessed, letting her expression slide into a shit-eating grin.

Andi groaned over dramatically. "Get it all out now, sister."

"All what?" Sammy asked, feigning innocence, before walking over to introduce herself to Damian, one hand out. "I'm Sammy—"

"Andi's beautiful Irish roommate who's into cars," Damian said, leaning forward over Andi to shake her hand warmly. "I'm Damian. We briefly met the other night."

"Yes, but that was before I knew you had a Pagani," Sammy said. She perched on the last remaining couch cushion like she wouldn't be here long, but Andi tucked her toes under Sammy's thigh because they were cold, and she knew Sammy's posture was lying. There was no way her roommate was going anywhere until she'd secured a future drive.

Andi listened to Sammy and Damian discuss cars, enjoying the easy way with which they spoke to one another. Two more murders were committed on the TV in the background, as they discussed RPMs or RPGs—Andi didn't really know or care. She just liked that two of the people who mattered to her had a thing in common. Sandwiched in between them on the couch, with Damian's arm around her, feeling the bass rumble of him speaking in his chest interspersed with Sammy's lovely lilt, she felt safe and warm and like maybe she didn't need the rest of her family.

Maybe she didn't need her uncle's answers, either.

Then there was a knock on the door as the sushi arrived. As they worked on appetizers, Sammy finally stopped pumping Damian for stats on his vehicles and eyed the TV. "Oh! I watched this one last week! That throat-slicing, brrrr!" she said and shivered, popping an edamame into her mouth to shell it with her teeth.

Damian looked between them both—mystified—and Andi laughed.

By the end of the murder show, which both Andi and his dragon were actually watching—his dragon fascinated by the fact that they would re-enact murders on TV for viewing purposes—and which, for some reason, her roommate was content to watch a *second* time, Damian saw Andi yawn. If it'd just been the two of them, Damian would've picked her up and carried her back to her bedroom, but he didn't want to do anything untoward while her roommate was watching.

"Did he ever confess to the other three?" Andi asked Sammy while loading all of their leftovers into one plastic clamshell.

"Not yet, the asshole. I looked it up on Wikipedia. But you know he did them," Sammy said, taking everything from Andi to put it into their fridge. "So," she announced, returning to the living room. "I'm going to bed now," she said in a leading fashion.

Andi grinned. "Damian...close your eyes, okay?"

He blinked between both of them. "Are you going to cut my throat?" he teased.

"Yeah, me and these chopsticks are going to get right on that," Andi said, sitting upright. "Also, don't listen." She put her hands over both his ears.

He heard the murmur of quiet conversation and some bargaining, and then felt Andi shudder with laughter before saying, "Okay, okay."

"Love you, girl...night!" Sammy said, then added. "Nice to meet you, Damian!" as her voice retreated down the hall.

Andi released his ears and reached for the remote, turning the TV off. "What'd I miss?" he asked.

"Usually we have a 'no strange men' policy here because this place is too small to be running into strangers in the morning. But, same as everywhere else, being rich has its privileges, and I basically promised her three rides in your car," Andi said, and he laughed. "It was that, or she was only going to let you spend the night so she could steal your keys."

"Just three rides?" Damian grinned. He couldn't say the idea of driving Sammy around filled him with glee, but if it made Andi happy—

"Three drives, rather," Andi corrected. "As in, you in the passenger seat. And you'd better buckle yourself tight. Sammy used to rally race."

Damian laughed. "Your roommate drives a hard bargain."

"Well, she knows what I'm worth," Andi said, beaming up at him.

"I do, too," he told her.

Her eyebrows arched. "And what's that?"

"Everything." He brought his hands up to catch her face and then kissed her.

If she had tensed even for a moment or pulled back, he would've stopped. He knew she'd already been through so much today, but her lips opened and her tongue met his as it pushed in, just as eager to taste him as he was her. His arms ran down to encircle her body, pulling her on top of him as they made out, listening to Sammy make politely quick trips between her bedroom and her bathroom down the hall, both of them freezing and quietly laughing as the faucet ran and Sammy presumably brushed her teeth, while his hands ran over the soft fabric separating him from the heat of Andi's skin.

Then they both heard Sammy's bedroom definitively lock, and the kissing began in earnest as she rose over him, pressing him back into the couch with her mouth as his hands slid underneath her top and up her ribs to cup her breasts, and he felt her shiver as his thumbs played over her nipples. She gasped and pulled her head back, whispering, "Bedroom?" but he shook his head. Confusion clouded her. "Why?"

"Because I want to fuck you here, princess," he whispered, kissing up her jaw. He knew why, even if he didn't want to say it— because he wanted to claim her every which way, in every space possible. He wanted her to know she'd been taken on every surface of this room. He didn't want her to look so much as sideways without remembering him in her and the way he'd made her feel.

She moaned as his lips reached the spot right below her ear, then whispered, "But it's kind of rude."

"Only if I don't buy you a new couch afterward," he said and nipped at her as he slid his hands down over the outside of her pajamas to cradle her ass and pull her splay-legged over him as he leaned back and pushed his hips forward, offering himself up for her to grind on. His cock was rock hard inside his jeans, and feeling the pressure of her grinding made him ache in a way that would've been intolerable if he hadn't known all the pleasures that could come.

"This is so high school," she whispered and giggled.

"Yes, tell me all about your high school boyfriends, so I can murder them for ever having touched you," Damian said, not entirely lying, looking up at her with a grin as she kept slowly rubbing herself against him.

"And here you were horrified by serial killers?" she laughed, then closed her eyes and made a soft noise of delight, as she rocked her hips forward, settling in. Then her bright gaze was on him again. "But, I didn't actually lose my virginity until I was twenty...because my mother would've killed me. When did you?"

He didn't have to stop to think. "Fourteen."

Andi stopped grinding and looked down at him with more horror than she'd shown for the entire time the TV show was playing. "That seems a little young."

"It was what it was," he said, pulling his hands away from her ass and putting them much more politely over the fabric at her hips. "My father decided that since I had my dragon, it was time. He put me in a room with a courtesan and locked the door and said he wouldn't open it for anyone until we were finished."

Andi gasped. "Oh, no."

"Exactly," Damian agreed. He ran his tongue along the line of his teeth, wondering what he should tell her. He'd never told anyone this story before, although he assumed that Max and Grim knew. "I waited a day. It wasn't even that I didn't want to have sex—although I am sure that up until that point, I didn't really even know what it was—but I was mad at my father for controlling my life like that... again. But then the woman got thirsty and begged me and...." He shrugged, staring over Andi's shoulder, fearing the look of pity that was surely on her face.

She took his chin in her hands and yanked him over to see her, and she was furious on his behalf. "That was not okay, Damian. That was awful. And you didn't do anything to deserve that."

And then I saved you, his dragon murmured, and Damian found that now that he'd started talking about it, he didn't want to stop.

"My dragon was there. It knew what to do, so I gave in to it—to this thing, moving inside me—making me like an automaton." He bowed his head at the memory.

Andi rose up and wrapped her arms around him, drawing his head to her chest where he could feel the soft fabric of her pajamas against his cheek and hear the thrumming of her heart beating. His hands rose with her and then wound about her waist, holding her tight, letting her stroke her hands through his hair and down his back, and then they just breathed together, each holding the other for support.

"If your father wasn't already dead, I would figure out a way to kill him," Andi muttered, possessively.

Damian snorted and shook his head against her. "I appreciate that. But it was a long time ago, now. Although when people wondered why I left the Realms—I have a hundred reasons why, each sadder than the next." He looked up at her and swiped a thumb against her perfect lips just because he wanted to touch them. "The thought of ever going back there is intolerable."

"Good," she agreed, wholeheartedly.

"Now...where were we?" he asked, grabbing the backs of her knees and pulling her back down.

She stiffened her arms against his shoulders, pushing away. "Are you sure?" she asked, her eyes searching his.

"With you? Always," he said, arching up.

"But you can't be serious, not after telling me that," she protested.

He reached up and cradled her head with a hand. "Andi...every time I do what I want with my body now, I win. And what I want right now is you."

She blinked at him, biting her soft lips, and then nodded, rocking carefully against him, and whatever blood had evacuated his cock during his memories now came rushing back.

"That's it," he whispered to her, biting back a grunt, watching her as she started to grind in earnest, tilting her hips forward and dragging herself up and down. "That's what I want to see." She closed her eyes and made small soft moans, and he relished the feeling of her heat on him even through the denim. "Rub your clit and pussy for me, Andi. Rub on me until you can't help it anymore. Come without me in you, get yourself hot and wet for me." She made a small whine and leaned harder. "I can't fuck you until you're ready for me, Andi," he whispered, arching up, giving her more of him to rub on. "I want your pussy to fucking ache to feel me."

She flashed him a pretend pout. "You're so dirty."

"You like it," he said with a grin. "Hurry up and come, so I can fuck you."

Her pout momentarily became real. "And you're mean."

He grabbed hold of her hips and stopped her grinding, and she looked at him, hot and flushed. "Not yet, princess. But, when I am... you'll like that, too."

She swallowed, and he could see her pulse pounding at her throat, and slowly and with great deliberation, he slid a hand into the waistband of her soft and chaste pajamas, fingers down the front of her stomach until he could crook them up into her soft folds. She gasped at his touch, and she was already wet enough to take him, which made his cock thump to be inside her, but first, he had a point to make. He pulled out his hand and licked his fingers clean, then reached for his belt with intent. *Yes,* his dragon urged him, already reading his mind.

She'd assumed he would pull himself out, but as he started freeing his belt from his waist, her eyes went wide.

"What're you doing?" she whispered.

"Shhh," he counseled, freeing his belt entirely, and holding it looped to the side like an empty bridle.

"Damian," she warned, squirming on his lap in fear, which made him even harder.

"Don't worry. I'd never spank you with it where Sammy could hear," he teased. "Do you trust me, princess?"

She sat there for a moment, considering—he knew she wanted him, he could still taste her on his lips, after all—but he also knew that this was like nothing she'd ever done before.

"I do." She said. "I think," she added.

"Good. Now, have I ever withheld an orgasm from you?"

Her eyes narrowed in curiosity, then she shook her head. "Not that I would let you, though," she muttered, and he laughed.

"Then trust me, princess. We're just taking a different path to the same destination is all," he said, holding up his black leather belt in front of her.

Andi looked between it and him, and then finally, hesitantly, said, "Okay," and offered up her hands.

Just her agreeing to try twisted the knife of his need inside him, and he fought not to rush her. "Thank you, princess, but not that. No...this way, we'll be ever so quiet and polite for your very understanding roommate, all right?" he promised, ignoring her proffered wrists to thumb the leather against her lips, running it around the back of her head where he buckled it and held onto the tail of the belt like a leash.

At that, her pulse went racing, much more than it'd been before.

"You still have access to safety. All you need to do is pinch me, and I'll stop, I promise. I'm not tying your hands." She frowned at him and made a sound like a question—likely to see if she could make a sound—and he smiled wickedly. "Open your mouth." She did so slowly, her brow furrowed, and he saw the full edges of her lips appear on either side of his belt's black leather. He pressed a thumb against it, creasing it in against her teeth. "Bite," he commanded and felt the pressure as she did so.

Then he leaned back to take her all in. "Goddamn," he whispered, and his dragon purred. His Andi in her white and teal striped pajamas was the very vision of innocence, only she was silenced by the black leather cutting across her face, straddling him, her scent thickening the air. Darkness roiled in him, the need to punish beaten out by the need to protect, but only barely.

He held the belt loosely behind her, and her eyes were as wild as her hair. "Are you okay?" he asked her.

One of her eyebrows quirked to let him know what she thought of that, and he laughed, grabbing her ass with his free hand and pulling it over him. "Let's get back to where we were."

She frowned, looking injured, but she placed her hands on his chest and did that thing with her chin, tilting it up so that he knew she ruled everything around her, even him, and that she was only humoring him was all.

"You are going to be such a handful," he murmured to himself, and she looked offended at that. "You are already such a handful," he amended, and he watched her chest rise and fall in a sharp laugh. He grinned at her, and his free hand went for the buttons of her pajamas, unsnapping them one by one as she bowed her head to watch him, then he arched his hips up, reminding her of why they were here. Her hands became small fists against his chest, and as he finished opening her top and reached to cup a breast, she finally began to grind again.

"Good, princess." He murmured words of encouragement, using his makeshift bridle to hold her head back and expose her neck to him. He fluttered kisses along it, and she writhed. Then, he started to lick and suck, sending her hips roiling. He bent her back as he leaned forward, bringing his mouth first to one breast then the next, working her nipples hard with his tongue as she gave a muffled moan.

She gave up on grinding him then, as one of her hands went between her legs and the other caught in his hair—he could feel her fingers working in between them, rubbing herself so hard, and he heard her breath catch. He tightened the belt behind her and pulled her to him, forehead to forehead, her riding him and touching herself, the hot scent of her filling the air, knowing that the same pussy that he was going to fuck was dripping for him already. He smoothed his cheek against hers, feeling the leather of his belt alongside his jaw as he went to whisper in her ear. "Does my poor, tortured princess need to come?"

She nodded strongly and made a muffled whine. She was so perfect and so his; she was his *mate,* and she needed *him.* He couldn't stand it anymore—his cock fucking hurt, and if he didn't get to feel it in her, he would die. He growled and reached between them, furiously undoing the fly of his jeans with one hand, shoving them down as she tensed and whined—so close, so close—and he let go of the belt to grab the ass of her pajamas with both hands to rip them off of her, exposing her to him as he reached between her legs to center himself as she still rubbed with her fingers, and then he was pulling her onto himself as she thrashed, and he pushed into her right as she was coming. He hissed as she quivered around him, pussy pulsing around his cock like it was trying to drink him down. He let out a guttural moan because *fuck*, entering her had never felt like this before, and her hips pulled him in with her spasms like she needed him inside her. Her moans were muffled by the leather, but he could feel her chest heave against him, and her hands were clenched into fists in his shirt the same way her pussy was grabbing him now. He swept one hand up quickly into her hair and pulled the end of the belt again as he finished the job, impaling himself inside her, feeling the echoes of her pulsing still.

Each time with her is always new, his dragon murmured, relishing the sensations the same as he did.

Yes, oh, yes, Damian agreed, as he felt her give a final tug.

"You couldn't wait, could you, princess?" he whispered to her when she was finished. A bead of sweat traced between her breasts, looking every bit like the precum he knew he was leaking inside her now, and she flashed him a guilty sex-glazed look. "No... don't apologize," he said, rewarding her with another thrust. "I love it when you come," he said, well aware of how quickly that phrase could've become dangerous. He thrust up into her again, so tempted to say more, now that she couldn't tell him he was being cruel. But somehow, he kept his head, even though his cock was buried deep inside her. "As long as you're only coming for me," he teased, but he knew he meant it. If anyone else so much as touched her, he would kill them. He swallowed, slowly pulsing in and out of her as she held herself still for him, her hands on his shoulders, keeping her hips in the perfect spot to arch along his length. He slid a hand beneath her breast, rubbing her nipple softly with a thumb. Her head rocked back, letting her still slightly damp hair cascade behind her. Her eyes closed, and at that moment, as she started to bob her hips against him, as he felt her soft folds parting to take him in, he realized the one thing his father's decision had stolen from him—he'd never gotten to dream about a perfect woman growing up. There had been no transition between innocence and lust, no time to figure out what he wanted or who he wanted to be with before he was given too many options and expected to take them all. He'd never been given time to dream or hope or wonder —until now.

With Andi.

Because she was the exact kind of woman he would've dreamt about, if he'd ever thought he could, the kind of woman he would've hoped to someday sate and hold tight. He wouldn't have known it before he'd met her, that such a small creature could control him, and yet now that he did, he needed her, and as she rutted against him, her teeth creasing the leather belt as she tried to moan around it, he knew *she* needed him.

His hand in her hair with the belt wound around it tightened, and he thrust up, hard. "Is this what you want, princess?" he whispered harshly, taking her more roughly now. He licked the fingers of his free hand, pulled one of her nipples with them, and was rewarded with a shudder. "Did the thought of feeling me inside you make you have to touch yourself and come?" Her own hands ran across his chest, grabbing and pulling his shirt up to touch his skin as her hips kept rocking. "Did my princess have to rub her clit for me? Waiting for me? Because she couldn't take it anymore?" Her brow rose, and she nodded, eyes wild while her hips still pulsed. He bowed his head forward, feeling the desperate urge to seat himself inside her and fucking claim her. "It's because you need me in you," he growled. He let go of the belt now and grabbed her hips and started to use her to fuck him, the belt's metal buckle clinking with each thrust. She gave a muffled whine, and he knew there would be bruises of his fingertips on her thighs tomorrow morning just as he knew she wouldn't mind because she was scorching him with her heat, her juices dripping down his sack, as she took his cock in again and again and he had to say it, he couldn't stop himself. "You were meant for me, Andi. Me and no one else. And now that I've found you, you're fucking mine."

Her nostrils flared, and her breasts heaved as she breathed in deep, suddenly holding herself still over him.

"Do you hear me?" he whispered hoarsely. She nodded, eyes wide and incredulous, and he caught a hand in her hair again, belt forgotten. He thrust deep inside her, and she moaned. "You need me because you're mine."

Him being able to say it out loud made all of him ache, a full-body agony, one that could only be healed by release. He felt her blood racing inside and out, for all that she was still now, and then as he thrust up again, he felt her match him. He made a low sound, and then they were together.

He didn't know how to explain it except her forehead was against his and her arms were around his neck and his hands were fucking her hips onto him and the metal of the belt chimed with each slick slap of her taking him right down to his balls. Each time he pinned her it felt like he was spinning the barrel of a gun, loading each chamber up, until everything was primed and then, oh, God, she was coming on him, her pussy somehow tighter right before her whole body shuddered and quaked, tears leaking from her eyes as she howled out, the sound muffled by the leather, and then he was coming too, his balls pulling tight as he shot round after round inside her. His cock twitched hard inside her tight little cunt with each load, as she rode him, he rode her, and they both died a little only to get to live more, or at least that was how it felt. And then he cradled her against his chest for what seemed like an eternity, relishing the skin on skin of it, the feel of her heart beating, the perfect sounds of her ragged breathing, until she pulled up and back, letting him slide out, and it felt like part of him was gone.

She still had the belt clenched between her teeth, and he reached up to pull it out, finding two perfect hemispheres of teeth marks upon it, and he purred, "Beautiful, princess," before showing it to her. "If you ever get the chance to bite me, bite me like that. Like you want to hang on," he said, then reached up to rub the corners of her jaw.

ANDI FELT his fingers touch the spot where she was sore and press in, and it was that familiar contact, albeit in an unfamiliar place, that brought her back to her body again.

She'd offered him her wrists first out of no small amount of guilt, and then it'd been a relief when he wanted to gag her, frankly, because then she wouldn't be tempted to tell him anything about her uncle.

But as they'd gone on, it'd morphed into something more—something hotter than she could've imagined. The belt had made her just the right amount of helpless. Shameless, too, when she remembered rubbing herself so hard for him. There was something about how raw it felt, being controlled by him, by letting him be in charge, especially when she knew she had a secret. She wanted him to punish her a little for holding back, and then at the end when he had to have her, and he fucked her so hard, so desperately, saying *mine, mine, mine,* her thighs were still quivering as her mind spun.

"Oh, God," she whispered, sagging against him.

His arms fell around her waist. "Good or bad?" he asked, nuzzling her hair with his chin.

She pushed back a little, looking around, as though her living room was unfamiliar. "As in, oh, God, that was insane." Damian rumbled contentedly beneath her, and then she focused in on him. It was hard because, before her orgasm, every single piece of her had focused on that one shared goal like she'd come with him right down to her very cells, but then afterward, it was like she'd exploded out into a million pieces. She needed time to collect herself back up again.

She breathed him in, the light musk she associated with him, some combination of deodorant, man, and sweat, and wondered if that was what her uncle meant when he'd said she'd smelled like dragon. "When would I ever get the chance to bite you?" she wondered aloud.

"I don't know. I might ask you to sometime. Or you might get really hungry." He nipped at her shoulder, and she laughed.

"You're joking, but there's like a whole Netflix category about that kind of thing, I bet," she said, blinking and rubbing her face. "Christ...Damian," she said, still figuring herself out.

"Are you okay?" he asked kindly, giving her a worried look.

"That...was, just intense, was all."

"How intense?" he asked her, continuing to be amused.

"Like, cult-leader intense."

"How would you know?"

"Also, Netflix."

He chuckled. She felt it start deep in his belly and then echo up through his chest, and he seemed so delighted at that moment, she wished she could take a photograph of him, to always have it with her and keep it for later.

"That's a new one," he said.

"Yeah, yeah, that's what all cult leaders say." Andi ran a hand through her hair and tried to straighten herself and then realized what, precisely, Damian had done to her brand-new pajamas. "Why do you have to destroy all my nice things?" she asked with a fake pout.

"Because I like buying you new ones." He swatted her ass gently, and she stood as he set himself back in his jeans. "And speaking of...." he began, looking down at the couch as he stood too.

"Absolute biohazard now. Yes, please." Andi placed a solemn hand on her chest. "On behalf of Sammy and I, we have always wanted a purple velvet sectional."

He laughed again. "I am completely willing to buy one, once you tell me what that is."

Andi grinned helplessly. His happiness was contagious, and so many other things too: addictive, dangerous. "I'll find one online and send it to you," she said, shimmying her pajama bottoms down.

"Aww," he complained quietly.

"What?" she asked, kicking them off and sweeping them up in hand.

"I was looking forward to eating you out through that hole."

"Damian!" she quietly hissed in her tiny living room, not all that far away from Sammy's bedroom door, scandalized.

"What?" he asked, pretending to be innocent.

"You...that's...kind of pervy!" she sputtered.

"Oh, yes, I'm the terrible, dirty, mean, pervy man who makes you come until you can't breathe. It's tragic, really," he said, looking smug as he threaded his bitten belt back through its loops, and Andi realized he hadn't offered her the belt in her mouth for her sake.

It'd been for his.

So that he could tell her all the things he wanted to, without any repercussions—so there'd be no possible way she could tell him he was being "mean" or moving too fast. She may have been high on endorphins, but she'd heard every word as he'd sworn he needed her and she needed him, and she'd seen the look on his face as he'd said them. Andi didn't believe in soul mates or anything like that, and life was far too complicated to think that you were going to bump into the one person out of seven billion who was your meant-to-be, *come the fuck on*—but if she wasn't meant to be with him when he could make her feel like that, for at least a little while, who the hell was runner up?

Andi tilted her head and took off her pajama top, so she was standing naked in front of him, and then held up one hand to count off the fingers on it. "Terrible, dirty, mean, perverted, boyfriend," she announced, upon reaching her thumb, and his face lit up from within. He beamed at her, and then he dodged around her, walking quickly down the short hall to her bedroom. "Where are you going?" she quietly whispered after him.

"To go rip access holes in all of your pants now," he whispered back.

She picked up a couch cushion and threw it down the hall at him.

· · ·

THROUGH SOME SUPERHUMAN effort after Andi cleaned up and Damian stripped, they got nakedly into bed and into a snuggling position without having sex again. She was proud of herself for turning her phone all the way off, seeing as the only people she cared about were currently under the same roof, but she understood why Damian had to leave his on, putting it carefully beside him on a nightstand before returning his attention to her. She sank into the sheets beside him, they were made of the same stuff her former pajamas were and pulled her hair through the strap of her nightshift-nurse-regulation blindfold.

"For the record, this is a sleeping blindfold for me, not a sexy time one. I'm embarrassed to say we need to stop for tonight," she admitted once it was on her forehead, and she was in his arms.

"Why?"

"Because I don't think anything left in me can top what we just did, and Damian, I'm so fucking sore—like, good sore—but still—"

"No, I mean, why're you embarrassed?" he asked. He shifted to lay beside her, holding her gently, softly stroking her elbow with his fingers.

She flushed. "I don't know. I'm not a tap out kind of girl. And, honestly, I'm not all that used to setting good boundaries and having them respected."

He tilted his head toward hers, rubbing her temple with his lightly bristled chin. "Isn't that what relationships are supposed to be about?"

"Yeah, call me back after you've had a few," she said and stuck her tongue out before pulling the blindfold down and snuggling in.

"Or maybe I won't have to." She could hear the hope in his voice.

"Oh my God, you are such a relationship virgin." She reached up and put her hand over his mouth to close it. "It's okay, I thought I would marry my high school boyfriend too."

He licked her palm, and she yanked her hand back with a yip. "I'm thirty-eight, Andi; it's a little different," he said.

"Mmmph. I'm almost twenty-eight, and I'm very, very jaded."

"Why?"

"Because," Andi said, tempted to leave it at that, but then figured she might as well take him at face value. She leaned back and pushed her blindfold up. "Because I've put out and then been ghosted. I've been ghosted without putting out. I dated one guy for eight months and even met his parents, and then he dumped me right before he suddenly became wealthy, and I've had a ton of guys try to go out with me because they hope that because I'm Asian, I'll be meek," and at that, she felt Damian snort beneath her. "I know, right? But when I started dating, it took a while to figure that shit out. I'm not an anime character...I'm not even Japanese!" She groaned and thumped her head against his chest. "And that's not even counting all the legitimately pervy guys who've followed me down streets or off the bus or whatever just...hoping." She shuddered, and Damian was very quiet in response. "Don't get any ideas or go off killing anyone," she warned him.

"I would never tell you about it. It's just that the streets around you would suddenly become littered with corpses," he said, and she wasn't entirely sure if he was joking.

"Officially, I'm a nurse, so don't joke about killing people. But unofficially, yes, please," she said. She made to reach for her blindfold again and then took a detour, looking up at him. "Okay, so how the hell do you get to thirty-eight without even trying this before? Was it because of your fucked-up childhood?"

"You could say that." He paused, apparently considering. "When I began...well, where I began," he started, and she felt him searching for words.

"You don't have to if it's too hard," she told him, spreading a hand out on his broad chest. He caught it in his own.

"It's just very different from your own is all. I was a prince, so the normal rules of Realms society didn't apply to me."

"Because your parents wanted to marry you off to other royal types?"

He shook his head. "No. They always knew I was too headstrong.

And while they would've appreciated me being cooperative, that's just not how it works. Because both of us...have to agree."

Andi realized he was talking about his dragon again. She turned in his arms, so her chin was on his chest, and her belly was on the mattress. "I take it that doesn't happen often?"

His golden eyes gazed down at her. "It has never happened before."

"But, you've had sex before."

"Countless times."

Her eyes widened. "Hmmm, maybe try counting? For me?"

"I honestly don't think I could. I said countless for a reason," he said, giving her a rueful smile, and she remembered all the images of him online with a different girl on his arm each weekend.

"Well," she swallowed. "I guess that does explain why you're so good at it."

"Thank you," he said simply. "In any case, though, Andi, none of those experiences compare to even one minute with you."

"Because you both agree. On me." She bit her lips and thought a moment. "What did he think when you were with all those other women?"

"We were passing the time. Who doesn't want to feel some pleasure? And I had more opportunities than most." Damian shrugged. "He's a predator. We both were, I suppose. We enjoyed the chase. So, you could say he—we—appreciated those women in the way a wolf appreciates a rabbit. Without thought, out of habit."

"And now?" Andi asked.

He looked past her, his eyes unfocused as he saw or spoke to something deep inside. "We like you wolf to wolf." His eyes brightened again on her. "As much as you infuriate me sometimes, Andi, and as human as you are...there's something fierce and sharp in you, princess." He inhaled deeply, studying her. "You make me feel like a little boy playing with a pretty knife. I don't even care if you cut me. The risk is worth the reward."

She flushed again, only this time with shame. He was in too deep.

Her going to see her uncle without telling him was definitely going to cut him. But she had to, no matter what it was they were to each other. How could she secure her future if she didn't understand her past? And if she found out anything she could use to protect Damian....

She reached up and brushed a lock of hair off his forehead, before twisting to regain her former position at his side. "Thank you, I think."

"It's a compliment. Knives are sexy," he said, pulling her close.

"Says the man who doesn't cook," she teased.

"I don't use them in the kitchen." He leaned over to kiss the crown of her head and tugged her blindfold down for her.

CHAPTER

TEN

Damian held onto her as she drifted off to sleep, intoxicated by her presence but utterly unable to sleep himself. His mind wouldn't stop wandering, and his dragon didn't help.

She is happy...yes? it asked him.

It seems so, Damian said, stroking one of his hands against her hip. He could feel his dragon trying to parse human emotions and struggling with concepts and words.

What is a boyfriend? Is it a mate?

No. Yes...well...it can be. Maybe. It's closer than we were, in any case. His dragon made a frustrated sound and settled inside him in the particularly vigilant way it'd begun to when he was around her. Perhaps distant and unobtrusive, but always watching. *You really do care about her, don't you?*

His dragon struggled again with the distance between their experiences. *I wish to fly by her side.*

But she can't fly, Damian told it, bemused.

If we were in the Realms, I would take her flying, his dragon told him, one hundred percent sincerely.

Damian shook his head. The only person he'd ever given a ride to was his sister. Austin had sent him a message a few hours ago that Ryana was unchanged. *It can't happen. We're never going back there, remember?*

I know, his dragon agreed. *Still. You have your dreams; I have mine.*

It was one of the few times that Damian wished he could interact with his dragon outside of his body, instead of being a part of it. It would be nice to give the thing a head pat now and then when it wasn't trying to impose its will on him or claw its way out of his mortal shell.

He arched his back, stretching a little, and looked around at Andi's small room. It was just like her—tiny, chaotic, with splashes of vibrant colors and emotions. The red rug beneath the bed looked a bit like a bloodstain in the room's dim light, and he wondered if that was intentional, considering her interest in violent TV. He scanned the book titles on her small bookshelf and didn't recognize any of the authors—except for her Stephen King—but he knew what the covers promised from their fonts and colors: fantasy, romance, adventure. Even before she met him, she wished for someone like him, and he found that charming.

On her desk was a scattering of paperwork—a framed photo of her as a child with another child and a woman, brother and mother, presumably—and the photo album her brother'd given her this morning, which he'd brought back through the mirror for her. He wondered if she'd ever look at it.

He wondered if she'd mind if he did.

He scooped her to himself tightly, thinking. He wanted to know everything about her. It felt like a moral imperative to discover who she'd spent her whole life being, now that he was so certain of their future. Once she began breathing softly, just this side of a light snore, curiosity got the best of him. He kissed her dark hair again and extricated himself gently so that he could reach the album and return with it.

She stirred in his absence, and he liked that—the moment of her running her hand across the sheet searching for him in her sleep almost meant more to him than her calling him boyfriend. One was a decision she'd made, but her reaching out over the space he'd just been was instinctual.

"Shh," he whispered, sliding himself back into bed carefully so that she could find him. A smile flitted across her lips, and she relaxed again.

He bent his knee beneath the sheets and propped the album up against it. Now that he was back, Andi turned to curl opposite him, tucking her back and bottom against his side, freeing his hands. He slowly opened the album, listening to it crack arthritically as though no one had opened it in years, and chunks of pages at the front were stuck together, so he started with the ones in the back.

The sepia-toned woman on the tombstone he'd seen in the cemetery was now here in color. Smiling, in a swimsuit, spraying a hose over two kids running back and forth outside—Andi and Danny —so full of life in the photo, he could almost hear their laughter. Other photos included Andi as a child with cake all over her face, she and her brother dressed up for Halloween. Andi was a princess—a fact that now he knew he would never let her live down—while her brother was some sort of Army man. School graduations, portraits taken professionally, Andi playing tennis, her brother standing proudly beside of what Damian assumed was his first legally-obtained car.

He grinned at the album, certain he'd made the right call. He just wondered where Andi's father was. After he'd left, had their mother snipped all his photos out? He knew what his own angry father looked like. Even after he'd died, their palace had had seemingly infinite painted portraits of the man. He went for the clump of pages up at the front of the album, caught his fingernails on their edge, tugged, and pulled.

The cellophane there protested opening, crinkling softly, all the while Damian monitored Andi for signs of waking up, but when she didn't, he felt empowered, looking at images that no one had seen for years.

Andi's mother, staring challengingly into the camera, sometime in the seventies, before Andi and Danny were born. He could tell it was her from her face. It was the same as the one on the tombstone in the cemetery, with the same steady gaze and well-placed birthmark. And he could tell it was the seventies because of the décor of the room around her and the clothing that she wore, but she looked no younger than she'd been when she'd been spraying the hose. Damian risked crinkling open another page, hopping further back, wondering if he'd find Andi's grandparents, but no, just another portrait of Andi's mother—same bold gaze, same birthmark location.

But...this photograph's background was the fifties. The collar of her dress, the apparent diner she was in, and the car he could see parked outside through the window behind her. If it hadn't actually been taken in the fifties, someone had put a lot of effort into mimicry. He frowned and moved several pages back—into the twenties. Black and white photos, tinted brown by time, all featuring Andi's mother. She looked like she was on safari. There was a downed rhino behind her, men already working at flaying the hide from the meat. She had a rifle slung casually over her shoulder as she gave the camera the same defiant stare he'd so often seen from Andi.

He flipped back. The same woman, in regalia he couldn't place with an ornate headdress. She had a fan in one hand, and her other hand rested on an elephant's skull with ornate claw-pointed jewelry on two fingers. He moved through the rest of the pages quickly.

It was always the same woman.

The *exact* same woman.

From the hair to the expression to the birthmark. Sometimes dressed in Western clothing, other times in what he assumed was Asian, looking directly at the camera, proud of the things that surrounded her—which were almost always skulls. The photo album in his lap contained a century and a half of photos, all of Andi's mother.

Is it possible? his dragon asked although they both knew.

Yes. Damian closed the album slowly.

Andi's mother had been some flavor of immortal, with additional lifetimes purchased by being a Hunter, in all senses of the word.

His own dragon seethed inside him, confused, chasing itself around in an imitation of his own thoughts. How could the woman he was mated to—the woman he loved—be the offspring of someone so...so hideous?

Clearly, Andi didn't know...did she? No. There was no way his kind and gentle Andi could've had any idea. Her upset stomach at the mere thought of it earlier tonight proved it.

But her brother had known. He'd chosen to take part in their family heritage, and somehow, because of his lineage, and willingness to sacrifice, right down to his own skin, he'd become a dragon.

A dragon. Someone like him, somehow...only, on the Hunter's side.

Damian tensed at the thought, his own dragon preparing for war, and Andi stirred beside him.

ANDI FELT Damian pull away from her in the dark and leave the bed. She supposed he was allowed to go to the bathroom, as long as he came back. She reached out to feel the space he'd left and then felt him return, shushing her fears as he crawled back in alongside her. She heard the sound of a book's spine crinkle and had to hide a grin. She'd always low-key dreamed of sleeping next to someone reading in her bed, and here it was, finally happening.

Then she felt him stiffen beside her. She pushed herself up on one arm and wiped the blindfold up. "Damian? What's wrong?"

She could see his brooding expression from the dim light coming from her bathroom. "I need to show you something," he said, sounding grave.

Andi scrambled to push herself to sitting, suddenly awake. "What?" She reached over to pull her nightstand light's chain, and then focused slowly on what he was holding. The photo album Danny had given her—the one she'd asked him not to touch.

"Damian," she said with a frown, already feeling disappointed.

"I looked," he told her.

"You mean you did literally the one thing I asked you not to?"

Now, he was frowning, too. "Yes. I apologize. But that doesn't change facts."

"What facts, Damian? That my whole family's a disappointment to me? Or...I guess that I am to them?" She rubbed the sleep out of her eyes and sighed.

"No, Andi, you need to see this," he said, tilting a page of the album her way.

She leaned forward with a sigh and saw her mother looking like an Asian Katharine Hepburn in Ye Olden Times safari gear. "So?" Andi protested as the rest of the photo came into focus for her sleep dulled mind, and she spotted the dead rhino in the background. "Oh, God...why would you show me that?"

"That's your mother, yes?" Damian pressed.

Andi forced herself to look at the image again. "It looks like her," she said, unwilling to be certain aloud—even though in her gut, she knew she was.

"This whole album, Andi...it's of her."

"Well, it's a photo album; that's what they're for," Andi said, sinking in on herself quietly.

"No...I mean...look at the difference between this picture and the next." He flipped back and forth between one old black-and-white portrait and the next.

"They've been made to look old."

"No. It *is* old. And this one too. And then there're all these," he said, quickly going from page to page like he was holding a flipbook, showing pictures of her beloved mother, over decades of time, almost always with skulls.

Andi put her hand to her mouth. "What is it that you want me to say?"

"Nothing, I guess. I just thought you should know."

"So, you're just showing them to me to hurt me?" She heard her voice rise and then lowered it for Sammy's sake. "Why did you look? I told you not to!"

Damian's brow furrowed. "Me looking doesn't change facts, Andi."

"No, but it was the one thing I wanted. The one thing!" Andi whispered harshly and then realized this was her only legitimate chance to push him back. "You've been my boyfriend for like, what, an hour and a half, and this is what you do?"

"Andi," he said, his voice low.

"No. I think you should leave, Damian." After looking at the photos, she needed answers more than ever, and she wasn't going to get any with him around. He reached to hold her, and she put an arm out to stop him. "I mean it."

He visibly held himself back. "What? Why?"

"Because," she said, sniffing back tears, trying not to cry. The tears were real, even if her reasoning was not. "Shit like this, Damian. It's why I said we should go slow."

"But you said earlier—"

"Yes, and I was wrong." Andi closed the album and set it down beside her, folding in on herself.

"Andi," Damian said, his voice soft. She could tell it was hurting him not to reach for her, and that hurt her too, goddamnit.

"I mean it, Damian. This is all too fast...I need to be alone for a little bit."

She watched his jaw clench before he asked her, "How long?"

"I don't know." She wasn't going to meet her uncle until two nights from now. She'd have to stay away from him for at least that long, so she apparently wouldn't reek of dragon. "Just...until my head clears. Two or three days. So I can make sure I'm my own person again." She raised her chin to look at him. "When I'm with you, I just get swept up and dragged along in your wake." That part wasn't a lie. Being with him felt like she was always on the verge of getting pulled out to sea. "I don't want you to go away, Damian, and I still want there to be an *us,* but I need a little space. It's not your fault, even! It's just who you are. I'm not used to this," she said, looking around at her brand-new sheets, and the tea things that they'd set across her chair to go to sleep, and him, taking up most of her bed even though she was sure he didn't mean to. "I'm not even used to having a man here, much less a dragon."

His golden eyes kept searching hers as he frowned. "Last night you wanted me to promise that I'd never leave you."

"Was that really just last night?" she asked, her question genuine. It felt like a lifetime ago now, and she shook her head. Everything *was* moving too quickly. She was messing things up, and she didn't know what to do. She was trapped between her need to really, truly know who her family even was and how and why they'd lied to her, her need to somehow glean information from her relationship to her very dangerous uncle to help keep her man safe, and trying not to break the pride of that said man—who thought he loved her after two short weeks. There was no way to win. Especially not when being around Damian made her feel like she might be able to love him, too. Andi made herself even smaller on the bed, like that could help her avoid the truth. "I don't know what to tell you, Damian. Maybe this is some fucked-up test, and maybe I'm an asshole. I just know that when I'm with you, sometimes I want to be yours so bad it scares me. I'm not used to this, okay? I don't *feel* like this. Ever."

He crowded her. "You don't have to be scared of it, Andi—"

"Please don't tell me how to feel. Not right now," she cut him off.

"Can you just trust me for forty-eight hours? That I'm not leaving you or going anywhere...that I just need to breathe?"

Damian rocked back and ran his hands through his hair, swallowing. "Probably."

"And can you honestly stay away from me for forty-eight hours without following me or sending people after me or peeking at me through any mirrors?"

He snorted. "Yes, princess."

"Are you going to hate me after forty-eight hours of waiting?"

"I could never. But I won't deny that the thought of two days without you hurts."

"It shouldn't," she said, knowing that it *was* a lie because it would hurt her too.

"But it will. Andi," he began, and then swallowed whatever else he was going to say, shaking his head. "How will I know if you're all right?"

"It's really me who should be worried about you instead, I think." She pulled the sheets up to her neck, hiding in them. "You can text me."

He groaned. "If I can text you, then what's the point?"

"The point is to find out if you can follow instructions," she snapped. "Jesus Christ, Damian, I'm asking you to do one thing. You want to tie me up and own me. I'm just asking for two fucking days for myself. Where you don't come through my mirror without asking or go through any of my things."

He inhaled sharply, clearly ready to unleash a retort, and then restrained himself. She watched his expression go blank, falling into the cruel kind of calm she didn't want to ever get used to, and a small part of her was panicking, thrashing, worried that this was the beginning of the end, and once again, Andi Ngo was fucking everything up. But either their relationship was real, or it wasn't. If it was, it'd somehow manage to withstand her bullshit, and if it wasn't, then she might as well fucking know now. So, she steeled herself to give him the same unforgivingly blank look back and said, "Please, go."

"As you wish," he said, getting up out of her bed to pull on his clothes. When he was done, he turned back toward her, and his icy façade had slipped. He looked haunted now and hurt, and her heart missed the smile he'd had with her all evening. "Am I allowed to kiss you before I go?"

Andi bit her lips. She knew if she kissed him, her resolve would break, and everything would be over. "I think that would be unsatisfying for us both, Damian," she said, which made him look even more wounded somehow, beyond what he could hide from her.

"Very well," he said. He departed for her bathroom and its mirror, and this time she didn't follow. She waited what felt to her like an awfully long time, and then stripped her bed, shoving his nice new sheets into a laundry bag, before putting everything he'd given her out in the hall and retrieving her spare set of penguin sheets out of her and Sammy's linen closet.

She couldn't keep anything that smelled like a dragon in her room, and that included herself. She walked back into her bathroom with still-not-entirely-dry hair for what felt like her fortieth shower of the day.

DAMIAN'S DRAGON gave him surprisingly little shit as they re-emerged into the green room of his castle on the mirror's far side.

Aren't you worried? he asked it as he strode through his house, heading for the stairs to check on Austin and Ryana.

No. She is frightened by the pull.

Damian grunted. *It's pulling me, too, you know.*

But you know what it is, his dragon told him. *I do not understand why you cannot tell her she is your mate.*

Damian inhaled deeply. He'd been about to when she'd told him she was afraid before she'd snapped at him. But if he felt like this, and he was part dragon, how much more disturbing must it be to be human and have these feelings and not know what to do with them, as they rushed in your blood and rang in your ears. Hell, if he hadn't had his dragon tell him what was going on back when they'd been together in his car, he still might not know. Might even still be afraid of being with her because it was a humbling thing to feel so exposed to someone. To be fully seen and heard. To have someone watch over you with love.

But what if she never admitted her feelings to herself? What if she always kept him at arm's length, or worse yet, he told her she was his mate, and she still pushed him away?

She will not.

How would you know?

Because it is our destiny to be with one another, his dragon told him. *At least for a moment in time.*

Damian paused on the stairs he was walking down. *How long is that?*

His dragon didn't answer; he felt it disappear inside him entirely.

DAMIAN TRAVERSED the rest of his house in a rush because he needed to stay busy, and burst in on his sister Ryana just as he'd left her, nestled in the hospital bed with her red bird guardian Lyka and his own 'magic-cat' Grimalkin at her feet, with Austin sprawled out on a couch across the room from the bed. He walked over to Austin, not knowing what to make of the numbers on the monitor screen that Ryana was attached to, and bit back a reproach. Of course, the werewolf had to sleep eventually. At least he was sleeping here.

"I'm awake, you know," Austin muttered, inhaling deeply and looking up at him. "Mostly. I've got all the alarms turned on." He swung himself upright on the couch. "And I figured between the actual bird and the bird-brain, if she woke up, one of them would let me know."

Grimalkin muttered something unkind about dogs and fleas in response to the insult but didn't move.

"How is she?" Damian asked, pulling up a chair. He reached over to pet Grim, setting him back to purring.

Austin put his head briefly in his hands. "I don't know. Either she'll get better or she won't. It's only been one day, though."

Damian nodded as everything he'd been through with Andi flowed through him in a rush. It felt like it'd been a year of a day—too long, but also, not nearly long enough.

"How's your nurse?" Austin asked solicitously after yawning and wiping his face with one hand. "Zach told me about what happened to her earlier tonight. I can't imagine what that'd be like, finding out that your entire family was filled with liars. I mean, wolf packs have fights, don't get me wrong, but at least when we're assholes, we're forthright."

"She's traumatized, yes." Damian put his hands between his knees and had a strange urge to confess. "Her brother gave her a photo album in the morning. She asked me not to look at it because she was mad at him, but I did anyhow."

"So, what?"

"Her mother was in the album. Surrounded in multiple photos by piles of skulls."

Austin's eyebrows rose. "Whoa."

"Yeah. It didn't go over well. Plus, apparently, her mother's been alive since at least the mid-eighteen-hundreds?"

"Hooboy." Austin let out a low whistle and gave Damian a long look. "That explains it, then. I don't have to be a dog to know you're in the doghouse."

Damian snorted. "How could you tell?"

"You're here, for one," Austin said. "And, I don't know, you've just got that look about you. Don't worry...usually, you're too tightly wound for me to read. No, I only recognize this," he said, waving his hand in Damian's direction, "because I recognize it from myself."

"How's that?" Damian asked as his brow rose on his forehead.

"You've got the look that says you were caught making a mistake. It's the kind of look I give women all the time, usually when they catch me out with someone else. Only yours is all sad and shit. Mine's more, 'I swear I didn't mean to, baby.'" He said the last like he meant it—like he was actually apologizing to a woman—and Damian groaned.

"Grim's right. You are a dog."

"Et tu, Brute?" Austin said, clutching his heart like he'd been stabbed. Damian rolled his eyes.

"In any case," Damian went on, "I don't have to have looks like that because I'm never in relationships. You can't fail to meet people's expectations if you never let them have any."

Austin eyed him. "Until now."

"Until now," Damian agreed slowly, as Austin continued to stare. "What?"

"You tell me," Austin said.

"Fucking hell, Austin—"

"You really like her. Obviously." The man was squinting at him, and Damian fought to maintain equilibrium.

"Yes, obviously. I've only come home smelling like her on multiple occasions. Congratulations, you're the werewolf version of Sherlock Holmes."

Austin moved forward to perch on the edge of his seat. "You've never given a shit about anyone romantically before...not even Guinevere."

"So? Maybe it's time for me to settle down," Damian said, and Austin started laughing. "What?" Damian said, getting angrier by the moment.

"Please. You? Settle? As if." Austin kicked back on the couch and gave a sharp snicker. "But if you're not settling, and if you're really *settling down*," he said as his jaw fell slowly open. "Holy shit, Damian, she's human! Does she know?"

Damian's hands clenched into fists. Werewolves could also find their mates, so it wasn't so unnatural that Austin could guess. "No, but if you tell her, I will gut you," Damian swore.

"Tell her what?" Mills asked, padding into the room barefoot with a yawn. She was wearing pajamas almost exactly like the ones he'd given Andi, and Damian had been so intent on Austin not figuring out what Andi was to him that her incoming presence hadn't even registered. She looked between them, sending the thick braid of her salt-and-pepper hair rolling across her back. "Hmm. Ryana's still out cold, so if you're talking about me—"

"We're not," Damian said definitively.

"He thinks Andi's his mate," Austin blurted out. Damian whipped his head to look at the werewolf, who threw his hands in the air. "I had to tell someone! And Zach's not up!"

"Goddammit, Austin," Damian cursed.

"Don't gut him," Mills counseled. "I mean, it's not a big surprise, really."

"Oh, so you've been talking to my dragon too?" Damian said, lowering his head to his hands.

"No, I mean, you're different around her, is all. How many times do I have to tell you that I can read your aura when you're feeling human?" She walked across the room to lay a warm hand on his shoulder. "It's okay, Damian. You two suit each other...I'm happy for you."

He looked up at her and found her smiling. "Does everyone know?"

"Not literally, no. But now that you've told the mouth of the south over there, chances are they will shortly," Mills teased, giving Austin a glance.

"I *can* keep secrets," he protested.

"I *can't* agree with you because I *can't* lie," she said, laughing.

Austin groaned, and Damian reached across his chest to squeeze Mills's hand. He found the thought of Mills thinking he and Andi were suited for one another somehow more comforting than all his dragon's talk of destiny. "What are you even doing up?"

"Jamison's snoring woke me, so I came down to get a snack."

"Just put a pillow over his head," Austin snarked.

"Or just wake him," Damian said, more reasonably.

Mills ignored Austin's comment. "Why would I wake him up to stop him? It's adorable. And it lets me know he's still alive."

"Do you worry about him dying often?" Damian asked. He hadn't even thought to add 'stopping breathing in the middle of the night' to his list of fears for Andi until now.

"No," Mills said with a shrug. "If he dies, I'll bring him back."

Austin and Damian looked to one another. "Now I kind of want to put a pillow over his head on purpose," the werewolf said.

"This is, perhaps, why you're single," Damian said.

"Eh," Austin shrugged. "Well, I guess no one *wants* a zombie Jamison wandering around."

"No one said anything about zombies," Mills said primly, sitting down on the far end of Austin's couch.

"If you could bring people back from the dead, why didn't you bring back Michael?" Damian asked her in all seriousness.

"Because I'm not entirely sure it can or should be done, or that I would be left whole after doing it. But if something happened to Jamison," she said, looking off into the distance, thoughtfully, "I would be forced to try."

Considering the things Damian had seen Mills do before, he said, "Understood. Although, let's hope it never comes to that."

"Agreed," she said, giving him a cordial smile

"What're we agreeing to?" Jamison asked, coming into the room with a plate full of cheese slices and a pile of crackers. Damian heard Grimalkin make a high-pitched whine.

"That you're a snorer," Austin told him.

"That if you die, I'll be forced to attempt to resurrect you," Mills explained. "So please, don't."

"Are we talking *Walking Dead*-style or *Dawn of the Dead*-style? Or *28 Days Later*?" Jamison guessed, moving to sit by Mills on the couch, between her and Austin. "Ooooh, would my robot arm be a zombie arm too?"

Austin pointed at Jamison, proving his point with his eyebrows raised, as Mills leaned in to kiss Jamison's cheek. "None of the above," she said, before reaching over to grab a piece of cheese.

"Only Mills is allowed to eat my cheese, Damian," Grimalkin clearly grumbled in his cat-language that only Damian could understand, from his spot on Ryana's bed.

"Which, oddly, reminds me...there's something I have to tell you all," Damian said, leaning forward, ready to tell them about the Heart of the Dragon he'd had Grimalkin hide in his Forgetting Fire's room earlier.

Austin rocked forward and looked at Jamison, "Damian thinks Andi is his mate."

"What. The. Fuck. Austin," Damian hissed.

"I'm sleep deprived!" Austin said chuckling. "Also, sharing good news is fun."

Jamison appeared caught between at least three different emotions. "Is this a high-five situation? Or a congratulations thing? I want to be supportive but not tacky."

"Does she know?" Mills asked Damian.

"No." Damian shrugged. "She's human."

"How does that even work?" Jamison asked, setting himself up a bite of cheese on a cracker. Grimalkin hopped up to all fours on the bed and attempted to stare the man down. "Mister Grimsley, did you want some cheese?"

Grimalkin turned to stare at Damian, ears high and fur bristled. "Tell him if he calls me that, there will not be enough of him left for Mills to save," Grimalkin growled, but then Mills cut in.

"Oh, no, no, Jamison...only I can call him that," Mills corrected him, as Austin gestured for the plate to be passed.

"Mister Grimsley," Austin said with a snort, as Mills handed the plate over.

"That goes double for him. I mean it, Damian," Grimalkin warned.

Damian made a time-out gesture with his hands, gathering their attention. "First things first: no one else except Mills is allowed to touch cheese in this house without prior permission."

"Why?" Austin asked, halfway through a bite.

"Damian, you can't tell them!" Grimalkin protested with a yowl.

"Because...reasons," Damian said, slicing through the air with a hand. "If you want it yourself, you can buy it. You can even buy it with my money, but if I buy it, it's mine, okay?"

Jamison's face lit up with a happy smile. "Andi really likes grilled cheeses, eh? No wonder she's mate material."

"Secondly," Damian went on, talking over him, "yes, she's human, and no, she doesn't know, so no one here needs to go and tell her. Not that you'd get a chance to anyhow because, as Austin somehow surmised, I am currently in trouble and over here, alone."

Austin clucked his tongue and rolled his eyes back in his head like he might go back to sleep. "Uh, with all your best friends and fighters, eating night cheese. This is hardly alone, brother."

Damian looked around the room at them, even at his sleeping sister, who he hoped for his sake did not wake up to the chaos of this. There was no corollary to this comradery in the Realms, no way he could hope to explain it. "Fair enough," he granted, relaxing enough to reach over to take a piece of cheese for himself. "Thirdly, and I meant to tell everyone this in the conference room earlier before you all decided that I was an asshole—"

"A fact which Andi seemed to agree on," Mills interjected.

Damian glared at her, and she winced apologetically with a shrug. "Yes, well," he recovered and continued, "my sister brought an object of power from the Realms through with her."

Austin perked up again. "What kind?"

Damian inhaled deeply, about to tell them, then heard Max loudly clearing his throat in the hallway.

"Is Grim still in there, Austin? Is there a reason that I can't get into the room with the Forgetting Fire?" Max said, coming into the room to find all of them present with a look of surprise, his blond eyebrows arched above his goggles. He was wearing black workout gear and looked ready to go outside. "Why is there a party without me?"

"It's a cheese party. This is the last of the cheese that the men are allowed to have," Mills announced, handing the cheese plate over to him. He took it, looking highly out of place, and Grimalkin began a snort-purring kind of laughter.

"Where are you off to this late?" Jamison asked.

"Running," Max said, plucking at his black shorts with his free hand, which made the paleness of his skin even starker. "I go out in the dark, so no one sees the goggles, or if they do, I can say they're night vision or some nonsense."

Austin took all of the bear-shifter in. "Christ, do people driving by you think they've seen a ghost? Should we be offering small children therapy?"

Damian pinched the bridge of his nose. "Max, the reason you can't get into the room with the main brazier of Forgetting Fire is because my sister brought the Heart of the Dragon through with her, and I had Grimalkin hide it there."

His old weapons master instantly began cursing. "You're kidding, right? No...you wouldn't...not about that."

"What's that?" Jamison asked around a mouthful of crackers.

"Trouble, I'm guessing," Mills said.

Austin leaned forward, put a hand to his mouth, and whistled loudly enough to make Mills cover her ears.

"What the hell, Austin," Jamison complained on her behalf.

"Look, if we have an impromptu meeting without Zach he'll feel left out, so whatever the fuck this is, hang on. Also, cover your ears again," he said, and then whistled one more time. They all heard a distant slamming door.

"Coming!" Zach shouted from somewhere above.

"Okay? So. Hold off," Austin said, looking around.

"Bad news is better with cheese at least," Maximillian grumbled, taking a slice from the plate he held.

Damian closed his eyes and shook his head. This...was insane. But it was good. And without Andi in his life right now, being here with his crew was the next best thing.

Zach thundered into the room shortly thereafter. "Whoa...why's everyone up? What'd I miss?"

"Dragons and hearts," Austin said, drawing a heart in the air with his forefingers like a schoolgirl, giving Damian a knowing smirk.

CHAPTER

ELEVEN

Damian gave them the truncated version of the story he'd told Andi, about his great-whatever ancestor having forged an alliance with a dragon only to betray it completely, stealing its power, but in doing so bringing a curse down on his house. And...that in the fight between Damian and his dragon, his dragon would eventually win.

"So, you're going to give the Heart over to us to study, right?" Mills asked when he was finished.

"Yes, but any time you open the box it's in, you'll have to warn me first."

"Why?" Zach asked.

"Because the box it's in is a magical dampener. When it's open, its effects work faster, and my dragon...." Damian inhaled deeply, remembering how wild the thing was when they were at the mall. "It lets it be more in charge," Austin grunted warily, and Damian nodded at the man. "Yeah. We don't always agree on things. It hurts. And it's hard to control."

"Which is why you've been making me work on that gun to kill you," Jamison stated.

"Precisely."

It doesn't matter what they attempt, his dragon told him. *The curse cannot be undone.*

"What happens if your dragon escapes while you're here and not in the Realms?" Mills asked.

"I...don't know," he said, right before his dragon told him, *I would open a rift and return,* and he blinked.

Is that something you can do?

His dragon seemed to ponder this. *I believe so.*

Damian frowned. If it could've opened a rift to go home, why hadn't it tried already any of the other times when it'd longed to do so and was almost in control? *Are you just telling me that so my friends don't murder you on sight?*

His dragon laughed at him. *I am not afraid of any weapon.*

"Damian?" Mills prompted gently.

"Sorry," he said, running a hand through his hair. "If it ever comes out, and you're sure it's not me, don't hesitate."

"That's grim, and not in the cat-sense," Jamison said.

"You've trained a gun on me before."

"Yes, but I have excellent trigger control," Jamison said, making his metallic hand clack between them.

"What if we just put you into a box that was a magic dampener?" Mills mused aloud.

"Like some sort of Ken doll?" Austin asked.

"No," Damian said. "I'll live my life. And we'll make it work. Or we won't. But I'm not pausing anything in the interim." *Except for these two days without Andi.*

"It's a heavy burden," Max said, the first time the man had spoken since Damian shared his story. He'd taken a spot on the ground, his back against Ryana's bed, and while Damian couldn't see his eyes what with the goggles, his weapons master's lips were in a thin, straight line of concern. Maximillian had been part of his father's court from before his mother's time, until after the dragon'd taken him. He'd seen his father change, losing himself bit by bit over time to his dragon, until there was no more human left. "We'll help you lift it, as best we can."

Damian nodded. "Thank you."

Zach stroked the dark stubble on his chin. "How did your father die? I mean, presumably, the heart was in the box over there as well, right?"

"He died in combat, as a dragon. It was at the end of a war that he'd started as a human, and to be honest, I don't even know if his dragon had a stake in things so much as it wanted an excuse to take a few thousand humans on." Damian and Ryana had toured the charred pit that'd been all that remained after his father's dragon had immolated itself to secure victory, taking out most of the magicians left on the opposing side. "I had hoped that distance would forestall things. Which it did seem to—"

"Until your sister messed up by bringing it over," Austin said, giving his erstwhile patient a worried look.

"To be fair, she probably didn't know I was going to save her," Damian said. Although she must've been hoping—there was a reason Lyka had come to his mirror for help. "I don't suppose you can talk to the bird?" he asked Grim, who had been creeping up on the cheese plate Mills had set down, scanning for crumbs.

Grimalkin fell to sit on his haunches. "I tried, Damian, but she's been very close-beaked. Thinking about whatever happened over there—it hurts her."

"Understood," Damian told him, and then to everyone else, "Grim says it's a no-go."

Max angled his limbs to rest his hands on his knees. "I still wish we knew what'd happened," he said.

"Me too," Damian said. "But I really just want her to get better."

"What's to stop us from opening up a mirror and throwing it back? Or launching it into space?" Zach asked.

Everyone else present looked at Damian expectantly. "It is a sought-after thing, and it cannot be destroyed," Max said on his behalf. "At least, that's what your father said, Damian," he added.

"Well, *we* haven't tried yet," Mills said.

Damian realized that this was yet another way that here, on Earth, he was doing the unthinkable. His father had only shown him the Heart once—after his dragon joined him. He didn't even know which vault of the palace it'd lived in, and here he was, willing to give it over to his five closest friends to experiment on. "My fate is still linked to it. I don't think I want it destroyed, so much as I want to be unchained. When it was in my stepmother's control, I could trust she'd keep it guarded, due to our mutual animosity. Now, though...." Could Mills really manage it?

"Launch it into the sun?" Jamison guessed in hope. "We own rockets—"

"Anything with enough magical power could open a rift between here and the sun. That's ninety-two million miles of opportunity, my love," Mills said, patting Jamison's knee affectionately. He caught her hand in his and interlaced his fingers with it.

"So, what's protecting it now?" Zach asked, doing an excellent job of project managing—even when that project was the object of Damian's eventual demise. Damian gave him a rueful grin.

"Grimalkin, and the fact that I'm sure the chaos back home is still evolving. They may not even know it's gone yet."

"I've made headway on Ryana's false-corpse, but if we knew what kind of attack they were under, it would help with authenticity," Mills said.

"Won't they know it's not her, though?" Damian asked with a squint and watched Mills bite her lips.

"Not if I do it right," she answered precisely. "But don't ask me how yet, please. I'm still working on it."

One of his eyebrows quirked up, but he acquiesced to her request. "Okay. But later?"

"Yes," she agreed emphatically.

"Have we gotten any more news from the trackers Andi placed?" Damian asked Jamison. The man closed his eyes for a second.

"The boat's parked at the harbor, and the car's at the airport;

both appear to be currently empty. So, nothing useful yet, but they've both got a few days of batteries left. I'll let you know if anything comes in."

Damian nodded, then turned to Zach. "And any news from Stella?"

"About that," Zach said, giving his brother a dark look.

"Here it comes," muttered Austin.

"I talked with her this evening after we returned. The Hunter we gave her didn't know much, except that there was an important meeting coming up in two nights. No location, though. He'd only heard it from other Hunters."

"I don't suppose enough of him's left for us to interrogate ourselves?" Austin asked archly.

"Doubtful."

Damian grunted. Maybe this brief separation from Andi was well-timed—he wouldn't have to talk her out of coming to stalk Hunters with them.

"I don't like the idea of Stella out there on her own," Zach went on.

Seeing as Damian currently intimately understood that pain, he nodded. "You want to bring her into the fold?"

"I do. As for whether she'd accept—"

"Or whether the rest of us would let her," Austin said, and Zach frowned at him.

"She's a loner. So far. But yes, I'd like to be able to ask."

"Is she trustworthy?" Damian asked, steamrolling Austin's concerns.

"I think so," Zach said.

"She stabbed you!" Austin protested.

Zach shrugged with a boyish grin. "I survived."

"Jesus Christ," Austin groaned, looking first at Damian, and then over at Mills and Jamison, clearly sitting together while beside him on the couch, before staring at Max. "Max, you and I are the only ones here not going soft."

Max quietly pursed his lips and scratched his chin. "No comment."

Jamison chuckled, Zach snickered, and Mills outright laughed as Austin groaned and stood, waving all of them toward the door. "Okay. Screw all of y'all. I'm tired. You don't have to go home, but you can't stay here."

"But we are home," Mills said, confused, though moving to stand.

"It's a saying," Jamison explained, sweeping the cheese plate up off the floor to follow her. Grimalkin had already licked it clean. The cat bounced back onto the bed and nestled himself in the crook behind Ryana's knee.

"Don't forget I've got a board meeting to get magicked up for in two hours, Mills," Zach said, filing out first.

"I could never," the witch told him truthfully.

"Mills, wait a moment outside, will you?" Damian asked as everyone else made their way out of the room and to their appointed floors. Then he turned to Austin, who was stretching himself back out on the couch. "Thank you for this, by the way."

Austin tipped the edge of an imaginary cowboy hat at him and turned toward the bed, eyes only half-lidded.

DAMIAN MET up with Mills in the hall, and she smiled up at him. "Did Andi like her pajamas? I like to think I have fantastic taste in cozy sleepwear."

"She did like them. Very much." He decided not to tell her what he'd done to them, for her sake. "Can you buy her a few extra for me? Also, she needs a purple velvet sectional, although I have no idea what that is."

Mills laughed. "I'll have Jamison pull up her apartment's blue-prints for measurements and send one to her."

"Thanks," he said.

She turned, walking for the stairs, assuming her audience was over, and he hesitated. There was already so much on her plate, he felt selfish asking her for more, and yet....

She turned around. "You can just ask it, you know."

"Is my aura a needy red right now?" Damian asked, gesturing to himself.

"No. It's more of a guilty green," she told him. "Whatever it is, I won't be mad at you, I promise."

Damian started walking with her until they were in the entry hall, and he could sit down on the stairs. Mills sat a few stairs up from him, moving the long braid of her hair, so it cascaded down the stairs beside her like a sturdy rope. "I was thinking when you were talking earlier—"

"I am sorry about Michael, Damian, really," Mills said.

"No, I get that. Michael wouldn't have wanted you to injure your-self to save him. Neither would Jamison, though," he said, giving her a stern look. "But let's not cross any bridges before their time; it was more about the breathing thing. Andi was very unhappy the other day when I had to go and leave her behind. And, as she took the time to remind me in exquisite detail, while there are a million ways that she could accidentally die when it comes to me, there's a million and one."

Mills nodded as he went on.

"So, I was wondering if there was something you could create or spell for me, to give to her—some sign of life. Just so that she knows I'm okay, even if I'm not with her."

Mills picked up her braid and started playing with the end of it, pondering. "What were you envisioning?"

"Something small. Smaller, the better, probably. And easily carried."

She nodded deeply. "Jewelry, then. And what are you willing to trade for it?"

He blinked. The question was very unlike her. "I can pay you, obviously, but—"

"I mean life-wise," she interrupted him. "A spell would just be like one of Jamison's trackers. Eventually, it'd run out of charge. If you really want her to know how you are, you will have to give up a piece of yourself to it." She paused to search for words. "It is a strange kind of magic you're asking for, Damian. On the verge of dark, almost, only you're doing it out of love...and don't tell me you don't love her. Remember who it is you're talking to. No, this is the kind of thing that has to be freely given, and in whatever quantity you deem fit. It's not prescriptive...it's unquantifiable."

Damian considered this. "When you say a piece of me...what precisely do you mean?"

"That's also up to you. It's the kind of thing you'll know when you know." She waved her hands with the braid in them. "I hate to be so vague, but this is that kind of magic."

Damian grunted. "How long would it take you to make?"

"A day or so. My part's easy, really; yours, not so much." Mills stood as he did, giving his chest a pat. "Just don't give her your actual heart. We need that to stay inside of you."

"I wouldn't want to curse her," he said with a snort.

Mills inhaled to say something, and then he could almost watch her swallow her words, as her friendly smile went close-lipped and tight. There was an instant in which he could've pressed her to make her say the thing she was sorely tempted to, but he had a feeling he already knew what it was.

That regarding himself and Andi and curses, it was already too late.

SHE SHOULD'VE KNOWN that without Damian around, the nightmares would come back. That might've been the only thing that could've changed her mind earlier if only she'd remembered. But she hadn't, so she woke up that morning after hours of being chased in her dreams by a half-skinned hound, sweaty and exhausted and alone.

She heard Sammy puttering and the scent of brewing coffee

wafted underneath her door. Andi got out of bed and went to a dresser to pull out an older pair of pajamas that she now knew were sadly insufficient and went out to see her roommate.

Sammy was surprised to see her. Her curly red hair was already up in a professional bun, and she was wearing her work uniform. "I didn't make enough coffee for three, missy," her roommate said, pouring the remnants of a pot into her thermos.

Andi waved her down. "He had to go home, and I should go back to sleep."

"You're working tonight?"

"Yeah. My schedule's all jacked up," she said, stifling a yawn.

"Did you sleep at all last night?" Sammy teased. "Before he went home, that is. Wait," her eyes narrowed, "did he go home just so he wouldn't have to let me drive?"

Andi snorted. "There was sleeping. And there was not sleeping. And I'm going to get us a replacement couch, I swear, and the drives are still on...as far as I know."

"You don't sound definitive," Sammy said, screwing her thermos cap on.

"I'm...not?"

"Oh my God, Andi," Sammy groaned, already mourning the loss of her time in Damian's Pagani. "What happened?"

"He's super intense?" Andi said, wincing. "And he's used to getting his way."

"Uh, that can be kinda hot. Assuming he knows what he's doing." Sammy gave her a look.

"It is, and he does, but...look, can we just hang out tonight before I go to work? Together? Like in the olden days of last month when boys still sucked?"

Sammy fished her phone out of her pocket. "I had plans for tonight, but this is me, canceling them for you," she said, quickly texting someone.

"Thank you. I owe you."

"Plus, you go into work at ten. I can totally swing by his place afterward," she went on, grinning.

Andi grinned back. "I'll take whatever I can get of you."

SHE WAITED until Sammy headed out the door and stood on their stoop, waving like a 1950's housewife until she got into her car and safely headed out. Then Andi scanned the parking lot for sleek black cars holding insane cannibalistic passengers, and finding none, she went back inside and locked the door.

She thought about plopping down on the couch, but that'd only bring back memories, plus probably make her smell like dragon. She did flip over the couch cushions. It was the least she could do until she got a new one.

It wasn't like Netflix could distract her with anything weirder than her own life right now, besides. She went back to her bedroom and pulled out the photo album, bringing it out to the kitchen counter and its much better light and began at the beginning of the photos.

It was definitely her mother. In all of them.

She'd always thought her mom was more mercurial than the mothers of her friends, but she assumed it was because of the different ways they'd been raised. She knew her mom was from a different generation and a different country...but now, a different century, too? Andi looked at the photos, feeling hopelessly lost. This page featured her mother standing in a cheongsam amidst a pile of skulls, her hair bunned up with beautiful floral hair pins, and strange pointed jewelry covering her last two fingers like she was some sort of evil-goth Chinese princess from one of the historical kung fu dramas they used to watch together.

Only, this had been her mother's *actual life*. No wonder she'd made fun of Andi for going briefly vegan in seventh grade.

But even though Andi knew it was her mother in each of the photos, none of them had the feel of her, until they got into modern times—until Danny and Andi started showing up in them as well. The photos then were looser, not as well framed, far more casual and blurry—but they were happier. All of them. The skulls were gone. Was that because her mother had had a change of heart, or if whatever it was they'd been killing was gone?

Without her mother to ask, her uncle was her next best bet. She had too much history with Danny to even think straight when she saw him, plus he had far too personal a stake in whatever the fuck this was. Whereas, yes, maybe her uncle had been a liar her whole life too, but seeing him didn't instantly send her into a blind rage.

Yet.

They were probably getting there, though.

Andi sank back on the bar stool she was sitting on. After she got her answers—answers that she was almost certain not to like—what would be left? Arguably, it wasn't even worth finding answers out if she knew it was all going to anger her. Curiosity killed the cat and all that, but at least the cat fucking knew.

She sighed, slammed the photo album shut, and carried it back into the bedroom with her, putting it carefully onto her desk before taking an Ambien and crawling back into bed. She set her phone's alarm for an aspirational eight hours later. There was no way she'd sleep that much, especially if she kept having nightmares, but since she was working tonight she had to try.

Just as she was about to drift off under the Ambien's spell, her phone screen flashed with a text.

Going to sleep now, Damian informed her.

Me too, she texted him back. The dots of him typing his reply began immediately.

Then good night, princess.

She smiled a little at the phone in spite of herself and texted back, *G'night, dragon,* before turning her phone off.

He was glad that he'd texted her.

He'd felt a fool, of course, worrying she wouldn't respond and all the things that that might mean. For a creature—and man—used to taking permission for granted, the delicacy of earthly courtship rituals was baffling. But Andi was of earth, and she deserved his patience.

It just killed him that these things took time because it felt like he was running out of it—ever since the Heart had reappeared. He could chase his fears away when he was with Andi or his crew, but alone, it was like he could feel the thing beating, despite the box, despite the room it was in not having doors. He knew he could put it into the middle of the Forgetting Fire itself, and it would neither burn nor stop.

So, he forced himself to concentrate on something slightly better —how he'd satisfy Mills's request, to give her something of himself to transmute for Andi. What would possibly work? For all the possessions he had, none of them felt intimate enough, and Sammy would be horribly depressed if Damian gave Mills his favorite car to crunch into a diamond.

I have a suggestion, his dragon told him, and showed him, flashing images of action across his mind. Damian considered it...and it felt right.

Yes, he agreed.

He lay down on his bed in his bedroom, watched by the darkened mirrors surrounding him like so many black eyes, and tried to imagine better places and better days, all with Andi, to fall asleep to.

Damian woke up later, not sure how much time had passed—it was light outside. And he was greeted by a text from Andi. *Up now,* sent from hours ago. *And I'd say thank you for the couch delivery, but we both know that it was Mills, wasn't it?* Her words sounded sharp to him until she followed it up with a grin.

I did tell her you needed one, so it's at least partly me. He texted her back. *Sleep well?*

Until they dropped the couch off, yes.

Sorry about that. I should've been more specific with my delivery request.

Eh. It's okay. Sleeping's hard for me, anyhow.

Nightmares?

Some, she admitted, followed by a frown. *But also working night-shift and being on the opposite schedule from the world.* He wished he could change the world for her when she added, *It can't be helped though. What are your plans for today?*

Not sure. Food, training, killing any monsters that pop up. You?

A little more domestic. I'm going to rest more, then go out with Sammy tonight, just us girls, don't get worried. Then, work, hooray. (That was a sarcastic hooray. They don't make an emoji for that level of sarcasm yet.)

Damian smiled at his phone, then shook his head. *You do realize we could have this conversation in person, right?*

Yes. But that would be cheating.

Who precisely is keeping score?

The Rock is. I'm looking at him here from my bed, and he's telling me to be strong. Damian snorted as she went on. *Vin agrees with him, by the way. They both think that less than forty-eight hours is nothing. Between sleeping, eating, me working, and you killing monsters, it'll be over in no time.*

Damian sighed. As much as he liked to claim it was his dragon that was the creature of action, he was too. This distance felt wrong, and it angered him.

I miss you, he admitted.

It felt like he watched the dots of her reply spin on forever before she finally stated: *I miss you, too.* But before he could get his hopes up, she continued, *We can both make it till midnight tomorrow night, though.*

While technically I know that we can, it is hard not to feel like this is punishment.

The dots circled again. *No. If I wanted to punish you, I'd send you nude photos.*

Desire poured through him, mixed with anxiety. *How many nude photos do you have?* he asked her.

Countless, she teased him. And then an image popped up—of the back of her hand.

Andi, he said, and finally went through the stupid smiling faces on his phone to send her one that had its tongue out.

She sent a string of laughing faces back to him as he noticed that the sheets in the background of her photo were changed from the ones he'd just given her. Why would she have changed them so quickly? They hadn't even defiled them yet. Or was that an old photo?

A new image loaded quickly—this time, of her chest. Her beautiful breasts were slanted slightly back by gravity; she'd clearly held the camera directly over herself and snapped it quickly. He knew it was a photo from just now because he could see a small spot inside her cleavage where his mouth had marked her yesterday evening, and the sheets were definitely back to penguins.

Look, Mister, when I send photos over, I generally expect some sort of response, flashed on his screen. *Unless you're too busy with your hands to type....*

He tapped the icon on his phone to initiate a call, and she picked up. "Speakerphone?" she guessed.

"Andi," he began, his voice low, ready to point out how arbitrary this entire thing was, and to ask her why she'd changed her sheets, then he remembered that he was trying extremely hard to be reasonable for ridiculous human definitions thereof.

"I'm not punishing you, Damian, honest," she said, defusing him instantly. "Maybe I'm punishing myself...I don't know."

"For what?"

He heard her sigh on the far end of the line, and he wished that he could hold her.

"I looked at all of my mother's photos. All of them. I mean, I really, really looked. And apart from the fact that my mother apparently lied to me my entire life, she was a horrible person. I guess. I think. I don't really know? And now that she's dead, I never will."

He could hear the pain echoing in her voice. "Andi...we are not the sum of our relatives."

There was a long pause, and then she said, "I'd ask how you can be so sure, but I think I know."

"I'm glad I shared enough family trauma with you then. And if I thought for one moment I was like my father, Andi," Damian said, stretching out on his bed, "I would kill myself without hesitation."

"Don't say that!"

"Well, the irony is that if I actually were like my father, I would never dream of doing such a thing. But if that's the reason you pushed me away, I understand."

"Thank you," she granted him. "But...I did mean everything I said last night. This morning. Shit, I don't know, time keeps slipping away from me. Whenever I was telling you, I just needed some room to breathe."

Damian grunted. "I like you breathing. So, please, do continue."

"Oh, see, now I wish you were here so I could shove you," Andi groaned. "Thanks for doing this for me, though."

"I do possess a limited capacity for following explicitly stated instructions," he said. "Even if it is hard sometimes to understand the human relationship process."

"Your dragon probably thinks I'm insane, doesn't he?"

Damian made a thoughtful sound. "No, actually, he trusts you. He doesn't understand either, mind you, but he's a lot more okay with that than I am," he said, and he heard Andi chuckle.

"I'm glad I have one fan, at least."

"Two for sure," he said with a smile he hoped she heard. "And maybe as many as six," he went on, thinking about the rest of his morning with his people. "Could be as high as seven, if my sister wakes up and you two get along."

199

"I hope so...on both counts," she said, and he thought he heard her smiling too.

Whatever doubts Damian had begun his phone call with had entirely evaporated after talking to her, and as much as he wanted to keep talking, this was probably his best chance to make a graceful exit from the conversation. "All right, princess. Get some rest and call or text before your shift tonight."

There was an unwarrantedly long pause on the far end of the line, before Andi said, "Hmmmph."

"What did I do now?"

"I sent you a photo, Damian. Technically, you're supposed to send me one back, for equitable blackmail."

Damian laughed. "What? I don't think I even know how to take pictures with this thing."

"You mean on all of your 'countless' dates, no one ever sent you nudes?"

"You're the first of my 'countless' dates to actually have my real phone number."

"No way. Wait...if that's true, who manages your pretend phone?"

"Mills. She just told me what I needed to know before I went out with anyone."

Andi started laughing hysterically. "Damian...I don't know how to break this to you, Mills has been holding out. I bet you've got a substantial amount of nudity on that thing."

"But...why?"

"Because that's what people do, Damian. Earth-people who don't have wings. And with all the vagina that you were getting thrown at you, oh my God," she said, giggling helplessly, as he blinked at his ceiling, trying to understand.

"So, wait...as your boyfriend...I could expect you to send me nude photos? Any time I desired?"

Damian didn't get an answer, just heard a rustling, and then a text popped up—a photo of the inverted V of Andi's thighs, covered by a triangle of dark purple underwear. He wished he could reach through the screen and tear them off.

"You are evil, princess," he said and heard her laugh even more.

"No, being evil is telling you that I might touch myself thinking about you when I hang up. I'll call you tonight and tell you all about it if I do, though; I promise. Bye!" she said, and then hung up quickly, leaving him semi-hard and staring at his screen.

"This is more difficult than I had imagined," he muttered to himself when one last text from her flashed across his screen—a photo of her hand placed seductively across her stomach, fingertips tucked under the edge of the purple fabric—and then a final text: *Promise if you go out fighting you'll come back safe to me?*

Always, he messaged her and put his phone down.

WHAT HIS DRAGON had suggested earlier was gruesome, but it felt right. And it was the last text from Andi that did it. She'd been so worried about him earlier—there was a chance that this distance wasn't just born of denying their pull, or her past, but also paranoia. Her needing to prove to herself that she could manage her fears alone. And now that it was light out, he needed to hurry if he was going to give Mills's magic time.

He got out of bed and went to the door that led to his dragon's bathing pond, which was fitting because this was where it seemed everything with Andi had begun.

This will hurt, his dragon warned him.

Pain is fine, Damian thought, as his dragon had once told him, before pulling off his clothes and folding them neatly at the water's edge. *I would rather hurt us now than her hurt later.*

So be it, his dragon said, as Damian relinquished control.

This time, it was like there was a massive beast below him and he dropped the reins—or some fantastic vehicle in which his foot was always on the brakes—and he'd just let it go. He closed his eyes as human, and within moments, he was gone, replaced by the monster always lurking inside of him.

The bathing pond, which'd seemed infinitely large as a human, now felt constraining, its roof in particular. Trapped inside of it, Damian felt his dragon's will surge, with all of its monstrous desires to fly and be free.

The Heart's proximity makes me stronger, his dragon rumbled gleefully. *I do not think you could stop me now if you tried.*

I thought we were in agreement? Damian said, tensing, mentally searching for the reins again and dropping his foot back down.

We are, the beast agreed, and reared up, the tips of its golden horns brushing against the room's cave-like roof. *For now.* And then it bent its head and caught its teeth beneath the scales upon its own chest and bit down.

His dragon's fangs weren't sharp—they didn't need to be. The creature had speed and crushing weight on its side. Which is why, as the thing bit down on its own flesh, Damian felt it through every nerve inside his body. It twisted its head, adjusted its bite, and continued, its muzzle filling with salty dark green blood and the heat of its own flesh, the sharpness of its own rough scales that he could feel across its tongue. It started snapping its neck, trying to yank the piece free, and Damian howled in wordless agony inside. He had never known such pain—nothing had ever gotten the chance to hurt him so badly before.

Do you wish me to stop? his dragon asked him, doing so, teeth still buried inside his own breast.

Damian reeled. *No. But...hurry.*

The beast growled and redoubled its efforts, and blackness came in at the edges of Damian's vision—a darkness shot with scattering stars. Damian wondered what would happen if he passed out with his dragon in control—what it would do, where it would take him—if this was at all like what it would feel at the end when his dragon finally won—as it whipped its head free and spit out a still bleeding scaled chunk of flesh on the sandy shore.

Damian sank to his knees in the void that he occupied when his dragon was in charge. If there were any reins available, he would not have been able to pick them up; he couldn't have fought his dragon now if he tried.

I am finished, his dragon announced before receding, folding once more into Damian's human form, leaving Damian gasping at the water's edge, his hand instinctively covering the bleeding wound above his heart.

ANDI DOZED AGAIN after sending Damian sexy photos to no avail. The fool had clearly taken her at her word and turned off his phone. She would have to sit him down and make him watch some romantic comedies, once she could think of any that didn't annoy her or have any elements in them that he could take too seriously out of context. Dating him was kind of like training a puppy if that puppy could also become a sixty-foot dragon. She snorted, rolled out of bed, and went into her bathroom. "At least I don't have to take a shower today," she told her reflection, hoping that Damian was being true to his word and not looking through.

"So, like, what kind of fun are we going for tonight?" Sammy asked, knocking on her door after she heard the toilet flush and knew that Andi was awake.

"Coffee casual," Andi shouted, working through her closet, pulling out some jeans and a cute shirt, and tucking her feet into sneakers she could also wear later at work. When she was dressed, she walked into the living room, where Sammy was already sitting on the couch Damian had delivered, in a bodycon blue dress and strappy heels.

"I said casual." Andi laughed, looking at the differences between them.

Sammy grinned. "Yes, but, after casual, comes—"

"A booo-tay call," Andi cut in, making fun of Sammy's Irish

accent. "And he's not going to care what you look like when you get there, trust me."

"But I do," Sammy protested, bouncing up off the couch. "I take professional pride in these sorts of things." She grabbed her purse and headed for the door, then gave Andi a sly look. "Nice couch, by the way."

"Thanks," Andi said, trying not to flush.

"Is there any way you two can fuck on the refrigerator next?" Sammy teased. "He's strong, and you're tiny; I know he can hold you up."

"I'm gonna hold you up in a moment," Andi muttered, loud enough to be heard, as she followed her snickering roommate out the door.

Not long after that, they were sitting across from each other at Jones & Shah Coffee, and Sammy was squinting at her over a steaming mocha.

"So...tell me why we got free coffee again?"

"The barista remembered me, and she really liked her iPhone," Andi said with a mysterious shrug. "I helped her with a problem." The problem of it almost being stolen by a former patient of Andi's, not that many nights ago.

"If you say so," Sammy said, giving up, but Andi was sure she'd circle back around later—Sammy didn't give up on anything. Ever. Dead engines, dead-beat men—their apartment would be full of feral kittens if she thought they could pull it over on their landlord. Her obstinate belief that she could make anything make sense was the main reason why she'd dated Danny for so long. As if reading her mind, Sammy reached out to touch Andi's hand. "So...any news?"

"Not yet. My uncle's working on it, though," Andi said with a tight smile. She hated lying to Sammy, but she had to. There was no way to explain that her brother, Sammy's ex, was now some sort of dragon-thing and that her uncle—

"Hey...you're not alone. I'm worried too." Sammy must've seen her fears flash on her face. "Just because we didn't end well doesn't mean I didn't care."

Andi flipped her hand to catch Sammy's. "Honestly, Sammy, if there's one true thing I can tell you about Danny, you shouldn't be wasting your time. I have to because I'm his sister, but one of us should get to escape scot-free." She squeezed Sammy's hand tightly and then let it go. "Tell me more about your smoking hot man? Or is he just a smoker?" she asked with a side-eye.

"I told him he had to quit or face my roommate's judgment."

"Did he sound scared?" Andi grinned.

Sammy grinned back. "Not after I told him you're five-three."

"Five-three-and-a-half, Sammy," Andi tsked. "And just for that, I'm not going to get fucked on the fridge."

"Fine," Sammy said, feigning petulance. "Stove? Please? Not on, but...like, I've always wanted a conduction range—"

"What? No!" Andi put a hand to her chest in mock horror.

"Why do you have to ruin all my dreams?" Sammy said, slouching in her chair dramatically, before perking back to life. "Wait...if you fuck in *my* shower...will I get better water pressure? Or faster heating?"

Andi cackled. "He's just rich, he's not magical," she said, even though it was the lie of the century, then stood. "I'll be right back, I've gotta pee."

JONES AND SHAH'S bathroom was gender-neutral and a single room, so you almost always had to wait in the hall outside. Andi knocked and found it occupied, so she crossed her arms and started reading the massive announcement board posted right outside while she waited. Another woman joined her, a feral-looking blonde with makeup shellacked on like armor, standing far, far, too close.

Andi put a hand over her purse and shifted her weight, wondering if the other woman would get the hint. When she didn't,

Andi gave up on being polite and physically scooted sideways, just as the door opened and a man stepped out. Andi caught the door as the woman moved forward. Maybe she'd never been here before and didn't know how it worked?

"Oh...sorry!" she announced, after glancing inside, ducking back into partial shadow.

"No, clearly, you need it more. I can wait," Andi said, making a sweeping gesture with her arm. The woman slunk forward, that was the right verb for it, she totally slunked—*or was it slanked?* Andi thought—darting in, grabbing the door out from Andi's hand and slamming it behind her.

A junkie. Probably. Andi looked back at Sammy and saw her waving the attentions of some Lurch-sized random guy away, using Andi's half-full cup of coffee as a prop, and knew she needed to get back to the table. Sammy was too hot for her own good tonight. *That smoking guy had better really quit.* The bathroom door burst open, and the woman prowled out, giving Andi an extended glare.

Andi caught the door again as the woman moved oddly as if to breathe on her, and in the distance, the man Sammy was trying to shoo away sat down. Andi let the door go and stormed over to rescue her friend. "Can I help you?"

"I don't know, can you?" the man said back at her, and she could smell the alcohol on him. Clearly, a drunken fuckwit.

"I was just about to round up the trash, darling," Sammy said, cracking her knuckles and leaning forward. Andi knew Sammy had a tongue on her like no one's business.

"You're not supposed to play with your food, Sammy," Andi said.

Then the weird woman from the bathroom line was there. "You... get the fuck out...now." She accosted the man without fear, despite the fact that he was three times her size. "You heard me," she said when he didn't move.

Sammy looked to Andi, who looked back and shrugged, and then the bathroom-line girl reached forward and caught the guy on his shoulder, Star Trek Spock-style, and practically picked him up with a pinch. He started instantly whining as she maneuvered him out the door.

"Who the fuck was that?" Sammy asked.

"No clue," Andi said, sitting down. It was odd, and now that she knew about Damian's life, her ability to calibrate local weirdness was all skewed. Was it a garden variety kind of strange or something that might come back to bite her—possibly literally—later?

"Well, it doesn't matter," Sammy said, brushing the incident away. Andi knew she had thick skin. She worked at a body shop; she got hit on all the time, whereas Andi usually only got hit on at work by people coming off of anesthesia and creeps on the bus. "Where were we...oh wait, were we talking about my man?"

Andi leaned forward with renewed intent, refocusing on the now, and how good it felt to lovingly hassle the shit out of her roommate. "That depends. Does he also do home improvements?"

"Possibly," Sammy said sagely while grinning like a fool. "I mean, he really is good at nailing things."

CHAPTER

TWELVE

Damian hadn't really considered what would come next after he hurt himself. First, that it would take him so long to heal—which made a strange amount of sense, he was a dragon, after all, and he had hurt himself on a dragon-sized scale—or how he would transport a piece of meat the size of a slab of beef to Mills to spell-with.

In the end, he gave up and called for Grimalkin to summon her. She came into the room shortly thereafter, looked at him—he hadn't put his shirt back on, as he was still bleeding—and then looked at the cast-off flesh with scales still attached that sat to one side.

"Damian...what did you do?" she asked, putting a horrified hand over her mouth. Damian wadded up his T-shirt and held it against his still bleeding chest.

"What you asked of me. I think. Unless I did it wrong. Don't tell me you need more." He'd survived it once; he could do it again, but it would be harder next time.

"No, that's like, vastly more than I need. I said something small. I don't need to make her a set of crown jewels."

Damian snorted. "Well, you also said it had to come from me. It did."

"Clearly," Mills said, eyeing him with concern. "Are you all right?"

"Nothing that won't heal quickly." Unlike his witch, Damian had no problem lying.

"My God," she muttered, walking around the piece of flesh's edges. "All right. I'll ask Grim to transport it up over to my lab once I get prepared. I'm going to have to redraw my ritual circle to hold this." She gave Damian a dark glance. "Do you have any idea what that would be worth to Hunters on the black market?"

"I'd prefer not to think on it...but yes."

She knelt down and put a thoughtful hand on a bloodied scale. "That's why this magic is dark, Damian. There's not that much difference between what I'm about to do and what they try to do with their talismans all the time."

"Except for the fact that I trust you," Damian said.

She flashed him a smile. "Indeed."

"Even if you have been holding out on me," he added. The pain was lessening now, even if the blood was not.

Mills tilted her head, sending her hair cascading over one shoulder. "How so?"

"Andi explained to me that you've probably been getting nude photos from prior women on my behalf."

He watched her flush redder than he'd ever seen. "Technically, you never asked, so I wasn't lying."

"Technically, I never knew," he said, giving her a bemused look. "Why didn't you tell me?"

Mills pushed her hair back with her clean hand. "Damian," she said matter-of-factly, "you know how the internet works, yes?"

"Yes," he agreed.

"Well, then, you already know how to see naked women any time you want. You just didn't need to see those ones in particular."

Damian laughed. "I might have liked to've had the choice, Mills."

She gave him a sheepish grin and shrugged. "None of them were right for you. I could tell."

"And this one is?" he asked her, not because he doubted, but because he wanted to hear her say it again.

She gestured to the still warm chunk of dragon flesh beside them. "Clearly," she said and whistled for Grim.

DAMIAN STUCK AROUND for long enough to explain to Grim what'd happened and what was required of him, plus also allay his guardian's fears about his health.

"That is a lot of blood, Damian," Grimalkin said, prancing around in concern.

"I'm fine." All he had to do was somehow make it without Andi until midnight tomorrow, and then everything would be better. He watched Grim disappear with the piece of him, Mills made her exit, and he went back inside to his bedroom. He grabbed his phone in case Andi had called, and made his way into his bathroom to clean up, finally pulling his shirt away from the gash his own teeth had carved in him, which set the whole thing to fresh bleeding, sending trickling trails of green blood down his chest.

"Dammit," he muttered, trying to look at the edges of the wound, grabbing a clean towel to blot up the blood and apply pressure. He probably ought to have Austin look at it, but then he'd have to explain what the hell he'd been doing, which would give the defiantly single werewolf an opening to tell him what he thought again. Maybe if he took a photo with his phone and sent it, that way, Austin could ignore it if he were still half-sleeping, or he'd only yell back at him in via text. Damian groaned, picking his phone off the counter where he'd set it down, striping his thumb up the screen so it'd turn on and found that he'd missed at least a hundred texts. All from Andi.

His stomach filled with acid, and his current pain was completely forgotten until the first text opened up to show him another revealing photo, this time her hands slightly lower beneath her purple panty's waistline.

He opened photo after photo of her, so many she might as well have made a video, and as he flipped through them one by one, he felt what blood he had left sink and make him hard. He could see the outline of her fingers as she pressed herself, her own wetness soak the center of her panties and then spread, the way she pushed her fingers deep inside herself, surely imagining they were him. He put the phone on the counter, blood forgotten, and opened his jeans quickly, his hand racing to stroke himself without conscious thought, imagining he was there. He saw her hips rise, and then her shimmy out of her underwear entirely, so that there was nothing hiding her from him and he could watch her fingers play her soft folds and rub her pretty little clit with her own juices and still reach to touch herself, deep inside. He felt his cock twitch and tense as he stroked faster, picturing himself with her, leaning forward, one hand on the counter now, letting each photo load in turn. The images in them were now further apart in time because he knew she was turned on. Her hips arched, and her fingers were buried in herself. He knew that she had come for him, just as she had promised, and he was going to lose himself for her. Even though she wasn't there, it was for her—for fucking ever and always. The last photo she sent was of her hand held up, fingers glistening, and he barely had the presence of mind to let his cum shoot into his free hand, striping his still slightly green-stained palm with silvery white. He grunted, seeing himself through, jetting everything in him out and then, dazed from his orgasm but determined to be with Andi whenever he could, he managed to take a photo of his own spill and send it to her, as he caught his breath.

She didn't respond, but he knew she would eventually, and that was enough. He rubbed himself clean with the towel, washed his hands, then went downstairs to see Austin in person.

212

"THANKS FOR THE RIDE, even if we both know it's only so you can get to Professor Ph.D.'s house faster," Andi teased, curled up in Sammy's passenger seat.

"Don't even worry about it...you're on the way," Sammy said, not rising to the bait, but she did lean over to give Andi's leg a motherly pat.

Andi grinned before getting serious. "You'll text me when you're home, right? Because otherwise, I won't know you've been murdered until morning, and that's way too long."

"Of course, I'll text you."

"What's his address? And his phone number?"

"He's off Lark street," Sammy said.

"Well, that's not going to help the cops much. Do you have a photo of him?" Andi inquired as Sammy laughed.

"Oh my God, for reals?"

"Says the woman who made me give her a safeword for a single date!" Andi protested, getting out her phone. "Speaking of, what's yours? Because fair is fair." She swiped her phone on and saw a text from Damian.

About damn time. She had not sent him all those photos for her health.

Then what Damian had sent her filled the screen, and she felt herself flush. She dodged to hide it from Sammy's prying eyes—but her roommate knew anyway, via best-friend-telepathy.

"What'd you get?" Sammy asked, peering over.

"Nothing!" Andi said, voice high, but she couldn't bring herself to close the screen. It was Damian's hand, clearly covered in cum, which was a good thing, but the palm beneath it was stained with green. He'd been out fighting and been hurt. As hot as the photo was, her stomach turned. If something happened to him while she was being stubborn to get answers from her uncle....

"That's a something look," Sammy refuted her.

"It's an, 'I can't share this in polite company' look."

"When the fuck have I ever been polite?" Sammy protested in her lovely accent and laughed. "But fine, I don't want to see your man's dick. I just want him to use it on you on the coffee maker. I want one of those pod ones."

Andi snorted. "Way, way, way too uncomfortable to fuck on top of," she said as she typed. *Hot as hell. But are you okay?*

His response seemed to take forever. *Never better. At work?*

She bit her lips, trying to figure out if she should pry when it was her own fault she wasn't at his side. *Soon.*

Have a good shift then, princess. Let me know when you get home tomorrow.

I will, she texted, *Remember your promises to me.*

Always.

ANDI WAS ALMOST calm by the time Sammy pulled into her hospital's roundabout. Going to work had a way of clearing her head. It was eight hours that she could use to get away from almost anything. Even if her own patients weren't busy, there was always something going on that she could throw herself into to forget everything happening outside the walls. All she had to do was make it inside the doors.

She was almost there when she thought she saw the reflection of someone walking up behind her in the security kiosk's heavy glass. Omar was sitting inside like he always did, the man behind the metal curtain, watching videos on his phone. She turned...and saw no one. Hanging out with Damian was making her paranoid. Or...Andi grabbed her phone and texted quickly: *You swear to God you didn't send anyone to tail me?* and was about to hit send when someone her own size tackled her, taking her down and into a wall of bushes.

She inhaled to scream, and a hand slammed on her mouth. "Say anything, and I'll snap your neck," someone hissed into her ear. A woman's voice, and then the sound of heavy breathing, as if the person holding her down was trying to inhale her. "You don't smell like anything special to me," the woman muttered. Andi kept struggling, but the woman predicted every move she made and held each limb in a grip like iron.

Andi went limp because clearly, she was better off playing along with whatever was happening...even if she could hear the singsong voices of other nurses going in.

"Are you going to scream?" the woman asked her.

Andi shook her head, and the hand released fractionally.

"Tell me how you're special," the woman whispered.

Andi asked, "Did Damian fucking send you?" at the exact same time. At the mention of Damian's name, the woman's insane grip slacked, and Andi whipped her head around. It was the woman from Jones and Shah again. *Fuck!* She should have known.

"He did, didn't he?" Andi said, stumbling upright. There were leaves in her hair and dirt under her nails, fucking hell. She dusted off her knees and pulled a stick out of her hair, and the woman was gone.

Andi stared at the text she'd almost sent him, him swearing he'd remember his promises: to keep himself safe and not lie to her. It didn't matter that she was lying to him—at least by omission—right now. He'd said he wouldn't send anyone after her. He'd promised.

"Andi?" she heard a familiar voice calling her name as she stumbled out of the bushes. Her favorite charge nurse, Sheila. "Are you okay?"

"Yeah," Andi lied, knocking more dirt off herself. "Just clumsy."

"Let me get this straight, you injured yourself right before you knew we were going to have a fight tomorrow?"

Austin was just as upset as Damian guessed he'd be. As the werewolf walked around the room, gathering supplies, Damian tried to explain. "It was for a good cause—"

"No, you keep your sex games to yourself; I don't want to hear it."

"Fine," Damian agreed, as Austin opened up a medical kit. "I assumed I would heal."

"So, why aren't you?" Austin asked, pulling on sterile gloves and picking up a cautery pen.

"Not sure. The proximity of the Heart, maybe."

"I wouldn't think it would weaken you."

Damian had considered this, wondering if he transitioned back into his dragon if he'd be healed—if the Heart had a vested interest in harming his human shell, trying to shove the inevitable along. His dragon was certainly quieter now that the thing it wanted most was close at hand. Damian looked down to watch Austin work, quietly zapping little pieces of him so they wouldn't bleed anymore. The room filled with the scent of ozone and cooking flesh, just like bacon, and Damian remembered what his bedroom had smelled like when they'd pulled Ryana through. "I spent my whole life avoiding it, so it's hard to say."

Austin made a noise, concentrating too hard to talk for once, and then Damian heard a rustle of fabric and saw a flash of brilliant red wings as Lyka flew up to the ceiling.

"Damian?" Ryana was pushing herself up, awkward with her injured wings splayed out behind her. Her eyes focused on him very slowly. "You're injured!"

"You're one to talk," Damian said, giving her a slow smile, gently shoving Austin's hand away. "What the hell happened to you?"

Emotions flittered across her face, just like Lyka's wings. "Oh, brother, it was awful," she said, gingerly making it to the edge of the bed, and then she spotted Austin and froze. Austin was staring at her, awestruck like someone had taken the suture kit he was about to use on Damian and had sewed him to the ground.

"He's a..." Damian began and then realized the word friend wouldn't have the same connotation for Ryana of the Realms that it did for him on earth, "general of mine. Anything you would say to me, you can say to him."

The word "general" shook Austin free, and he flashed Damian a glance that let him know he'd never live that down.

"He's the one responsible for keeping you alive," Damian pressed on.

"You were an easier patient than him, trust me. I have no problem leaving, however," Austin said, as he backed toward the door.

Ryana flung her arm out to stop him. She'd gained weight since Damian had seen her last, and it suited her. It made her more imposing. It felt to him like in his absence, she had come into her own. "No. If you're his general, then you need to hear this too." And then she began scanning her bedclothes as Damian realized what she was looking for—the Heart.

"I found it," he told her.

Her gaze rose up to meet his. "I'm sorry."

"I am too." Damian picked up the chair he was sitting in and turned it to face her and then waved Austin back toward his chest to continue his work. "What the hell happened?"

It was fitting that Austin was intermittently hurting him as she talked. The Realms had always hurt him. Why should now be any different?

"She ruled in peace for a time, Damian," Ryana told him. Her hands were nervously smoothing the sheet on her lap, and Lyka had created a nearby nightstand for her with ice water and hot tea.

"I find that hard to believe," Damian said. His stepmother excelled in casual cruelty.

"As do I. And yet...for a time...there *was* prosperity. Everyone was expecting her to fail, so there didn't seem to be a need to rise against her. I think the countries of the Realms were waiting, honestly, for someone else to take the risk. Everyone was so divided and had so many wounds to lick after father's last war. Then, when things weren't so bad, there didn't need to be a rush. Father's generals stayed loyal, and the ones who didn't, she had the Kagaroth kill quickly."

"What changed?" he pressed, looking down to inspect Austin's work. The werewolf's fine sutures on the muscles he'd torn had brought the edges of his wound close enough for it to begin healing on its own.

"The prognosticators," she said. "A few cycles ago, they started prophesying the next Conjunction."

Damian laughed. "You're kidding." Prognosticators were crazed men and women who were entranced by the movement of the assorted Realms, who ate little and drank less, sitting and watching their orrerys, reading signs and portents into what was essentially unknowable.

"I am not. It was just one or two at first, but then all of them started babbling about it. They don't know when it'll happen, of course...just that it will."

"As everything will in the fullness of time," Damian snorted. "You mean to tell me the Kagaroth couldn't catch them?"

"They caught the first few hundred. My mother had them executed in elaborate ways, but that didn't stop the rest of them from talking. And once the general populace knew, it was too late."

"So, then...war?"

Ryana nodded. "Skirmishes on the borders at first. A botched attempt at poisoning, which led to the execution of most kitchen staff. I lost my favorite baker," she said with a sigh.

Damian felt the free hand Austin was balancing with on his chest tense and was darkly bemused. He'd tried to explain the Realms to his friends—people who he could truly use that word for here on Earth—but it seemed they didn't get it until you mentioned losing a person's life casually like it'd been a mere possession.

"But then it escalated, and here we are," Ryana said. "Wherever here is. Earth, right?"

"Yes. A horrible non-magical place, full of interesting, occasionally magical people," Damian said, giving Austin, who was finishing up, a nod. "But that doesn't explain the Heart, Ryana."

His sister inhaled and exhaled. "It's what the invaders were looking for. My mother knew where it was, of course, but she wouldn't show me. When we heard they were making their final push, my mother whispered which vault it was in in my ear, and I ran."

Damian's eyes narrowed. "Why?"

"I thought," she began and licked her lips, hesitating. "I had to touch it. To find out."

And Damian realized exactly what'd happened. His sister had gone and opened the box it was in and shoved her hand inside and tried to make a pact with the object herself, and it'd denied her in the most brutal way. Damian pushed Austin away and stood. "You thought? It almost killed you, and it will kill me!"

"You weren't there, Damian!" she shouted back at him, rising to stand herself, teetering. Her injured wings fluttered behind her, what was left of them, as the green of her eyes sparkled in her still-swollen eye sockets. "They were at the gate! If it had worked—"

"If it had worked, you would've been cursed the same as me," Damian snarled, angry at her for taking her chance.

"Maybe we should just calm down," Austin began, trying to be the voice of reason, and Damian and Ryana both shot him wilting looks.

Ryana readily refocused on Damian, the bruises on her face still sallow in the library's low light. "Damian, what was left for me, without it?"

Damian inhaled to refute her, but he couldn't.

"That's right. You know what would've come to me. Either it worked and I sold my soul to a dragon, or I would die horribly in the worst imaginable way. You've seen what torments the Kagaroth dream up. I doubt our enemies would've done any differently to destroy a potential queen."

"You could've come to me. Earlier."

"And hidden here, with you?" Ryana scoffed. "My mother was happy to see you go, but we both know she'd move the Realms into a Conjunction herself to reclaim me. She may not know how to love me, but I am her blood."

"And just where is she?"

Ryana frowned, sitting back down on the bed, flaring her wings awkwardly out around her. "I don't know. I touched the Heart, and things went black."

"And it was Lyka's decision to come find me?"

Ryana looked up and communed with her guardian for a moment, Lyka's melodious chirps filling the air before Ryana responded with a snort. "Do you remember the time you saved her from Bruud?"

Damian's eyes narrowed. His stepmother's guardian, given to her when she married their father, was a horrible skinless hound. Appearing half-skeletal, half-exposed-muscle, whatever The Snake ordered, her beast Bruud obeyed. It was clear the guardians had been fighting, though Damian had never known why, and Ryana had been too young to talk. He'd just walked into a room full of blood and feathers and chased the hound off. "Yes."

"Well, Lyka did too. Plus, she says things were bad."

"That they were," he said, softening. "When Lyka summoned me, I opened up all my mirrors. Each of them showed utter destruction."

Ryana rocked back. "All...of them?"

"Down to a one. I have not opened my mirrors since."

"That's good, though, right?" Austin guessed, interjecting himself. "If it's so chaotic over there, they may not know what has happened to you or the Heart yet."

"That's what we're counting on," Damian said, nodding.

"How so?"

"I've got another...general, working on something to save you. I should have news of it in a day or so."

"To save me? But I'm here."

"It's complicated. I'll explain later if she manages to bring it to fruition."

Ryana's eyes widened. "How many generals do you have?"

"Many. And Maximillian, too, you remember him, and—" Damian was about to say Grimalkin's name when the cat bounced in to lay on Ryana's lap.

"Oh, Grim, how I've missed you!" Ryana said, picking the cat up for a hug. Lyka chittered overhead, and Grimalkin chattered back. The bird flew off, and Grimalkin chased her. "I guess some things never change," Ryana said with a smile.

"It doesn't seem so," Damian agreed.

AFTER AUSTIN SAID it was okay for both of them, Damian gave Ryana his arm and took her on a quick tour of his home—which would now be her home as well. Lyka and Grimalkin worked on an equitable arrangement and changed the spatial reality of one of the existing rooms so that it became the spitting image of Ryana's expansive room in the Realms as befit her status, plus or minus her actual things, some of which couldn't be magically recreated so easily.

"I miss my books," Ryana said, looking at her empty shelves.

"About that," Damian began, remembering the destruction of the palace library, and how fond his sister was of reading. "The fires... there was devastation—"

"I'm not ready to hear about that, yet." She shook her head and held herself. "Tell me happier things instead. Tell me about the books that this world has. I haven't read any of them, obviously. Will reading them all take quite some time?"

While Damian could read, it wasn't a pastime for him like it was for Ryana...and Andi. "I think so. There are libraries here twice the size of father's, and," he said, before pulling out his phone, "you can keep a million books in this."

She squinted at it. "No. How?"

He grinned, remembering what it was like when he came over, and the world had been a lot less complicated then. "There's a lot to show you. Earth is different. But, trust me, once you're feeling up to it, there are things here that you'll enjoy." Being in her recreated room was the closest he'd gotten to the Realms in two decades. He sat down on one of the chairs and looked out her window, pleased that the view outside was still the roll of his own familiar hills. "Although Ryana...there are a few things we need to talk about, first."

"Understandably," she said, looking at herself in her new mirror. She was still wearing the dress he'd recovered her in, scorch marks and all. She smoothed her hands over the generous curves of her body. "My goodness...I'm a sight. If I went out looking like this—"

"You can't," he said gently. "Earth isn't like the Realms. Everyone here is non-magical, for the most part, so much so that they don't even recognize that magic exists."

She sniffed. "How pathetic."

"They have other charms," he said. "But...even though Earth may seem safer...it's not. We're currently at war with a group of non-magical enemies who know magic exists and want it for themselves. If they caught you, they'd strip your wings for the leather."

She rolled her eyes at him like he was her mother. "Do they not have leather here?"

"Not that's inherently magical, brought straight from the Realms." Her amusement curdled into horror, as he went on. "So, you have to promise me, should you ever leave the house, you can never go without hiding your birthright. And never alone. Not until you're more used to this world."

Ryana frowned. She'd displayed her wings proudly her entire life in lieu of a crown. "I would have to be normal?"

"You would never *be* normal, Ryana. Only appear it. For your own good." Although that did bring up a good point. Ryana was used to waves of servants seeing to her every need and everyone knowing who she was and catering to her whims. He knew his sister wasn't evil, but she was spoiled in a way that earth couldn't accommodate.

"Fine. What else?" she asked.

"There was an attack on me not that long ago. Someone from the Realms paid an earthly assassin to stab me. It didn't work, but I need to know who you think would've tried."

She frowned even deeper. "It could've been almost anyone, Damian. There's been unrest brewing for a long time—"

"From inside the palace, though?"

Her eyes widened. "I don't know. Not many people had access to the mirrors, or knew how to find you, besides—"

"Well, they didn't find me. They found someone else who had a mirror and brokered a deal for the assassin to find me. But the man with the mirror claims not to know who they were." Thoroughly interrogating Rax was one more thing on Damian's exceptionally long To-Do list. "And since when have there been liquid portals? Lyka used one to bring you through."

"Oh, you brilliant bird," Ryana muttered, even though her guardian was nowhere near. "Those are thanks to me."

"What?"

"No one spent more time in the library than I did, Damian." She began pacing. "As the unrest grew, it wasn't safe for me to leave the palace, so I didn't. I always enjoyed reading, so I indulged, and there were books in father's libraries with completely unsafe magic to perform. A Kagaroth had to put a fire in my hair out, and I inhaled sulfur more times than I'd care to admit, but, at least, I was doing something. Contributing in my own way. And when I figured out how to create the liquid that could be used like mirrors, I hoped it would change our course. But it takes so long to make even a little, and it can only be used a few times before it loses its integrity. Did Lyka use a bladder of it to bring me here?" she asked him, and he nodded. "Well, then. That was all that I'd made of it over the past several months."

"Who knew that it existed?"

"Why?"

"Because that was how they tried to kill me."

Ryana was horrified. "Oh, brother, I never would've let it out of my sight if I had known. But...how?"

"In the form of a knife. The liquid was pressed into a blade."

"Devious," Ryana said.

"It's gone now, but who had access to it?"

She winced. "No one...and everyone. I was the only person who created it, but I always had my guard with me, watching. They knew the experiments I was doing, as did my mother and her generals. And I didn't always have the same guards."

"So, any of them could've learned to make their own?"

"Oh, no," she said, shaking her head. "I doubt any of them would have the skill, but..." she said, sinking down. "I didn't weigh my repository. Someone could've stolen some from me, easily. It never even occurred to me. I thought I was developing a new kind of spycraft, not an attack on my own family. I wasn't even done perfecting it yet. How did you survive the attack?"

"They stabbed the wrong man."

Ryana looked him up and down. "How?"

"Not everyone on earth knows who I am."

"I find that impossible."

"Yet, it is true," he said. "And since it seems like you'll be staying, eventually that will happen to you, too. You'll be able to move among them, and no one will notice a thing."

She looked out the window like she was an explorer surveying new terrain. "I find the idea of that somewhat thrilling. I never wanted to be a commoner, mind you, but I did envy them their freedom."

"You'll enjoy a lot more of it here. Not having people bow to you all the time will be an adjustment," he teased. "But if I overcame it, you can as well."

Her brow crept up her forehead. "And there's no *phellaran* or *grodobu*?" she asked, naming mythical creatures from the bedtime stories their nannies read them growing up—one a giant bird that snatched bad children up in its beak to swallow whole, the other a thing that crawled out of tunnels it dug beneath your bed at night to bite your head off.

Damian chuckled. "Not that I know of. Just occasional intrusions from Unearthly when rifts open. My people and I take care of those."

She looked at him again. "Are you genuinely happy? Serving others? Or do you do it just to fight?"

"Maybe it was all fights when I started. But...I...." he began and paused. Was he happy without Andi by his side? Perhaps not, but now he knew what happiness was.

"There's a woman, isn't there?" Ryana asked.

He groaned. "You know, people from earth say I'm hard to read."

"Yes, well, they don't know you like I do. Even if I haven't seen you in an age. Does she suit you?" Ryana asked.

"I feel that she does. She is perhaps not so sure yet."

Ryana blinked. "What?" she asked as he spread his hands. "I cannot believe that."

Damian knew she was being literal. There was no world in which she could imagine a woman denying him—or a man denying her. "And yet, it is true."

"No. That's simply impossible," she said, trying to make sense of things. "Unless...oh, Damian, no." And even with the swelling around her eyes, she still managed an eye roll. "She's a human, isn't she?" She read his face again and exclaimed, "Just like father! Why would you involve a mere human in anything you do? How do they even begin to comprehend you? For all that my mother's atrocious, at least she suited him at the end. Have you even told her?"

"I had to. You bringing the Heart here forced my hand."

"Yes, well, I'm sorry about that, but maybe it's for the best, so she can get out now."

"*She* is not going anywhere. Except where *she* desires to be," Damian said, his voice going low in warning.

"I may have never met your mother, Damian, but I heard stories."

"I have not used the Forgetting Fire on her even once, and I never will."

"And I'm sure our father swore the same," Ryana said, putting a hand to her head like he pained her. "I don't know why I thought you'd have more common sense after you were smart enough to leave."

Damian stood and crossed the room to her. He knew there was no way he could explain his relationship with Andi to her, not when he couldn't even try to explain that Austin was a friend. "Let's not argue right now, Ryana." He matched her hand on her head with his own, affectionately. "I'll explain more later. You should rest now."

"I feel like I just got up," she complained, but she gave him a tight smile. "And I need to bathe, at the least, before sleeping."

"Please do. And have Lyka consult with Grim regarding any other accommodations you require. Rest tonight as much as you like, and I will introduce you to all of my generals tomorrow."

"Your generals, and your woman?" she pressed.

"Yes. Late tomorrow night. I promise."

She sighed, but nodded into his hand, and then rose to see to her bath as Lyka flew in.

CHAPTER

THIRTEEN

A ndi spent the majority of her shift going for ICU MVP. IVs were placed, endotracheal tubes were suctioned, medications were crushed, poured, hung, teeth were brushed, and if there was a patient that needed cleaning, no matter the mess —even that one GI bleed, shitting blood—she helped clean them. She even managed to make sure that there were no expired IV lines in use on the floor.

Sheila caught her pacing by halfway through the night. "Are you trying to make ten thousand steps or something?"

"Why?" Andi asked innocently, holding empty suction canisters.

"Because it's either that, or you're on uppers." Sheila cocked an eyebrow at her; she had seen Andi earlier, looking disheveled outside. Andi didn't want her charge nurse thinking she'd been getting high on something before coming onto her shift.

"No," Andi quickly lied. "I went to Jones and Shah before our shift and had a Vietnamese coffee."

"It's three a.m."

"I had the biggest size."

"That stuff is rocket fuel." Sheila snorted. Vietnamese coffee was treated like the gold foil it was wrapped in was real gold come three a.m., but few nurses were brave—or stupid—enough to drink a whole cup on their own if they ever wanted to sleep again. "You should know better."

"Look, just because I'm the most awesome nurse you have here doesn't mean I'm immune from having made bad decisions." Andi grinned at her.

Her charge nurse considered her again for a long moment and then laughed. "Well, cut it out. You're making the rest of us look bad."

"Fine, Mom," Andi said in a particularly teenaged voice, which made Sheila laugh even more and let her pass.

IT WASN'T until she'd taken a rinse-off shower the next morning, with her hair safely up to save her blue streak until she could get Sammy's help to freshen it up again, that she got into bed to text Damian. The only thing she held off on was taking an Ambien. She'd made a couple impulse purchases on eBay before while drifting off to sleep before on the drug, so she knew how powerful it was. If she was on it, she wouldn't trust herself not to tell him secrets.

Home. Safe. In bed.

If she'd been smarter, she would've just set her phone face down instantly, pounded the Ambien, and closed her eyes, nightmares be damned. But she wasn't. She hesitated for a crucial moment, and he texted her back.

Ryana's up.

And now she was glad she hadn't taken the Ambien, as she sat higher in bed. *Is she okay?*

She will be now that she's here.

So did she tell you what happened back home?

The usual, he quipped. *And that place isn't home anymore,* he corrected her.

Sorry..."*the place that you hate where you came from*" *takes too long to type.*

My only home is at your side.

Andi rubbed a hand over her face and swallowed. When he said things like that, it didn't even matter if he'd had her followed. Which, maybe he hadn't? It'd have been unlike him to not confess after being outed, she thought. Then again, maybe that strange woman hadn't reported her failure to do *whatever* to him.

But suddenly, she was glad she hadn't sent the text in her drafts —because if the woman had been freelancing as an attacker/asshole somehow, there was no way Damian wouldn't be over right now, laying atop her as she slept—for her own safety—and possibly other things.

And there'd definitely be no way he'd let her out of his sight long enough to go meet with her uncle tonight.

Normally I would have things to say about that, Damian...but I had a long shift. I'm going to go to bed now. I'll text you when I'm up again, though.

Good night, princess. See you at the stroke of midnight.

When he put it like that, it made her feel like a reverse Cinderella. Like she was the normal girl right now, and then in a few short hours, the clock would strike, and her princess-like nature would be revealed.

G'night, dragon, she texted back, with an emoji blowing a kiss.

HER NIGHTMARES WERE standard issue at this point. Was it wrong to be jaded by things that happened in your sleep? If that were a thing, how come those kids in that Freddy Krueger movie couldn't manage it? Blah-blah-blah-chasing, terrorizing, the sensation of falling, the feeling of being rendered limb from limb by some sort of skinless demon-dog. There was really only so much of it a girl could take. So, when Andi woke up and still felt exhausted—that was just something to slap coffee on, like a liquid bandage—she dabbed foundation underneath the dark circles around her eyes.

She wouldn't want to disappoint her family now, would she?

Up, she texted Damian simply. *See you in a few short hours.*

See you in a few long-seeming ones, he texted her back, and she set her phone down. From here on out, she needed her wits about her, and Damian was too distracting.

Andi looked at herself in her mirror, praying that Damian was good to his word and not looking back, because if he saw her, he'd instantly know something was up. She was wearing all black for the occasion—black flats, black slacks, and a black silk blouse. It was one of the nicest shirts she owned, a great irony seeing as she'd never wear it again if she could help it because the last thing she'd worn it to was her mother's funeral. She fanned her hair out over her shoulders, gave her makeup another once-over, and went out to sit on her brand-new couch to wait for the driver that would surely come.

ANDI DIDN'T RECOGNIZE the man who knocked on the door or the car that was waiting. Just as well, because if her uncle had sent Elsa and the car she'd tagged previously Damian might've known what was up. But her uncle had probably guessed as much, and he'd known Andi wouldn't pepper some random man with questions.

Instead, she sat silently in the back of the car, biting on her lower lip, trying to figure out what she'd ask. It was hard. There were so many things, and each question could lead to others, unfolding in her mind like reverse origami as she tried to prepare herself for all possible scenarios—until the car stopped.

They were there.

Wherever *there* was.

She looked around. The car was parked in front of a warehouse on a block of warehouses that all looked abandoned. The kind of place she knew from watching TV with Sammy, you could wrap a body tight with a tarp, and no one would find it until it was flyblown.

I've already worn this blouse to one funeral, what's another? she thought, and got out of the car.

The man lead her silently into the warehouse they were parked in front of, through doors and down ill-lit halls until they reached a door that he gestured she should open. She wiped sweaty palms on her thighs, and then pressed in.

"My dearest Andrea," her uncle said, as her eyes adjusted to the low lighting.

"Uncle," she acknowledged him, allowing herself a quick look around. He was surrounded by a series of low tables which had designs carved upon them underneath glass tops, and many more chairs, but they were the only people in the room so far.

He walked over to her, equal to her in height, and stood close enough that she could've touched him if she wanted to—but she didn't. Not anymore. No more hugs, no more closeness, just answers.

"You came alone as promised."

"I did." She felt foolish for admitting it at the moment, but it was too late now. "Because you said that there were things that you could tell me. About Mom."

"Yes. So many things. Did you finally look at the gift Danny gave you?" The photo album didn't feel like a gift to her. She nodded, and he continued. "Then you must be burning with questions if I know you."

"Not questions," she denied him. "Just one."

He laughed. "Well, then, this will be a short trip. Ask."

"Did she enjoy lying to me as much as you do?"

Uncle Lee looked like she'd punched him. Her whole life she'd been smaller than everyone else, pocket-sized, bite-sized, whatever you wanted to call it. She couldn't fight him with her hands, but she could with her tongue, and it was so satisfying to see her land a blow on him.

"Your mother loved you, Andi," Uncle Lee said, sounding affronted on her mother's behalf.

"Such an odd way she had of showing it. By hiding all of her past from me, especially the part where she apparently lived for over a century and used to hunt down creatures that could talk."

"It was a different time," her uncle said, as he folded his hands together sagely. "And it was over a century. Many centuries, actually."

Andi blinked.

"Go ahead," her uncle said and gestured to the chair across from him. "Sit."

Reluctantly, Andi sat down.

CHAPTER

FOURTEEN

Damian stared at the last text from Andi on his phone. There was so much more he wanted to say to her, but typing it didn't make sense when all he had to do was wait until midnight to get to speak to her in person. He got up, showered, and had Grim summon everyone shortly for a meeting in their conference room to introduce Ryana, which would be a damn sight more comfortable than their meeting in the library the prior night.

Mills entered first, looking smug, walking around the table to his side. "I did it," she crowed, holding her hands clasped in front of her. "And, if I may say so myself, it came out very nicely." She opened her hands to show him what they held.

Nestled in the center of her palm was a smooth, smoky gemstone that looked like it had a live coal trapped inside. It was wound with what looked like platinum wire and on a simple silver chain. He picked it up, and the coal glowed brighter like it was reflecting the fire inside his dragon back at him.

"She'll love it." He could already imagine Andi wearing it, the warm stone sitting at the notch of her throat.

"It's the most magical object I've ever made, Damian. Utterly one of a kind."

"I should hope so," he said, giving her a smile, as everyone else filed in.

AUSTIN AND RYANA were almost last, having some shared conversation in which he made her laugh. She made a grand entrance with her injured wings, and Austin winced on her behalf as she carefully cleared the door. She'd worn a sparklingly beaded cream-colored gown and makeup that covered most of her bruises if not the swelling, and she'd clipped her auburn hair to all be the same length, falling just below her chin. Lyka summoned a backless chair for her, as Austin chose to sit nearby. Damian was not a fool. It was easy to see how Austin was putting himself in her proximity. He rather wished he could warn the werewolf about her temper and how incompatible they'd be, but suspected Austin would take that as a challenge. In any case, if he kept puppy-dogging around Ryana, he'd learn soon enough.

"All right, everyone," he said, with the necklace for Andi still safe in his hand. "As some of you may have noticed, my sister is awake now."

Ryana arched her neck gracefully and looked around the room. "I look forward to making all of your acquaintances. But—"

"Ryana!" Max burst into the room with an armful of magenta amaranth flowers draped over his arm. Joy flooded Ryana's face at seeing him there.

"You remembered!" She clapped her hands as he came to present the flowers to her.

"I remember you making the entire convoy stop to pick them for you until your carriage was full enough to sleep on them." He grinned at her. "These are probably a different kind than those were, but they look very much the same."

"The servants were picking purple petals out of the carriage for weeks," Ryana said with a laugh. "Mother was so upset!"

Damian took a stealthy glance at Austin, who seemed mystified. *I don't need to warn him about a thing. He'll learn soon enough.*

Max hovered for an ingrained moment and then lunged forward to sweep her into a hug. Ryana's wings flexed and battered at him, and her arms flailed before finally finding awkward purchase around him, the same as he had her.

"Max, I'm a princess!" she protested, but she was laughing.

"I know, but this is how we do welcomes on Earth." The weapons master pulled back. "I want to hear all about home. What happened at the end? And all the gossip before that. Is General Eshever still in charge—"

"In due time," Damian cut in. "In addition to Max, these are...the rest of my generals."

Ryana rearranged herself on her chair and looked around, spotting Mills first. "And what is your name?" she imperiously demanded. Damian knew she wasn't being unkind, just used to being obeyed.

"Millicent," Mills said. "Although everyone calls me Mills. I'm a witch."

"A witch general. Excellent!" Ryana said delightedly, scanning down the table. "You...general with the metal arm! What magic makes you work? Are you an automaton?" Jamison looked an appropriate combination of amused and horrified.

"That's Jamison, and...Ryana...I was explaining things earlier, so they'd made sense, but in truth, these are my friends," Damian said.

"Except for me," Austin corrected him. "I am totally a general."

"A general pain in my ass," his brother Zach snickered.

"Are you both wolves?" Ryana guessed, looking between them. "Or are they *chevoni*?" she asked Damian and Max with a frown.

"No," Max answered her quickly. Chevoni in the Realms were far worse—they were closer to hyenas than wolves, had a taste for blood, and had a strange type of group telepathic sentience.

"We're just average, cuddly werewolves," Zach said with a tease. Austin gave him a stern glance that said, *Back off.*

"Not average and not cuddly," Austin clarified, pointing to himself.

"As long as you've got all your skin, I don't really care," Ryana said with a laugh that made everyone else around the table check out their neighbor to make sure they'd all heard the same thing.

Damian pinched the bridge of his nose, unwilling to explain her reference to Bruud. "In any case, I'm going to need all of your help acclimating Ryana to earth in the coming weeks. Where are we with your alternative plan, Mills?"

The witch's lips pulled into a serious line. "Still working on it. I've got a rather extreme plan that requires a willing volunteer."

Damian snorted. "I'm sure we can manage that."

Mills tensed. "I'm not so—"

Then Jamison cocked his head to the side and announced, "Hold up." His eyes got that far away look they did when communing with his electronics. "I think we're going to get a location on that meeting, Damian. The car at the airport is moving."

"Back to Andi's?" Damian asked with concern.

"No. It circled around, presumably to pick someone up, and is now heading east."

Mills reached under the table and hit a button so that the wood in front of her opened and revealed a terminal. "Let me know when they land, baby."

"Zach, Austin, Max...gear up. Get the tour bus ready," Damian commanded, and the men quickly filed out.

Ryana watched all of the excitement with glittering eyes.

"Triangulating coordinates...likely destination: warehouse row," Jamison announced.

"Recently bought by Bright Star conglomerate, go figure," Mills muttered, now working on her own terminal. "I'm uploading schematics for all the buildings on the block in case they move while

236

inside, but no guarantees if they're up to date. Evil empires don't keep up to code."

"Ready!" Austin's voice echoed from outside, piped in from the SUV.

"Load up," Damian announced. Mills slapped her terminal shut, and Jamison stood, both of them jogging for the door. Damian almost followed them, until his sister blocked him with a wing.

"Where are we going?" she said with excitement.

"We're going to attack an assemblage of Hunters. You're staying here."

"Oh, no, no, no," she protested, and Damian was hesitant to shove her injured wing aside. "I'm coming with you."

It was a terrible idea, and he knew it, but maybe, if she saw who Hunters were and how "wars" worked on earth, it could be instructive. Just as long as his people could keep her safe.

"Fine," he grumbled, and she folded her wing in with a grin.

"Remember what I told you," Damian said, running flat out for the SUV as she followed him. Her sparkling gown was entirely inappropriate because she thought she'd just be meeting his "generals" tonight, but he knew if he gave her a chance to change, the meeting would already be over.

To her credit, she hopped twice and pulled her delicate sandals off, finishing up the last of the run barefoot, and she'd already magicked away her wings by the time they jumped into the car.

Austin gawked at her as she sat down. *How convenient that there was an empty seat beside him, again,* Damian thought. "Where did they go?" the wolf asked her.

"Wouldn't you like to know?" Ryana said with a laugh.

The second his door was slammed, Max pulled the SUV into drive and started gunning for the gates.

"Any new news, Jamison?" Damian asked.

"Nothing on my end other than an address."

"And the tech in the building is so old I can't connect to it," Mills complained. Then she whispered, "Oh, shit."

"What?" Damian pressed.

"Well, if it isn't our old friend, the janitor," Jamison said, giving Mills a look.

"He's never going to let us hear the end of this, is he?" she asked him back, before glancing back to Damian. "The man you wanted tagged two days ago at the mall, who's been as boring as wallpaper paste since, is on his way to our same location—with his cell phone in his pocket." Mills rubbed her hands together in glee.

"Then, you're right. I never am going to let you hear the end of it," Damian said with a satisfied chuckle.

"It was a horrible risk," Zach complained.

"A calculated risk," Damian corrected him. "Not made in haste— nor in error, apparently."

Ryana just kept looking between all of them, one after the other, beaming a smile as bright as the beads on her dress. "This is all so exciting!"

THE JANITOR BEAT them to the location, but he walked in. Mills piped the microphone from his phone through the SUV's system so they could all listen in to his low-level, forced-to-stay-outside-the-club-house enforcer-small-talk with others of his stature. Max slowed their SUV to coast as Jamison pulled up views from outside.

"Fifteen cars parked, so at least fifteen targets, not counting drop-offs," Max announced with his magical eyes.

"Definitely more. A lot more," Mills said, her eyes closed, trying to track fragments of too many conversations.

"Any luck on voice recognition?" Zach asked Jamison.

"Hard to get a clear sample from inside this guy's pocket,"

Jamison complained. "Let's hope he's a Pokémon fan and decides to see what's around to catch, eh?"

Then the ambient sounds quieted. They heard the sound of a solidly closing door and the throat clearing and a rustling of fabric as the man presumably adjusted himself nearby.

"Fuck, fuck, fuck," Mills hissed.

Austin reached into one of their lockboxes and pulled out a weapon. "I bet I can make them talk again."

Damian put a hand on his wrist to hold it. "They all went in… they've all got to come out."

"After doing what nefarious things?" Ryana asking out of prurient curiosity rather than altruism, before reaching for Austin's gun.

"Later. I promise," the werewolf said, pulling the weapon away.

Just what Damian needed. Austin arming his sister. He closed his eyes and tried to concentrate on the here and now, as they all heard the sounds of more fabric, as the phone was freed from whatever pocket it'd resided in, and a distant voice grew louder.

"Our janitor's nosy," Mills said. "Yes. Go for it. Lean in."

Everyone in the SUV was holding their breath collectively, even Damian, so they all heard it at the same time, clear as day: "And this is my esteemed niece, Andrea."

Damian froze, as inside his chest, his heart—a dragon's heart, possibly made of crystal, just like the cursed one in the box—skipped a beat and shattered.

THANK you for reading DRAGON FATED!

Here's a brief excerpt from the next and final book in the series, DRAGON MATED!

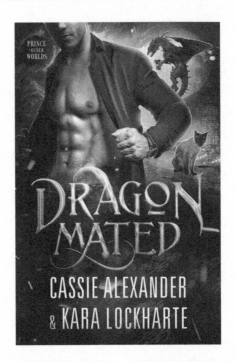

Then they banked and began to slow down, into a stomach clenching spiral like a roller coaster's highest turn. She shrieked and laughed, tempted to fling her arms up but too scared she'd drop Damian's clothing, until his wings flared out and she realized they were going to land someplace that she knew—the top of Damian's castle.

The beast made a nimble landing, considering two of its four paws were still holding her. After coming to a stop it slowly splayed its fingers out, releasing her to the castle's rooftop cobblestone. She stumbled forward, breathless. Her eyes were dry, she was freezing, and her body was shaking from the adrenaline. "I loved that!" she shouted, whirling, to see him and finding Damian standing naked there in all of his chiseled, brooding, perfection. It'd been two days since she'd seen him—two days too long—and her eyes soaked him in all at once. His broad shoulders, muscled chest, arms that could probably throw someone to the moon—Stella wasn't wrong about that—

and below that the slight V of his flat stomach leading directly to his heavy cock. Andi rocked with ache from missing him, even as she blushed to see him so exposed. "I love," the words left her body again, her excitement priming her to repeat things, only this time there wasn't wind to rip them safely from her mouth. "Flying. I love flying."

Damian walked over to her, unashamed of his nakedness, and took his clothes out of her arms to put back on. He started with his slacks. "Yes. My dragon also loves flying," he told her, although there was something faintly accusatory in his tone. "You should see your hair."

She quickly pulled her wind-whipped hair into a bun. She could make out the same injury on him as his dragon had. "You should see your skin," she frowned, trying to lay a hand on his chest but he moved back, quickly buttoning his shirt back up.

It was very unlike Damian to be dressing in front of her unless he had someplace to be. "Where are you going?"

"Why do you care?"

Andi blinked. "Are you...mad at me?"

"Yes," he said flatly, pulling his suit jacket on. "But I'm also mad at myself."

For what? Andi's head tilted, imagining bad things instantly. "You heard what I told your dragon, right?"

"I did," he said, straightening his cuffs. It was a reflexive maneuver, she could tell—like he was nervous—and anything that made him nervous made her doubly so. His brow creased in disappointment, and he made a thoughtful noise before speaking again. "I told you once you were a pretty knife, princess. Well, congratulations, tonight you cut me."

"Damian—" she began, as he squared off in front of her.

"You called me your boyfriend and then pushed me away for days so you could do what you liked. You hurt me. On purpose."

"I had to lie to you, you know that—"

"No, actually, I don't."

241

Andi crossed her arms. "You know, I could get used to your whole dragon's not-talking thing."

He snorted. Wind struck up and brushed his straight black hair into his eyes. "You don't actually have a defense, do you," he said, pushing it back with one hand.

"I was doing what I thought was right. I deserved answers, Damian, and I wasn't going to get them with you at my side." Andi hugged herself, angry at him and herself in turn. *At least we have that in common tonight?* "I didn't want to do it, you know. Do you think I enjoyed lying to you? Being scared, knowing that I had to go see my crazy family alone?"

His eyes searched hers, stepping forward as she retreated. The sky had been dark and cloudy when they'd flown through it, but that was nothing compared to the storm Damian brought with him now. "But you did it anyway."

"And I came straight to you to tell you everything!" She threw her hands up in exasperation. "Even knowing it would piss you off!" The stone of a castle parapet was at her back.

The corners of his lips cruelly lifted, taunting her, as she realized she was trapped. "Why?"

"Why what?"

"Why me, Andi?" He moved to stand so close to her that they were almost touching.

Andi blinked and blurted out, "Because you're the person I tell things to." She was surprised by how wrung out she felt after fear with her uncle, the elation of flight, and the stomach-churning queasiness of fighting now. It left her with few defenses.

"Why?" he pressed again. "Why am I that person?"

She bit her lips and shook her head. "I don't know!"

They were toe-to-toe and he was breathing hard and she didn't know what he wanted from her as he bowed his head toward hers. "Lie to me again, why don't you, princess."

"I love you," she said. She didn't think she meant it at the time. She was just pissed off at the way he was treating her and had

242

thought of the worst possible thing for her to say. She watched the words hit him like a slap.

But then...oh, but then, it was like she'd uncorked a secret reservoir, the place where she'd been shoving her emotions with him all along, trying to dole them out into societally acceptable pieces, not letting herself get too hopeful or appear too wanton. But now that the lid was off and the words were spoken, she could feel it all jumbling together inside her like a science project volcano. His eyes searched hers, his expression more wounded than anything any monster could've done to his chest.

"I don't believe that's a lie for a moment," he whispered, leaning down.

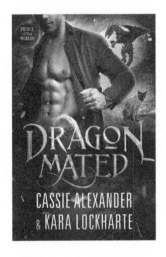

Click here to find out what happens next in DRAGON MATED!

ALSO BY CASSIE ALEXANDER

PRINCE OF THE OTHER WORLDS (co-written with Kara Lockharte)

(Andi & Damian's story)

Dragon Called

Dragon Destined

Dragon Fated

Dragon Mated

WARDENS OF THE OTHER WORLDS (co-written with Kara Lockharte)

(each book is a standalone)

Dragon's Captive (Sammy & Rax)

Wolf's Princess (Austin & Ryana)

Wolf's Rogue (Zach & Stella)

Dragon's Flame (Tarian & Seris)

...and don't forget to join Cassie's newsletter for access to an exclusive Andi and Damian prequel story, *Dragons Don't Date*, plus *Bewitched*, a Jamison and Mills novella!

THE DARK INK TATTOO SERIES

Blood of the Pack

Blood at Dusk

Blood by Moonlight

Blood by Midnight

Blood at Dawn

Cassie's Stand Alone Books

The House: Come Find Your Fantasy -- a choose your own adventure erotica

Rough Ghost Lover

Her Future Vampire Lover

Her Ex-boyfriend's Werewolf Lover

The Edie Spence Urban Fantasy Series

Nightshifted

Moonshifted

Shapeshifted

Deadshifted

Bloodshifted

Sign up for more news from Cassie here!

ALSO BY KARA LOCKHARTE

Dragon Lovers

Betrothed to the Dragon

Belonging to the Dragon

Bonded to the Dragon

Dragon Lovers Complete Vol. 1

The Space Shifter Chronicles

(Science Fiction Romances)

NOVELS

Wanted by the Werewolf Prince

Taken by the Tigerlord

Desired by the Dragon King (coming soon)

SHORT STORIES

The Boy Who Came Back a Wolf (free to newsletter subscribers)

The Lady and the Tigershifter

In Search of Skye

ABOUT THE AUTHOR

On her own, Cassie's a nurse by day and writer by night, living in the Bay Area with her husband, two cats, inside a massive succulent garden.

Whereas Kara's a California transplant by way of NYC and is still, to this day, searching for the perfect bagel (although the no-snow and strawberries out here help to make up for it.)

Don't forget to sign up for Cassie's newsletter for free books and bonus content! https://www.cassiealexander.com/newsletter

Follow Kara on Facebook, www.facebook.com/karalockharte or get a free book at her website, www.karalockharte.com/signup

Made in United States
Orlando, FL
16 June 2023

34203049R00157